Fantasmagorical
By Annmarie McKenna

Welcome to Fantasm Island! Leave your inhibitions at the door and let your fantasies soar.

That's what the brochure said anyway. A week long fling with a stranger. Where's the harm in that? Take a compatibility quiz and a slew of other health tests, sign a strict privacy agreement and give license to any sexual fantasy you've ever had. Evan Knight couldn't wait.

Gabe and Lance have been searching for their perfect third for what seems like forever. One look at the woman he and his best friend and lover Lance have chosen to claim during her time on the island, and Gabe thinks they may have finally found her.

But what if Evan isn't interested in more than the fling she signed up for? Or worse, what if she can't handle two men who are into each other too? Gabe and Lance have one week to convince Evan that the three of them belong together...and they'll use every bit of seduction in their arsenal to make sure when the fantasy ends, their reality together will only just be beginning.

Warning, this title contains the following: explicit fantasmagorical sex, graphic language, ménage a trois, and hot nekkid man-love.

Take Me

By Mackenzie McKade

One tempting heiress. Two sexy cowboys. Three means fun beyond her wildest dreams—until her Cord starts to unravel.

Thoroughbred rancher's daughter Caitlyn Culver has always wanted playboy Cord Daily, even after her daddy threatened to bankrupt him. But winning a racehorse in a poker game means Cord is no longer just a cattle rancher. He's come back wealthier and more wicked than ever.

Snaring this cowboy won't be easy for Cait, and keeping him will be even harder. Still, his sexual antics and taste for ménages won't scare her off. She knows the best way to snag a man like Cord is to pretend indifference. So when he comes onto her in the barn, she plays along—only to leave him tied to a ladder, aroused and unfulfilled.

It's payback time.

Cord seeks out Cait and brings along his playboy cousin, Dolan Crane. The two cowboys are enough to set her body afire. She's bound and determined to resist their sexual allure, but ends up experiencing a night beyond her wildest fantasies. Now Dolan wants Cait for himself. Cait's father wants Cord's racehorse. And Cord wants Caitlyn to choose—her father's money or her cowboy's love.

Warning, this title contains the following: explicit sex, graphic language, ménage a trois, and BDSM.

A Scorching Seduction
By Marie Harte

Duty wars with affection when Racor's greatest spy must decide who to trust, the evidence against her sexy suspects, or her heart?

Lt. Col. Trace N'Tre and Assassin Vaan C'Vail are hiding out in the only place the military can't touch them—on a pleasure planet in an island resort owned by Vaan's cousin. Gathering evidence on the outside, they know it's only a matter of time before they'll have to face their accuser, a high official in the Racor government.

Unbeknownst to them, Myst, Racor's greatest spy, has had her eyes on them for some time. The puzzle of these two alleged traitors doesn't fit, and Myst has made it her mission to find out why. But when the tables are turned and she's caught spying under the planet's hot summer suns, pleasure and affection confuse the issue, making her wonder who to trust—her heart, or the evidence against her lovers.

Warning, this title contains the following: explicit sex, frank language, ménage, m/m action, and hot sweaty adventure.

Honeymoon Castaways
By Dawn Halliday

Newlywed Catalina Robinson thinks it's not possible to be more satisfied...but then she learns what it's like to love two men.

Cat has just married Dave Robinson, the man of her dreams. Their Best Man, Andreas Bailey, is flying them to their honeymoon resort in Barbados. But over the middle of the ocean, something goes horribly wrong...

Cat, Dave and Andreas find themselves stranded on an uninhabited Caribbean island. Though she's never thought of him as more than a friend, Cat finds herself connecting to Andreas in a way she never expected and is shocked and aroused to learn that her husband feels the same way. Together, the three of them discover a heat and passion uninhibited by the conventions of society. But will they ever be rescued? And what will happen to their unusual relationship once they return home?

Warning, this title contains the following: explicit sex, graphic language, ménage a trois, voyeurism and skinny dipping.

Sins of Summer

A Samhain Publishing, Ltd. publication.

Samhain Publishing, Ltd.
577 Mulberry Street, Suite 1520
Macon, GA 31201
www.samhainpublishing.com

Sins of Summer
Print ISBN: 1-59998-775-9
Fantasmagorical Copyright © 2008 by Annmarie McKenna
Take Me Copyright © 2008 by Mackenzie McKade
A Scorching Seduction Copyright © 2008 by Marie Harte
Honeymoon Castaways Copyright © 2008 by Dawn Halliday

Editing by Sasha Knight
Cover by Anne Cain

Fantasmagorical, 1-59998-579-9
First Samhain Publishing, Ltd. electronic publication: July 2007
Take Me, 1-59998-592-6
First Samhain Publishing, Ltd. electronic publication: June 2007
A Scorching Seduction, 1-59998-572-1
First Samhain Publishing, Ltd. electronic publication: June 2007
Honeymoon Castaways, 1-59998-581-0
First Samhain Publishing, Ltd. electronic publication: July 2007
First Samhain Publishing, Ltd. print publication: April 2008

Contents

Fantasmagorical

Annmarie McKenna

Dedication

I have to dedicate Fantasmagorical to all those manlove writers whose books and ideas somehow wormed their way into my head. I hadn't meant for my two heroes to be gay but I guess that's what they wanted ☺. To all the manlove writers out there, you guys rock!

Chapter One

"Dayum." Evan Knight's duffel bag dropped to the ornate tiled floor with a thud. Sweat beaded her upper lip and rolled off her body everywhere else. Her forehead, the small of her back, between her breasts. "Look at all those chests."

"Makes you want to dive right in, doesn't it? Part the sea of male specimens." Kiley came to a stop next to Evan, so close their shoulders rubbed. She leaned over as if to whisper, but what she said could have been heard on the mainland. "Which one do you want?"

Evan smiled. "I don't know, I don't care, but it better be that one." She pointed none too shyly at the most gorgeous man she'd ever seen in her life. The same half-naked man currently surrounded by a throng of other women.

"Mmm," Kiley sighed, clearly not paying any attention to Evan's god of choice. "Methinks I like the redhead stroking his... Oh my God. Have you ever seen one that big? It's huge!"

Evan reluctantly removed her gaze from the sandy-haired Adonis. "Wow. That *is* impressive."

Kiley clasped Evan's hand and tugged them both toward the man in question. Evan guessed it was okay to leave her bag unattended for a few minutes. Fantasmagorical was a private resort after all, only invited guests and the employees were permitted on the property.

Before they even reached the man, Kiley was already talking. "That is beautiful."

"Thank you." His green eyes lit up and Evan watched them touch on every inch of Kiley's hourglass figure before settling on her face.

Evan snorted. He didn't even look at her. Too bad, because he *was* rather yummy.

"Is it as soft as it looks?" Not one shy bone in her best friend's body.

"Absolutely."

"So big. May I touch it?" Kiley's fingertips were already stretching toward the object of her fascination.

"If it would please you."

She hesitated. "Will it bite?"

The corners of his mouth quirked. "I would never allow it to hurt a guest, my sweet."

Jeez, looked like Kiley had already been claimed. A sharp bark of laughter followed by several female giggles made Evan turn to the man who'd first garnered her notice, and sigh. Probably no way in hell of attracting that particular Adonis's interest. Not with that many women already vying for his attention. Besides, she didn't have the perfect shape of Kiley or, apparently, the wiles of any of his groupies. But he was built to the specifications of all her fantasies, she whined to herself.

"Suck my cock."

The loud squawk dragged Evan's gaze back to Kiley, who practically cooed.

"Oh my God, he's so cute," Kiley squeaked in delight. The girl had a thing for tropical birds, and she thrust a hand toward the bird once more to stroke the plumage of colorful feathers on top of the cockatoo's head. His owner laughed one time before his face turned serious.

He took a hold of Kiley's chin. "I believe you've been claimed."

A rush of fire pooled in Evan's belly at the intensity in the redhead's gaze. Kiley whimpered.

Who wouldn't?

"Do what Milo said. Drop to your knees and suck my cock."

Evan's heart pounded and she swallowed. Where was the man who would talk to her in the same guttural, commanding tone? The one who would tell her to drop to her knees and suck his cock. The one who was the reason she'd come to this resort in the first place—to experience domination with absolutely no consequences.

She watched, mesmerized, as her best friend in the whole world slowly sank to the ground in sudden submissiveness, her gaze never leaving the man's.

Holy shit. The brochure had been right. This place was every fantasy wrapped into one picturesque, private island, beachfront resort.

Evan forced her fingers not to rub her throbbing clit as the man spread his thighs and set the cockatoo on a perch beside him. Kiley moved to the ties that held a loose pair of cotton pants together over an impressive bulge.

"Eyes on my face," he demanded.

Evan licked her lips. This was so not fair. Why did Kiley get to go first? When was it her turn and why could she not stop watching? She'd never felt so liberated in her life. Perhaps knowing she was safe in this controlled environment made her feel this way? Both she and Kiley had had to undergo extensive testing before even being considered for this once-in-a-lifetime experience.

And damn, when you weren't getting any at home...

Kiley nimbly untied the loose knot at the bottom of the man's six-pack. She pulled the waistband toward her with one hand and reached inside with the other to extract a rather stunning erection.

The sweat on Evan's skin increased tenfold, as did the moisture pooling between her thighs.

Kiley's open mouth moved forward, ready to take on the plum-shaped head glistening with what seemed to be several drops of pre-come. Evan was suddenly glad she wasn't Kiley because she didn't think she'd be able to take a cock the size of his.

The tip of her friend's pink tongue darted out to lick the slit when two hands settled on Evan's shoulders.

She jumped with a shriek only to be hauled back against a hard chest. Her heart slammed into her ribs, threatening to break them as a hand, liberally sprinkled with light brown hairs, covered one breast. The hardened nipple was rolled and tugged on just to the point of pain and released with a pluck.

Evan moaned in desperate need and rested her head on whoever held her. She didn't care who he was, only that her body clamored for him.

Warm breath caressed her ear making her shiver in direct competition with the stifling heat of the air.

"I think you need a couple of your own cocks to suck on."

Evan bit her lip. Cocks, plural?

Chapter Two

Gabe Lariet had recognized her as his the second she'd walked in the door. Her long, dark brown hair was caught up in a haphazard ponytail that had worked itself loose in the oppressive heat of Fantasm Island. He itched to rip the offending elastic off so he could see the thick strands flow over his thighs and belly when she sucked him off.

Or better yet, over Lance's cock while Gabe buried himself in her pussy. A pussy he knew by the tremble of her body and the scent of her essence was already wet and preparing itself for them.

He pressed his erection into the small of her back and she melted into him. She was tiny compared to him. More than a head shorter. They would need to be careful not to hurt her the first time they took her together. And make no mistake, they would most definitely fuck her at the same time. They'd shared women many, many times over their long friendship, especially since discovering some time a few years back that what would make them whole would be a third. A woman to complete their circle.

He plucked at the woman's distended nipples through the thin cotton of her shirt as she watched her friend take a good amount of Zach's length down her throat. It looked like the friend could do some major sucking but she didn't do anything for him. His taste ran to a certain petite brunette who would fall to the floor if he took a step back right now.

Gabe supported her with his arm across her smooth tummy and continued to palm her breasts with the other. They were small, but damn if her nipples weren't hard as rocks.

"I'm claiming you," he growled in her ear, glancing around at her face in time to see her eyes slide shut. She pursed her lips and nodded acceptance.

There weren't always matches at Fantasmagorical. He'd never had it happen to him, but occasionally it did happen that a guest wasn't claimed for the entire week. In those cases, the guest's name was put into a pool and they were then paired by the day. They spent their week being doted on by several different employees who'd been hired for the sole purpose of keeping unclaimed guests happy.

Gabe and Lance, on the other hand, had made lots of women happy. Women looking for a ménage or a break from their traditional bedroom antics. They'd even had several return customers to the island who'd asked for them specifically, but they'd yet to connect with one on a spiritual level. The day would come eventually, either here on the island or back at home in Florida. And when they found her, they'd keep her forever.

Fantasm Island, owned by his own eccentric billionaire uncle, got its business through word of mouth. Usually women, sometimes men, came to the resort ready for intense sexual freedom. Anything goes. Guests were tested both physically and mentally and only those who passed with flying colors were invited to come.

"I'm claiming you too." Lance's voice rumbled beside him. The woman jumped in his arms and twisted to see who'd spoken. Her eyes widened to quarter-sized disks and she gasped. She looked around him at the group of women pouting after Lance.

"You're ours," Gabe said and tugged her toward the rear exit. "Get her bag," he threw over his shoulder.

"Already taken care of."

"But my—"

"Your friend is being well taken care of too, by Zach. Believe me." Gabe took one elbow, Lance the other and headed to their quarters. If he didn't relieve the tension in his cock soon, it was liable to explode before he got inside her.

Palm trees lined all the pathways coming to and from the main resort building. Parties, dinners and dances were held at the big building. Smaller huts housed specialty rooms for any fantasy a guest could think up. If they couldn't find what they wanted, the situation could be created.

"I can't wait, Gabe." Lance drew to a stop along the balustrade outside.

She squeaked when he backed her up to the concrete ledge and trapped her between his hands, which he rested beside her.

"You are beautiful." He nuzzled her throat. "What's your name?"

She gave a hysterical little laugh and tilted her head back to give Lance better access. Gabe moved to the other side and added his mouth.

"This is really weird." She moaned.

"But what you want, right?" Gabe whispered, licking along the vein.

When she paused too long, Lance said, "Answer him, sweetheart."

"Yes." The word hissed from deep in her lungs.

"From now on you answer us the first time." Gabe placed a hand at her waist and slid it beneath her shirt. Lance's met his at her breasts so they each held one. They manipulated the hardened tips simultaneously.

She made a disparaging sound but didn't balk at their command. It was part of her profile. She wished to be a submissive in every way that mattered sexually. Of course, her profile only provided a photo, not a name. All the "employees" were given profiles for each guest. It allowed them to claim the guest that interested them the most the minute they walked in the door.

They weren't given a name in case the guest desired to stay somewhat anonymous. If things didn't work out, both guest and employee were allowed to trade at a mixer later in the week, or, if things were really bad right from the start, the owner would see to it the guest was directed to another employee. He wanted everyone to be happy.

"This one time will be your only warning. From here on out you will be punished. Do you understand?" Lance demanded.

"Yes."

"Good." Lance pulled his hand from her shirt and tugged the fabric up and off her body, leaving her naked from the waist up.

"Make sure you leave the bra off all week," Gabe growled and cupped her mound. Her head fell back when he gave a tight squeeze. "The panties too."

"We want to be able to touch you, to fuck you, at anytime. Day or night." Lance pressed his lips to hers and coaxed them open.

Gabe watched her tongue dart out and tentatively touch the tip of Lance's. His cock jerked behind the fly of his jeans. That tongue would be lapping at his erection very soon.

18

"What's your name, honey?" Gabe asked, adjusting his jeans around the persistent hard-on.

She broke the kiss and looked back and forth between the two of them before swallowing and licking her lips.

"Evan Kn—"

Lance placed his fingers over her open mouth. "First names only, sweetheart."

She nodded.

"Good. I'm gonna strip these shorts off you, set you on this ledge and eat your pussy until I'm full. You are to do nothing. No screaming, no touching."

Gabe helped divest Evan of the rest of her clothes, sticking the tiny, white lace panties smeared with her cream in his pocket. "Up you go, honey." She was the most fucking gorgeous creature on the planet and he and Lance were about to get to know every intimate detail of her body. Damn if life wasn't good.

Chapter Three

Holy shit. Was she really doing this? Letting a stranger, *strangers,* strip her naked and go down on her? In public? With the man who'd been surrounded by women? The same one she'd pointed at when they'd first walked in. And his friend. Two gorgeous men presenting her with the opportunity of a lifetime, because it was for damn sure this kind of thing would never happen in her real life.

Evan's heart raced in anticipation and a healthy amount of fear.

Another couple had sequestered themselves in the corner and were...actually fucking. Evan had never thought of herself as a voyeur but it was hard to avoid it here. She had to admit, it turned her on. This place was incredible. More than lived up to its reputation.

The blond knelt and spread her thighs with practiced ease. For a second, she balked, unsure she could really go through with this. A ménage a trois had been her ultimate fantasy. The first one she'd listed on the countless number of forms she and Kiley had filled out.

She hadn't really believed it would happen. For all her bravado and talking big, she was scared to death now. Except for the three-quarters of her body that said, "You'd have to be the most stupid girl in the world to turn down two red-hot blooded American males who both appear to want you."

Who cared if this is exactly what they got paid to do?

The man's—God, she didn't even know his name—hand slid the length of her thighs, widening them as he went.

"I'm Lance," he said, reading her mind.

She swallowed for the billionth time and nodded. What a moron. She'd been reduced to swallowing and nodding as if she had no tongue.

His head came closer to her apex. Her clit seized and flooded with blood. Sucker was probably sticking straight out like a miniature hard-on. A pink tinge colored her cheeks as his breath fanned over her skin.

"She's blushing, Lance."

The dark-haired god's name was Gabe. She remembered Lance calling him that at least. He'd been the one to grab her from behind.

Evan licked her lips and watched in wonder as her knees fell apart magically on their own. Lance insinuated himself in the space with a sly smile.

"You think she wants this?" he asked Gabe.

"I know it. Look at these nipples." Gabe flicked at one distended nub and Evan had to bite her lip to keep from moaning.

They'd said no screaming which was likely to become very ugly for her since she was a screamer.

Lance's long tongue shot out and licked her slit and she did it. She screamed. A short, staccato burst of sound that had both their heads lifting.

Shit. Shit, shit, shit. She pressed her lips together and prayed to God they wouldn't stop.

"You were warned, sweetheart." Lance rubbed a circle around her clit with his thumb. She squirmed and couldn't squelch the whine.

Gabe flexed his hands. She swallowed.

"How much honey you think will flow from that pretty pussy when I redden her ass?" Gabe murmured, never taking his eyes off hers.

"More than I can lap up." Lance licked the length of her slit from asshole to clit and ended the pass with a swirl over the taut bundle of nerves. "Sweet fucking honey."

"Maybe I should have a taste."

Evan mewled. Gabe leaned at the waist and planted his face between her thighs. His tongue traveled the opposite direction, ending at the tightly puckered hole in back.

Jesus. She'd never been touched there, but it had been another experience she'd written on her most-wanted list. Evan hadn't imagined someone's tongue being there though. Her back arched, forcing her pussy into his mouth, and she squeezed her eyes shut.

Velvety smoothness slipped into her channel. She opened her eyes. Two tongues tangled together at her pussy, slipping through her folds and rubbing against one another.

Her groan rent the air.

"I think we've got us a noisy one, Gabe."

"Mmm." He stood, licking her cream from his lips like he'd just devoured barbecued ribs and was savoring the last of the sauce.

Oh Lordy. She'd never last.

Those lips took possession of hers. She tasted herself on him and opened to receive his tongue.

The man could kiss. She lost herself and lifted her hands to cradle his face, keeping him right where she wanted him. There was definitely something to having two men pleasure you at the same time.

Lance returned to her pussy, eating her like a starving man. He made no attempt to cover his slurping noises or the growls that erupted from his throat. Every time the tip of his tongue came into contact with her clit, she jerked.

Gabe added his fingers on her breasts to the assault. He tweaked and pinched, rolled and pulled, engorging the buds until they were rock hard. When he broke contact between their lips, a tiny sob slipped out of her mouth.

Evan sucked in a breath at the gleam in Gabe's eyes. She glanced down to see the same look in Lance's even as he continued to lap up every millimeter of her pussy. His top lip was covered in her slick juice. It was the most erotic thing she'd ever seen. Her previous lovers had only done such things in the dark.

Gabe chuckled once and latched onto one of the nipples he'd just made stand at attention. Her hands, which had fallen to his shoulders, slipped off to dangle uselessly at her sides.

Lance sealed his lips around her swollen clit and flicked his tongue back and forth, around and around, up and down. The pattern kept her orgasm just out of reach.

Her spine and neck went noodly and she started to fall backward.

The nipple popped from Gabe's mouth. "Whoa, honey." He pulled her forward and rested her forehead on his chest before returning to stroking her breasts.

"Please," she begged. Anything to come. So close...

"Shh. Soon. Lance likes to take his time."

A finger joined Lance's mouth, swirling and getting lubricated in her slick opening. It stabbed into her and she screamed again, loving how it felt in her long-since-used sheath.

Another chuckle sounded above her. Evan didn't care. She was delirious in the sensations bombarding her. If she got punished, she was sure she'd love it too.

She glimpsed down, catching just enough of a peek of Lance to see him add a second finger to the first, stretching and preparing her for, she hoped, their cocks. A second later, he did something so amazing with his tongue, she exploded.

If Gabe hadn't been holding her she'd have flipped over the balustrade and landed on her head. He wrapped his arms around her and soothed her through the most intense orgasm of her life.

Lance's hand tightened on her thigh, keeping her in place, as he continued to taunt her spastic clit until her breathing returned to normal.

Sweat clung to every inch of her naked body. Breathing wasn't easy in the soupy atmosphere of the island anyway, let alone after the climax she'd just had. Now, completely sated, all she wanted to do was take a nap.

Gabe's chest rumbled against her cheek as he scooped her up and started walking with her. "My turn."

Chapter Four

Lance led them to a bungalow set off the main path and hidden behind dense tropical foliage. It was their private residence for when they were on the island, one they'd never brought a guest to, but there was something about Evan. Something he'd felt after seeing her picture and reading her profile. Even then he'd wondered if she might be the one he and Lance had been waiting for. Lance must have felt it too or he would have headed straight for the bungalow assigned to her.

Evan sighed contentedly and melted into Gabe's arms. The woman was more than incredible. Heaven only knew why he felt this way. It wasn't like him to let a woman affect him like this. He and Lance would have to sit down and do some serious talking later, because he for one didn't want to see their time with Evan end.

And he'd only known her for about fifteen minutes. Well, a couple of weeks now, if rereading her profile twenty-nine thousand times counted for anything. Just thinking about the hours he and Lance had spent pouring over her information made his dick hard. It was as if they couldn't help themselves. Something about her had stood out to them like no previous guest had. She was beautiful, yes, but there had been a look in her eyes, a combination of shyness, passion, desire and vulnerability. They could have described her with a million different adjectives based on her picture alone.

The fantasies she'd written about had been concise. She knew what she wanted and they'd liked the determination they could read in her words.

"The bed or the couch?" Lance asked as he unlocked and threw open the door.

"Bed," Gabe grunted. He strode down the short hallway and into their bedroom. A second later he deposited his precious bundle on the edge of the mattress. Lance dropped her clothes in the chair in the corner and then yanked the cords on the blinds. Sunlight flooded the room.

Evan's gaze took in everything from the hooks on all four posts of the bed, to the vast array of toys laid out on a series of shelves on the far wall. She shivered in the air-conditioned room. Her nipples stood out like twin rockets ready to go off at any second.

Gabe reached for the buttons of his fly, drawing her attention. Her nostrils flared with her sharp intake of breath.

"You want to see this, honey?"

She nodded shyly.

"Let me help you." Lance stepped up behind him, and Gabe dropped his hands, never taking his gaze off Evan's face.

Her eyes widened. Lance reached around Gabe's hips and fondled his cock through the thick denim. He hissed out a breath and rested his head on Lance's shoulder. The man handled his cock in the most exquisite way.

A button popped, then a second. Lance slid his thumb over the swollen head of Gabe's dick, spreading the drop of moisture and torturing him. He lifted his hand to the back of Lance's neck and squeezed, telling him without words he wanted more.

Lance lifted his thumb to his mouth and licked off the pearly sheen of pre-come. "I fucking love how you taste," he said, nuzzling his chin into the crook of Gabe's neck and shoulder. He attacked the next few buttons and Gabe's cock sprang free.

Gabe reached for his erection, intent on soothing the pain caused by the massive amount of blood rushing to it, but got his hand slapped instead.

"Mine." Lance wrapped his fingers around the base and tugged, making Gabe's knees weak. "Evan, come over here and get on your knees."

Evan gulped and moved slowly off the bed, as if in a daze, unable to turn away from the scene unfolding in front of her. She'd probably never expected this. Hell, Gabe hadn't expected it. Yeah, he and Lance had fucked and sucked each other dry. No secret there.

What they hadn't done was outed themselves with a guest before they knew for sure the guest was ready to see them this way.

Another drop of come seeped out when Evan knelt to the floor and crawled the distance between them. Her breasts swayed, and her hips made a sensual dance across the few feet. She was the most erotic creature he'd ever met.

After a long, drawn-out prowl, Evan finally reached them and rose up on her knees.

"Link your hands behind your back."

Without hesitating, she did what Lance demanded. The action thrust her beaded nipples forward. Lance tugged again, his hand tight around Gabe's circumference, wringing a groan from him.

"Gabe has a beautiful cock, don't you think?" His hand traversed the length with a slow, meant-to-make-Gabe-suffer fist.

"Yes," she whispered, staring at it like she'd never seen one before. Her tongue darted out to lick her lips and Gabe's heart nearly stopped.

Lance's erection pressed into Gabe's thigh. At least he wasn't alone in this anguish.

"That's it, sweetheart. Get those lips nice and wet." Lance's fist constricted over the mushroom-shaped head before sliding back down.

"Move closer." Lance nudged Gabe's feet, spreading his legs, and reached between his thighs to cup his balls. His fingers rolled them and pulled with the perfect amount of pressure to make Gabe's breath catch in his throat and his eyes roll.

"Suck his cock." The guttural command made Evan jump. She leaned forward and Lance guided the purpled head between her sweet lips.

"Fuck," Gabe groaned.

Her tongue lapped over the velvet skin. He wanted to take a hold of her head and fuck her mouth. Instead, Lance slapped Gabe's cock against her chin and lips, teasing him. Gabe hissed. Another pull on his balls had him standing on his tiptoes.

"Stand still, Gabe." Lance licked his ear and bit at the lobe. "She can't suck it if you're jumping all around."

"Fuck you," he panted.

Lance chuckled. "Later." He released Gabe's cock and twisted Evan's hair in his fingers to guide her back onto the rigid length. "That's it, Evan, suck it."

Her lips pressed over the head and sucked as if he were a straw. "Jesus Christ," Gabe bellowed, rocking back on his heels.

"More," Lance ordered.

She took more. Nearly half. Her cheeks sank in as she drew on him. Her mouth was made for fucking. Just like he knew instinctively her pussy would be. Gabe thrust his hips until he touched the back of her throat. For a second she gagged, then controlled it by breathing through her nose. Her eyes never closed and nothing on her face showed she didn't want exactly what she was doing. He backed off, giving her the freedom to set whatever pace she desired.

"Make him come, sweetheart." Lance still held her head, but Gabe could see she was the one doing the moving, not Lance.

She took all she could and withdrew, pausing to swirl her tongue around the tip before plunging again. The parry-and-retreat dance had Gabe ready to explode in seconds.

"His balls are drawing up tight, Evan. He's ready to come. Can you swallow?"

Her gaze searched his, not in fear or disgust, but almost...permission?

Gabe nodded, his teeth clenched, fighting to hold his orgasm at bay.

She slurped him in again and held him there against the back of her throat. Her tongue and cheeks worked at him. They didn't need to.

Gabe let out a hoarse cry. Lance still grasped his nuts. His come shot down her throat as she sucked him dry, leaving him panting and shaking where he stood.

Chapter Five

Evan stared at the bamboo-looking ceiling fan and sighed, more content than she'd ever been. Who knew coming here to be doted upon sexually could be so...*fandamntastic.*

When she and Kiley had left St. Louis to come to the secret island, her dreams had been nothing like this. A little slap and tickle sure, but not blow-your-mind, wham-bam-thank-you-ma'am, now let's do it again.

For the first time since arriving several hours ago, she wondered how Kiley was faring. Surely not as well as her because, holy crap, Gabe and Lance knew how to please a woman. And she was damn glad she'd changed her mind at the last second when filling out those forms. Putting down her fantasies of not only being with two men but also submitting to them, had seemed monumentally over-the-top embarrassing at the time.

Now? Whoa, momma.

Her nose itched. Of course. Why wouldn't it? She turned and rubbed it on her upper arm. Not an easy task with her arms stretched above her head and secured to the headboard.

In fact, her nose wasn't the only thing bothering her. A few more minutes and her bladder was going to protest in a not-so-pretty way.

After tying her wrists, Gabe and Lance had left her, saying they'd be back. Hadn't said when though. She made a popping sound with her lips and returned to studying the room.

The fan above should have created at least a stir in the air. It did nothing in the soupiness that made up Fantasm Island.

Besides the charming, hotel, island-resort-type fan, the rest of the room screamed, "I am man", which was a little more than strange. She expected a more generic setup. This room felt lived-in, not occupied by a different guest each week.

Personal items adorned the dresser in a disheveled manner. A piece of cloth stuck out of a drawer, keeping it from closing all the way, and nothing felt like it got a daily maid cleaning.

What the hell kind of place was this? Okay, to give the guys credit, Evan normally hung the "Do Not Disturb" sign so the maids would leave her stuff alone, but she couldn't ever remember actually taking her stuff out of her suitcases and putting them away in the drawers. They must have brought her to their own room instead of hers.

Evan twisted her wrists in the satin-lined shackles and wriggled her body on the silk sheets. Normally they would feel heavenly on her naked skin. Right now, they sucked. She was sweaty, not only from the one-hundred-and-sixty-degree heat from hell, but also the raunchy lovemaking she'd been subjected to. Every fiber stuck to her body instead of sliding sensuously against it.

The door opened and her heart thudded in anticipation. Bad. Very bad. She shouldn't be feeling anything for either one of these men. Not when she would never see them again after this week. Okay, so that wasn't exactly true. She should feel sheer gratitude toward them. She should hit her knees and bow while exclaiming, "God bless you for making me feel so goddamn good."

"Time for a little snack, sweetheart." Lance entered the room, kicked a stray shoe out of the way and laid his burden on the nightstand. It was a tray filled with the most delicious-looking fruits, cheeses, crackers, and some kind of dip, she guessed, in small ceramic cups. Her stomach rumbled.

"I think our little sexpot is hungry." Gabe laughed, joining Lance beside the bed.

Odd how normally Evan would be totally mortified lying here in the buff, tied to the bed and being stared at by two men. She found it hard to be when their appreciation of her body was clearly written on their faces. Nor was she the least bit embarrassed by their chosen bisexual lifestyle. Hell, she hadn't felt anything but absolute excitement when Lance had taken hold of Gabe's cock earlier.

It was fucking erotic seeing two men who obviously loved each other, touching each other sexually. The way Lance had handled Gabe was reverent, not play. Evan could see no one would ever come between them in the simple way they looked at each other. At one point she'd seen that gaze directed at her... She mentally shook her head, clearing the ridiculous notion they wanted more from her than this week.

She would never have guessed they were gay in a million years, but if they wanted her to share in their experiences, who was she to stop it? Her pussy clenched just thinking about them together. She wanted to see them do more than touch. She wanted to be a *part* of them doing more than touching.

First things first. She was almost afraid to ask, but damn it, she had to pee.

"Um, is there any way I could...you know?" She jerked her chin in the direction of the bathroom she saw through an open door.

Lance picked up a piece of ripe, orange melon and sucked the juice off it.

Shit. She squirmed, trying to rub her clit with her thighs. Nothing happened. She needed fingers. Or a tongue. If he was going to do things like suck the juice off fruit, then he damn well better be sucking the juice off her clit soon too.

"Damn, honey, I'm sorry." Gabe leaned over her and unlocked the shackles.

Evan couldn't resist. His nipples were right there, why should she? She poked her tongue out and flicked at the brown disc. His breath hissed, but he stayed where he was for another moment, giving her the chance to kiss the now-distended nipple.

She saw Lance's hand come between them and watched his fingers work on the opposite nipple. Gabe moaned. He dropped his head and Evan seized hold of his hair with her freed hands. She pressed her open mouth to his chest and worked that nipple for all it was worth.

Lance's hand moved and suddenly it was tugging on her nipple. She let go of Gabe. He stood, a grin tugging at his lips, and reached for her hands to pull her into a sitting position.

"I believe I should spank you for that."

"We'll add it to the list of offenses." Lance stared at the nipple he pulled toward him.

The slight pain had her womb clenching. She couldn't take her eyes off the sight either. He twisted and pinched, reddening the tip and bringing it just to the edge of painful before retreating then starting again.

Nipple play had never done it for her before. She just hadn't gotten the attraction. They were boobs. So what was men's fascination with them?

If he didn't touch the other one soon, she'd kill him.

Lance lifted the weight of her breast in his fingers and smoothed his thumb over the skin. "Go use the bathroom and then we'll feed you," he said softly.

She shivered at the tender look on his face.

God, please tell her she wasn't falling in love with two men she'd only met a very short time ago.

Chapter Six

Gabe had just finished gathering the supplies he needed when Evan stepped tentatively out of the bathroom. Her skin glowed in the sunlight. She must have freshened up a bit because when he'd released her from the bed, her skin had been coated with dry sweat.

"Come." Lance beckoned her with his tone of voice alone. Gabe nearly dropped the butt plug he held and went to him too. The man could have the most dominating tone at times. His cock stiffened.

Evan's chin lifted and she strode over to Lance. Good girl. She wanted this, otherwise her steps would be shy, her demeanor subdued.

Lance offered a bite of juicy pineapple which Evan took none too shyly. They laughed as she inhaled the fruit and licked her lips.

She smiled. "Sorry. I was hungry."

"I can see that." Lance patted the space beside him on the mattress and proceeded to feed her, alternately giving her bites and nibbling on her lips.

Gabe joined in, dipping the fruit into the creamy concoction and rubbing it on her nipples, then licking it off. She tasted better than anything on their tray. When they were through,

Evan was wet between her thighs and practically begging to be taken.

"On the bed on your elbows and knees. I want that tight little ass of yours in the air."

Evan swallowed, her eyes round when she looked at Gabe and saw what he had in his hand. He had to give her credit for overcoming her initial reaction of uncertainty. She turned and climbed on the bed.

Lance crawled up after her and planted his gorgeous naked self by her head, spreading his legs on either side. When she lifted her gaze, she stared at almost nine inches of perfect, rock-hard cock.

"It's my turn to feel your pretty mouth on my cock."

"Mmm-hmm."

He tucked the hair falling in her face behind her ear and stroked her cheek. "While you're sucking me off, Gabe is gonna start preparing your ass to be fucked."

Gabe heard her breath hitch from where he stood several feet away. Her glance jerked to him, partially panicked, partially intrigued.

"Eyes on me, sweetheart." Lance had his hand wrapped around his thick erection—the same erection Gabe loved being fucked with—idly stroking its length.

He knew exactly what Evan would feel and taste when she finally took it in her mouth. Gabe's cock jumped. He palmed it and spread the drop of pre-come over the swollen head.

Evan's tiny puckered asshole called to him as her hips wiggled when she bent to take Lance's cock.

"Fuck yeah," Lance ground out, watching her face as she went down on him.

Gabe knelt between Evan's feet, spreading her knees farther apart. The sweet scent of her drenched pussy wafted up to him. He couldn't resist pushing his fingers into her channel and then bringing those digits to his lips to taste her. Damn, but she was the sweetest thing.

He caught Lance's look over her shoulder and sucked her cream from his fingers. Lance's eyes glazed and he inhaled sharply.

Gabe swiped his spit-laden finger down her crease and pressed against the dark pink hole. She whimpered, but leaned back, silently asking for more.

The tight ring fought the intrusion. Gabe laid a hand on the small of her back. "Relax, honey. Let me get this in you and I'll fuck you nice and slow."

She moaned.

"Ah fuck," Lance spat.

Gabe chuckled. The vibrations of her mouth must have felt good on Lance's cock.

"Push out, baby, let me in."

Evan thrust against him and the tip of his forefinger slipped past the natural barrier. So fucking snug. She'd eat his cock alive whenever he took her there.

She clamped down on him when he tried to move, blocking his way.

"Every time you do that, I will spank you. Relax." He smoothed his hand over her butt cheek, showing her just where he'd lay a smack.

Lance tugged on her hair. "Stop thinking about your ass and suck my cock, Evan."

That did the trick. She went to work on Lance, and Gabe withdrew to pick up the lube and the plug. Evan gave a little sound of distress and maneuvered back toward him.

"Not goin' anywhere," he murmured. He slathered a good amount of lube on the thick, hard plastic plug that measured about an inch and a half in diameter. He could have started smaller. Would have, if he'd been at home and had a lot of time to train her to take something in her back door. As it was, he had less than a week now, and this was something she'd stated on her forms she wanted.

No fucking way would he deny her this or anything else she had on her list.

Gabe jerked his gaze to Lance. His lover had his lips pressed together and his hands white-knuckled in her hair as she moved up and down on him. She took an impressive amount of cock in her mouth.

Did he feel anything beyond the sweet suction of her lips? Could he sense like Gabe could that she might be the one they'd been waiting to find?

Her hips squirmed into his erection, reminding Gabe what he was supposed to be doing. He edged the lube to her opening and squeezed. She squeaked and jumped, dislodging Lance from the back of her throat to stare at him with shocked, wide eyes over her shoulder.

"Hey, come back here." Lance tugged her head back down with a petulant look on his face. Gabe smiled.

He held her still with a hand on her back and worked the dildo in slow increments into the puckered opening. Evan helped by pushing against it, effectively drawing it in. She groaned as the entire length settled inside her, and her hands fisted in the sheets. Gabe stared at the flared base, mocking him with its position. He wanted to be the one sunk into her depths.

Soon. For now he'd settle for her pussy instead.

"Getting close here, Gabe," Lance panted.

Close? Fuck, he was about to come just looking at her ass up in the air.

Gabe snagged a condom from his stash on the bed and rolled it on before lining his cock up with her pussy and thrusting home. Evan sighed as if she were more than familiar with the fullness. Unbelievable. She'd been tighter than a fist even without the plug. He didn't want to move. He wanted to stay planted inside her sheath for an eternity.

Another scary thought. He'd never thought this way with any other woman. Evan was going to change his and Lance's lives forever. He could feel it.

He pulled back, working against her as she tried to keep him inside by contracting her vaginal muscles, and slammed in again.

Gabe felt like a horny teenager, ready to climax after two thrusts.

Fuck it. He grabbed her hips and drove into her. She grunted with each shove and didn't need to work on sucking Lance. The force of his movement was enough to make Lance's eyes roll back.

He reached under and flicked at her clit. The little bud was standing up proudly. His touch was all it took to set Evan off.

And her orgasm was all it took to set him off, which lit Lance up like a Roman candle.

Minutes later as they lay in a sweaty heap of tangled legs and arms and heaving chests, Gabe leaned over and kissed her cheek just as Lance kissed the other one. Lance's hand stroked the forearm Gabe put on his hip, effectively trapping Evan between them.

The three of them were good together.

Chapter Seven

Evan squirmed in her seat, the unfamiliar fullness of the butt plug wreaking havoc in her mind. This morning, Lance had shoved a bigger size up inside her. Okay, maybe shoved was a little harsh. Especially when he'd topped off sliding that sucker home with one hell of an orgasm.

And what had Gabe been doing while Lance manipulated her ass? Alternately sucking her nipples and Lance's cock. She'd never imagined seeing two men together being so unbelievably erotic, but holy crap. They could touch each other any time they wanted to in her presence.

"My God, Evan, is this not the most fantabulous place in the galaxy?" Kiley dropped the little purse she never left home without and gingerly sat in the chair next to Evan.

Good. Looked like she wasn't the only one getting her ass worked over.

"So which one did ya get? I heard that some of the guests got two. Can you believe it?"

Evan slouched into her chair and popped back up when the plug slid deeper. In a minute she'd be able to pull it out of her throat.

"You got plugged too didn't you?" Kiley laughed. "The look on your face is priceless."

"If mine is, so is yours, Ki."

"Don't I know it." Kiley squirmed in her seat. "I'm used to it though. Remember, what's-his-face used to like screwing me there." Her face scrunched up in distaste.

Evan chuckled. "If you didn't like it, why'd you let the redhead do it?"

"Are you kidding me? I'll let Zach do anything he wants. The man is pure magic with his hands. And his mouth. And his ginormous cock." Kiley squirmed again. "Damn it," she snarled. "I'm not supposed to touch myself but just thinking about him makes me tingle all over."

Crossing her legs, Evan groaned and dropped her head back. "Did you have to mention tingling?"

"You're not allowed to touch either, are you? I knew this would be good for you. You needed to get out of your stupid little vanilla zone."

"I can assure you that nothing your friend has done could be considered vanilla," Gabe rumbled from behind her.

With a gasp, Evan twisted in her seat. Both Gabe and Lance had arrived.

"Ladies." Lance nodded at Kiley. "Spread your legs, Evan," he said without even bothering to turn to her. Lance sat at her left side. Gabe snagged a chair from a neighboring table and slipped it between her and Kiley, sandwiching Evan.

Her cheeks heated as her knees fell apart of their own volition.

"Jesus, Ev, you are seriously holding out on me." Kiley leaned around Gabe to stare at Evan with wide eyes. "Did I not just say some guests got two guys? Why didn't you just say, yeah, me."

"Because you didn't shut up long enough for me to answer you," Evan replied sweetly. One of Lance's big hands settled on the back of her neck and caressed gently. Her eyes slid shut and she melted into the bliss. "Uhn. Keep doing that," she begged.

He stopped. She whimpered.

"What was that, sweetheart?" His breath feathered over her ear giving her a shiver.

Damn. She should have known to keep her big mouth shut. It just felt so good. A slow rub on her neck or in her hair had always been the most relaxing thing to her. Now she'd probably never get it again. And she was pouting.

Great.

Eyes still closed, Evan felt a hand on each thigh.

"I believe she asked you not to stop," Gabe mused.

Lance snorted. "She didn't ask." He nipped at her earlobe. "She begged." He traveled his hand up her belly to rest it on her breast. His thumb flicked idly across her nipple.

Evan bit her lip. Heaven help her she needed more.

The cool glide of what smelled like cantaloupe skimmed her lips. "Open your mouth, honey."

She did and Gabe pushed the tiny piece of fruit past her teeth. Before she could bite down he followed the fruit with his lips and tongue, licking the juice from her lips. Evan opened her eyes just in time to see Lance move in too. Their mouths met in a three-for-all and her womb clenched.

A tight pinch to her nipple had her moaning aloud as she chewed and swallowed the small piece of melon.

"Holy shit, you guys are hot." Kiley's exclamation jerked Evan back to reality.

Mortified, she swung her gaze around the room. She squeaked when Gabe's hand journeyed to her core and his finger slipped inside.

"Shh," he soothed and burrowed deeper, bumping against the plug and drawing her cream out. His thumb circled her swollen clit, bringing her so close to orgasm.

No way could she have one here. Not in front of all these people eating breakfast. Her screaming would most definitely garner attention.

"Please don't—"

Lance covered her mouth with his, cutting her off.

"Stop?" Gabe laughed. "I won't."

She tried to squeeze her thighs shut but they prevented her by trapping each knee with one of their own. "Uh-uh," Gabe whispered. "Right here, right now."

"I can't," she hissed.

"You can and you will." Lance added his fingers at her pussy. They took turns filling her with their fingers and plucking her clit until she couldn't stand it any longer.

"It was one of your fantasies, sweetheart. To be made to come in public. Relax."

Who the hell had held a gun to her head? She'd kill them for making her write this fantasy.

Of course, she'd have to kill herself then, because no one other than her own inner voice had forced her to write the words. Her breathing grew more erratic with each passing second.

"Come for us."

She exploded, screaming out and thrusting her hips into their hands like a sex fiend.

Evan slumped in the chair when Gabe and Lance pulled their hands from beneath her skirt, smug looks on both their faces. If she weren't breathing so hard or so exhausted she'd tell them what they could do with those smug lips.

Bastards.

"I thought I told you not to touch yourself, Kiley."

Evan glanced up. Zach stood above her friend, practically clucking his tongue at her.

"Oops," Kiley said.

Evan knew she wasn't a bit sorry.

"Suck my cock," the bird squawked and Kiley got up to kneel at Zach's feet.

Chapter Eight

Evan was more beautiful than any woman had a right to be. On her belly sprawled over the bed, one leg bent at the knee, the other straight, her hair spread out across the pillow. Gabe's gut twisted, and his cock hardened. How could he possibly need her again? And he did *need* her. His desire had long since passed the want mark.

"What are we going to do, Gabe?" Lance stood in the doorway, hands holding the top frame. The position pushed his chest forward, accentuating his pecs.

For a minute, Gabe stared at the man who meant more than anything to him. As a quasi-brother, a friend and a lover. Lance had been with him through thick and thin. Now they faced one of the biggest decisions of their life.

He glanced back at Evan. Was there any way in hell she'd agree to their offer?

"She's perfect for us. You know that, right, Gabe?" Lance murmured, keeping his voice low so he didn't disturb her.

Gabe nodded. "Question is, how do we tell her?"

Lance cracked the length of his spine before letting go of the doorframe and sauntering over, his erection tenting the seam of his loose shorts. With one of his long arms, he traced the tiny bones along Evan's back from her neck to the crease of her ass.

Evan moaned in her sleep and tucked herself into a ball to ward off the obvious chill Lance's fingers left behind. Tiny goose bumps prickled her smooth skin and Gabe smiled.

"She's fucking gorgeous," Lance growled softly. He looked up and snagged Gabe's gaze. "You are too." He reached out and took hold of the back of Gabe's neck to pull him closer.

Gabe didn't hesitate. This was Lance. Their lips met, their tongues danced. Gabe wrapped one hand around Lance's hip to steady him. The other one went to his cock. He covered the thick length through the cotton, squeezing with the exact amount of pressure he knew Lance liked so much. This is why they'd never taken on a male client. Each of them felt to do so would somehow be akin to cheating. They were looking for a woman, not another man.

Lance groaned and dropped his forehead to Gabe's shoulder. His hands came around Gabe's back in a tight hug, leaving just enough room between them for Gabe to manipulate Lance's shorts and uncover the hard cock he held.

"Fuck, I need you inside me," Lance hissed.

"Yeah," Gabe kissed along his jawline. "Me too, I want that."

"Couch?"

"Fuck no." He gave a firm tug on Lance's cock, making the other man's knees nearly buckle. "Here. We'll know one way or the other if she can't stand who we are when she wakes up."

"You're right." Lance nuzzled his cheek on Gabe's then slid his hands down to slip off Gabe's shorts.

When they'd each divested the other of their scant clothes, they fell on the bed at Evan's feet. Lance landed on his back and settled Gabe between his legs, wrapping them around his waist. They thrust against each other.

"Now, Gabe."

"Then you gotta let me up so I can get the lube," Gabe hissed.

Lance nodded and reluctantly released him. A few seconds later Gabe returned, already slicking the velvet smooth skin of his cock. The tip glistened with pre-come and Gabe watched as Lance swallowed, a shit-eating grin on his face.

Lance grabbed hold of his knees and pulled back, spreading himself. His asshole puckered, beckoning Gabe like nothing else. Except for Evan now. He turned his head and glanced at the woman quickly filling the strange void in his and Lance's life.

"You're killing me here, Gabe." Lance's hoarse words demanded his attention.

He knelt between Lance's thighs and lined himself up with the heaven he knew he'd find tunneled deep inside Lance's body.

"Do it," Lance snarled. "Quit fucking staring at me and do it."

Gabe smiled. Lance tended to get a little anxious when it came to this. He liked it quick and hard. There was no doubt in Gabe's mind Evan would be awake before either one of them came.

He thrust home. Lance threw his head back and fisted the sheets. Gabe took Lance's cock in hand and mimicked the action of his hips. Fast and furious. Lance and him were record setters when it came to fucking each other. Each knew how the other liked it best.

Gabe pressed in, withdrew, pressed in, aiming for the sweet spot deep inside, but staying just out of reach. It pissed Lance off no end, but made it that much better when he finally did hit it. He looked down between them. Lance's balls were drawn up tight, his breath coming in shallow pants, his eyes squeezed shut.

He was close. And so was Gabe.

Gabe hammered into Lance making him shout and arch his back. Sweat dripped from his forehead and coated his chest.

"Oh, fuck," Lance yelled, his neck corded in what looked like pain. Gabe knew better.

He flicked at a distended nipple and Lance's head shot off the bed.

"I'm gonna come, Gabe."

Gabe smiled. "Was there ever any doubt?" he gasped.

He slammed into Lance's ass once more, driving them both across the bed, and came in long hot spurts, coating his passage. A millisecond later, Lance shouted and Gabe found his chest splashed with what he knew to be salty-sweet come. Still embedded in Lance's body, he collapsed onto him. Neither could move.

"The next time you do that, I better be between you."

Gabe jerked his gaze to Evan to see her wide-eyed and staring at them. Her nipples were taut and ripe as berries, and she leaned on one elbow.

Lance grinned. "Anytime, darlin'."

Looked like they had their answer.

Chapter Nine

Shit. Shit, shit, shit. Evan hadn't meant to say those words out loud. From the looks on their faces she was about to get it. Whatever *it* was.

Gabe's smile stretched wide. He carefully withdrew from Lance's body, leaning over to kiss his lips when Lance hissed at the extraction.

"Damn. I fucking hate when you pull out."

Gabe laughed. "We'd look a little stupid walking around with my cock stuck up your ass."

Evan's pussy clenched picturing it. Hell, she had a gay friend. The lifestyle had never bothered her in the least bit. Richard and his lover were very open in front of her but she'd never witnessed anything like Gabe and Lance together.

They were truly made for one another. Both athletic, gorgeous and one-hundred-percent alpha. Any woman in the world would kill to have a shot at just one of them. Yet here she was, naked, in their bed. She had to wonder why they did this.

"Fuck each other?" One of Gabe's eyebrows shot up.

Shit. She'd done it again.

Lance's hand stroked Gabe's hip. Evan watched, mesmerized by those long fingers, remembering them deep inside her vagina, and groaned.

"No," she murmured, looking back up to Gabe's face. "This." She gestured around the room. Lance sat up, curling himself around Gabe's back and lazily fondling his lover's softened cock. It didn't stay soft long. Evan licked her lips.

Gabe's breath hitched audibly and his hand curved around Lance's thigh. Evan found herself wanting more than anything to be a part of what they had. What would happen when she had to leave in a few days? Somehow she knew a section of her heart would be left behind.

Gabe shrugged and let out a strangled gurgle when Lance rubbed his thumb over the tip of his cock. A heartbeat later Gabe reversed their positions so Lance was sitting between his legs. He mimicked what Lance had been doing to him by taking hold of Lance's quickly hardening erection.

"My uncle owns it," Gabe breathed. Lance arched into Gabe's chest, spreading his legs to give him better access to his balls.

Caught up in watching them, Evan did a double take. "So you do this just because you can? I'd think any woman in the world would jump to take you both on." She shot her gaze back to Gabe's wandering fingers. Lance tilted his hips. His heels dug into the mattress between her feet when Gabe touched the rim of his still slightly open asshole.

"Not looking...for just...anyone," Lance panted.

Gabe bit down on Lance's shoulder and pressed the tip of his finger inside his anus.

"What does that mean?" Evan asked, gaze glued to the scene before her.

"Come here, Evan."

She jumped at the command in Gabe's voice, but moved nonetheless, scooting her butt across the couple of feet that separated them. He'd done a damn good job of changing the subject.

"Spread your legs and put them over ours."

She did, forming a diamond between them. She smelled her juices and was tempted to touch herself.

"Uh-uh," Gabe growled. "Ours." His hand never stopped moving on Lance's cock, making it longer, thicker, harder.

Evan felt her ears go red. How did he know?

"Move closer. I want to watch you fuck Lance like this. Up," he urged, helping her to sit on their outstretched thighs until Lance's cock lined up with her pussy.

Gabe let go of Lance's length. He hissed out a breath, watching Gabe trail his fingertips through her slit, testing her, making sure she was ready.

Evan leaned back, ready to brace herself on Lance's knees.

"No," Gabe barked, then softened. "Come forward. Put your hands on his shoulders."

"Let me—"

"Shh..." Gabe cut Lance off with a finger across his lips. "I'm in control here." He slid his hand down Lance's throat, over his chest and toyed with one nipple.

Evan bit her lip. Harder when Gabe lifted his hand from her sopping pussy to ring one of her nipples with her cream.

"Scoot up a bit. Let me guide his cock into you," Gabe whispered.

She shifted so she was on her knees and raised her hips. Lance's cock nudged her entrance. Gabe directed the fat head through her slippery folds and slapped it against her clit. Every muscle in her vagina spasmed in response.

"Come down slowly."

Evan lowered herself inch by agonizing inch, impaling her body on Lance's.

"Look at that, Lance. Watch her sweet pussy sucking you in."

Lance's nostrils flared with each harsh breath, and his belly quivered. "Fuck yeah."

"Ride him, Evan."

Evan rose up on her knees and started pumping her hips, stroking his penis in a nice, even rhythm.

"That's it, baby. Feels good doesn't it, Lance?"

With every downward movement, the thick head of his erection bumped against her g-spot. She pursed her lips. There wasn't enough friction on her clit though. She needed more, her fingers, something.

Gabe read her mind again. His thumb settled on the tiny bundle of nerves, not moving, just pressing. Sliding up and down against it was enough.

"Her little clit is like a rock, Lance. She's gonna explode soon."

She watched Gabe nip at Lance's ear. Her breathing nearly drowned out his words. She dropped her head back and upped the pace. Lance's thighs were solid beneath hers, the muscles taut.

"I'm gonna come," Lance cried.

"Not yet." Gabe surrounded the base of Lance's cock with his finger and thumb and squeezed. The action prevented Evan from taking all of his length as well as prolonging Lance's agony.

Sweat beaded his forehead and chest.

"Gabe," he snarled.

Still cupping Lance, Gabe returned his thumb to her clit. Sparks ignited in her womb and seconds later, Evan screamed her release, slamming down one last time and holding herself rigid while her pussy pulsed around the cock deep inside.

"Now you can come," she heard Gabe command and then Lance shouted too.

Thick jets of semen splashed her womb. Evan curled into Lance's chest and Gabe's arms came around both of them, hugging them close. She and Lance were breathing heavily but she swore she heard Gabe say, "I love you. Both of you."

Chapter Ten

Rays of sunlight filtered through the palm trees, kissing Evan's mostly bare skin, adding to the already stifling heat on the island. A giggle followed by a squeal sounded from the far end of the pool drawing her attention yet again. The couple had been going at it, making lazy love for a good thirty minutes now.

And for twenty-nine of those minutes, Evan had been peeking at them from behind her sunglasses. She wondered when she'd become such a voyeur.

No, she didn't. She knew exactly when it happened. The second she'd walked into Fantasmagorical Resort and seen all those warm, semi-naked bodies, she'd transformed into some sex-starved addict. Watching other people *in flagrante delicto* was a high like no other. Okay, not as high as some of the orgasms she'd had at the hands of Gabe and Lance but still, a heady feeling.

Evan sighed and dropped her head back. What the hell was she going to do about them? There were only two days left before she had to leave Fantasm Island and she was nowhere near ready to let go.

What exactly did she want though? To take this relationship back home? To stay another week until she'd fucked them out of her system? Did she even have any options?

The rules expressly stated that guests were forbidden from trying to contact their matches after their stay.

Was it different for the owner's nephew? Isn't that what he'd said? "My uncle owns it." Which led her down another path. What in the shit were they doing here? Getting their jollies fucking a different woman each week, more than likely. They didn't seem to be the type though.

Demanding, coercive and outright male, yes, but in it just to get their rocks off? She didn't believe it. They could do that anyway with as potent as they were.

Evan couldn't help but think she'd never find anyone else who made her feel so...whole. How had it happened? She'd come here to relax, indulge in a no-strings-attached affair, find out what non-vanilla sex was really like.

In her heart, she had never expected to not want to leave when the week was up.

She thought back to their last time in bed. Sticky with sweat and come, smelling of sex and clinging to each other, she swore she'd heard Gabe mutter, "I love you, guys. Both of you."

A figment of her imagination? Hearing what she wanted to hear?

Evan wiped the tiny droplets of sweat from her belly and off her shoulders and arms.

"Might as well be in a sauna," she muttered.

"You got that right, Ev. Damn it's hot. Shoulda stayed inside."

Evan laughed as her friend sat in the lounge chair beside her. "Zach finally let you out?"

She sniffed. "He didn't have a choice. He got called to some kind of employee meeting. Something about switching up the matches at tonight's mixer."

Evan's heart thudded, and her stomach rolled. "Switch it up? What the hell does that mean?" She swung her legs to the side and sat up.

Kiley shrugged. "I wasn't privy to anything else. I wouldn't mind doing something a little different for one night though. That is why we came here you know. To partake in our fantasies. Besides, you got two guys. I wouldn't mind having a threesome."

Evan knew she looked like a fish with her mouth opening and closing the way it was. What could she say? Kiley was right. Still didn't make Evan want to share her guys with anyone else. Tonight or any other night.

Whoa. Time to step back and look at the big picture. She was on an island somewhere in the Caribbean having fantastic sex with two men she'd never met before. In two days, she'd go home to St. Louis to her boring job as a buyer for a car leasing company. There'd be no more mind-blowing orgasms or commands to suck a cock.

Instead she'd be forced to endure plain old vanilla sex whenever she could find it with some date she met at a gathering of friends.

Suddenly, her life looked bleak. Evan stared at her hands in her lap and willed her eyes to stop watering.

"You're right," she said, lifting her chin and squaring her shoulders. "We came here to have outrageous sex, and we've done that. In spades."

"So spill. What's it like to do two guys at the same time."

Evan smiled. "It's the most incredible—"

"Suck my cock."

Kiley dropped her chin to her chest and Evan laughed. "Does that bird say anything else?"

"No," Kiley answered, flexing her jaw. "And if it weren't for the fact that Zach reciprocates most deliciously, I'd kill it."

When Kiley made no move to drop to her knees, Evan turned, looking for Zack. "Where is he?"

"The bird?" She pointed to a tree near the door. "Over there."

"Ah, so he squawks even when his owner isn't around."

"Yes. So three more days, huh, then back to the grindstone."

Evan flopped back down, covering her eyes with one arm. "I guess so." She nearly choked on the words.

"What's wrong? I had to practically drag you here and now you don't want to leave? The sex must be spectacular."

"It's not just the sex." She groaned. Besides, the sex was way more than spectacular. More on pace with a nuclear explosion. "It's like I feel a...connection with them."

"What?" Kiley squeaked and transplanted herself from her lounger to practically on top of Evan. "You like one of them?"

Evan cringed. She could hear the excitement in her friend's voice. She'd never live this down.

"No." That much was true. She didn't like one of them. She liked both of them. And the like was bordering on something far more complex. Damn it. She wished she'd heard exactly what Gabe had said.

"Oh," Kiley said, dejected.

"I like them both."

"Aahhh."

Evan jumped at Kiley's girly squeal.

"I knew it. I could see it in you the other day."

"Great. I wonder how many other people can see it in me."

Chapter Eleven

"No. Hell no," Gabe yelled, his neck corded.

"Fucking hell no," Lance agreed.

"Boys, it's not up to you. Maybe Evan wants something different. You've got to let her make her own choice."

Gabe scowled at his uncle Silus across the room. "And if she doesn't want it?"

His uncle sighed and slumped deeper into his seat, throwing his pencil on the desk. "You've never questioned my rules before, Gabe. What's different now?"

Gabe looked at Lance and they both turned to his uncle.

"She's..."

"She's what?" the older man barked.

Lance dropped into the chair across from Fantasmagorical's owner. Gabe watched his lover and best friend eye the man who'd practically raised Gabe as his son instead of a nephew when Gabe's dad had died way too young. Silus had treated Lance the same way since Gabe and Lance had met in the first grade. They'd been closer than two friends were meant to be from day one and Silus had supported them both even after they'd shared with him their true feelings for each other.

"She's different," Lance said simply.

Gabe's uncle snorted. "I see." He sat forward and folded his hands in front of his mouth. "Different how?"

Gabe cleared his throat. "Different in that we want to keep her." No use keeping it a secret. "You've known from the get-go Lance and I were looking for a third. We both think Evan is the one."

Silus looked between his nephew and Lance. "And what does she have to say about this?"

Gabe sighed and dropped his head back to stare at the ceiling. What did she have to say? How the hell would they know? So far they hadn't exactly delved too deeply into their backgrounds with her. She didn't know they were searching for the one woman who would complete their lives and thereby fill a void. "We haven't really asked her yet," Lance answered, saving Gabe from the task.

"Hm." The grandfather clock in the corner ticked loudly in the otherwise silent room. "You know it's in the contract—all three of you signed, by the way—that there is to be no further contact off the island. It saves our guests from possible, *uncomfortable* situations when they leave."

Gabe nodded, Lance grunted. They both knew this.

"So do you think she'd be amenable to an arrangement outside this resort? Because I've got to tell you boys, I don't want a lawsuit brought against me because my own nephew can't keep his paws off a woman." He slapped his hand on the desk, catching the lead of the pencil and causing it to flip into the air. It landed on the carpet about five feet away.

All three men stared at the point where it stabbed into the ground, eraser end up.

"Your mother would kill me if you had a restraining order brought up against you, Gabe."

Gabe shifted his gaze. "Evan wouldn't do that."

"How do you know, boy?"

Lance bailed him out again. "We don't, for sure. We're going on our instincts here, and you know as well as we do they've never been wrong before."

Silus audibly growled and his lip curled up on one corner. "I don't know," he wavered.

"There's nothing to know about, Uncle Silus. We know she's the one we want."

"And if she doesn't want you, what will you do? Kidnap her? You can't make someone love you, Gabe."

Lance cleared his throat. "I don't think we'll need to make her love anybody. I think she already does."

Gabe jerked his head toward Lance. What did he know? Lance gave him a subtle nod, an indication they would talk later. First they had to get off Uncle Silus' radar.

"Hmph. She said those words to you, boy? Women tend to be a little touchy when it comes to men telling them how they should feel."

Lance chuckled. Gabe smiled.

"We know that. Evan is no different. She doesn't take shit from either of us," Gabe assured him.

"Unless it's in bed," Lance muttered.

"Good." Silus nodded. "I wouldn't want you with some female who cowed under both of your dominant ways." He sat back again and contemplated them. "Fine. But here's the deal. You have to offer her the opportunity to go tonight to the switch. If she wants to, knowing she'll have a different partner if she does, then I guess you'll have your answer. And," he continued when Lance and Gabe both let out a big breath, "you will tell her what will be happening at the party. You can't just ask her if she wants to go to a party or stay in your room when you've got her distracted and otherwise occupied, if you know what I mean."

"Shit," Gabe snarled.

"Fine." Lance brooded.

"Great. Now get the hell out of my office and leave me in peace."

They stood and headed for the door but not before they heard Silus grumble, "Now I gotta hire two new employees."

Chapter Twelve

Evan knew something was up the second she walked in the door. Gabe was perched on the arm of the sofa, his arms crossed over his chest, and Lance was sprawled in the armchair, legs spread wide, hands behind his head. Both wore a look of serious rumination on their faces.

Her heart pounded. Were they getting ready to tell her they were tired of her? That tonight she would be with some other man?

She steeled herself for the inevitable. They had no hold on her here. They were employees on a resort island for God's sake, not her lovers back in St. Louis. Gabe's uncle had paid them to do a job. A job which required them to be at a different woman's beck and call every other week or so.

Evan wasn't delusional. She had known their relationship would end when the week was over, but damn it, she still had two days left and she sure as shit didn't want to spend them with anyone else.

She wiped her sweaty palms on her shorts and licked her lips, prepared to fight for the right to stay with them. Maybe it was up to her if she wanted to switch. Maybe she was borrowing trouble before she knew the facts.

"Is there a problem?" Evan croaked. She sounded lame even to her own ears.

"There could be," Gabe all but grunted.

Lance held out a hand and crooked a finger. Neither took their eyes off her as she swallowed and walked toward them. She could no more ignore his summons than she could grow wings and fly. Evan stopped when her knees touched his. His hand grasped hers and tugged, throwing her off balance so she landed in his lap.

Only then did Gabe move. He stepped in behind her, sandwiching her between them. He bent and lifted her to tuck her knees between Lance's hips and the arms of the chair. Might have been more awkward if the chair hadn't been so wide, but this felt perfect.

She braced herself with her hands on Lance's chest and glanced back at Gabe. His eyes, like Lance's, were filled with an intense possessiveness. Her breath caught in her throat. How could they look like they did and want to give her away tonight? It didn't make sense.

"We need to talk," Lance said, diverting her attention off Gabe and back to him.

This was it. Her heart sank. She sat back on Lance's knees. *Now's the time to save yourself the humiliation.*

"So, I hear there's a mixer tonight." Evan almost choked on the words. "A little switcheroo."

Lance's eyes widened in disbelief for a split second before narrowing into dangerous slits.

Gabe's hands pressed on her shoulders, bringing her back into contact with his front. His chest rumbled and he dug his thumbs into the tense muscles at the base of her neck. She nearly melted into his touch, but she had to show some bravado here.

If they were going to let her go, she wasn't going to show them how much it hurt. She stiffened and straightened her spine.

Gabe's hands gently pulled her back. "Relax," he whispered.

She could have sworn Lance gave him a visual warning over her shoulder but then the look was gone.

"There is," Lance continued. He steepled his fingers and tapped them against his chin.

Her throat was so dry she could probably spit cotton. His mouth worked, pressing his lips together and apart as if he didn't know how to say what he wanted to.

Evan could do this for them. It might break her heart, but that's where she was headed no matter what. What difference did two days make? The inevitable would happen now or then. Perhaps it was better to get it over with.

"How does it work? Do I get picked out of a lineup, my name pulled out of a hat, what?" Tears threatened to break free from their tenuous hold at her eyelids. Couldn't Lance see how much this was killing her?

Lance's nostrils flared. This time she did not imagine the hurt that crossed his face. Gabe's fingers squeezed into her flesh almost painfully.

"So...this is what you want? You want to go and be fucked by another man? We weren't enough for you?" Lance fisted his hands. His face was pinched in anger.

Evan sucked in a breath at his vehement suggestion. She shook her head sharply one time.

"Lance," Gabe barked.

"How could you say that?" she rasped. The tears fell unchecked. Lance grasped her upper arms. He pulled her forward out of Gabe's hold and hugged her to his chest.

"Christ, I'm sorry, baby." He rubbed his hand along her back.

She could feel him shaking. And then it occurred to her. They didn't want her to leave either. They wanted her to stay but tonight's event was out of their hands. Evan pushed herself up and looked between both her men.

"I don't want to go tonight," she ground out. "I thought you wanted me to, I thought maybe you were tired of me. I know how many girls you go through."

"Jesus," Gabe hissed. "Stand up." He helped her stand in the chair with one foot on either side of Lance's thighs.

Lance's hands wandered the length of her legs as Gabe unfastened her shorts and pulled them down with her bikini bottom. Balancing her, they pulled the offending material off each foot and guided her into Lance's lap again. Next came the shirt and bikini top, leaving her naked between two completely clothed men.

Hmm. Serious case of *déjà vu* from the first day on the balustrade.

"Let's get one thing straight," Lance snarled.

Too late. There were already two things straight. One between her legs and the other pressed into her spine.

"We don't want another man to touch you ever again."

Evan gasped. Lance's hands fumbled with his jeans. Gabe's circled her and toyed with her nipples. She moaned and leaned her head back on his body. Lance slipped a finger through her slit. She clenched her thighs and bit her lip, knowing she was wet.

"And if we ever see another man touching you, things are bound to get ugly." Gabe's teeth found her earlobe and bit. She whimpered. He tugged on her nipples, twisting them and making them hard, beaded pebbles.

Her tummy flipped over. Were they serious? Did they want more than this week like she did? She couldn't think. Not when a long finger slid into her pussy and curled to stroke a sweet spot deep inside her.

"You know, Lance, I don't believe this beautiful woman ever received a punishment this week, do you?"

"I think you're right." Lance's guttural reply made her pussy clench around his finger. She arched her back and lifted her arms around Gabe's neck. A second finger joined the first. Lance thrust them in and out of her, drawing her juices out and spreading it closer and closer to her asshole.

He hadn't touched her clit, but it hummed and begged to be played with. She would explode if he did, she was so sensitized right now.

"Bend over, honey. It's time for me to pinken this pretty little ass of yours."

Evan panicked until she felt Lance's arms around her middle. He brought one to tangle in her hair and his lips touched hers. Then she lost all thoughts of being scared.

A solid smack rent the air followed by a sharp sting. She yelped and tried to pull away but Lance held fast. The burn brought another round of tears to her eyes, but something else she couldn't determine, too.

"That one is for screaming," Gabe said, his hand soothing the hurt away then slipping between her folds to spread her moisture from her clit to her anus.

Another smack to the other side. Her cry this time was caught by Lance's lips where he devoured her mouth. The tingle moved, spreading from her ass to points south. Her pussy flooded. Again, he moved her juices, lingering on her pucker in the back, spearing her with the tip of his finger.

"That one is for touching yourself."

She opened her mouth to protest, but Gabe smacked her ass again.

"Uh-uh, honey. I saw you. Don't lie to me." His breaths came faster and harder. Lance's cock bounced around her nether lips. She tried to trap him there. Lance yanked his hips further into the cushion away from where she wanted it.

Gabe slapped her a fourth time. She hissed as flames licked down her cheeks and zeroed in on her clit. She wiggled her ass back and forth. Anything to get him to slip the hand that soothed onto her pussy another time so he could douse the fire there.

"And that is for thinking we could *ever* let you go," he said grimly.

Her heart soared. She rolled her forehead back and forth on Lance's chest. His hands roamed her bare skin.

"No. I don't think that anymore," she breathed. "Never want you to leave me." She heard the rasp of a zipper and fabric being jerked off, then two hands settled on her abused butt cheeks.

"Can you take us both?" Lance murmured, his hands spreading her cheeks so Gabe could continue preparing her tiny hole. Something cold replaced the heat of her spanking. It had to be lube. She didn't know where it had come from and it didn't matter. They could keep it tucked under the chair for all she cared. As long as it was available when they needed it which, apparently, it was.

Evan nodded vigorously. "Yes, please."

"Sit on my cock, Evan," Lance demanded.

She did, lowering herself until the head of his thick cock lodged inside her pussy. He lifted his hips and brought her down at the same time, impaling her on his entire length. His eyes slid shut, his head fell back on the chair. She clamped down on him and he hissed.

"Do it now, Gabe, I'm not gonna last."

Gabe leaned over them both. One hand rested on the arm of the chair, the other guided his cock to her back entrance. "Deep breath, sweetheart, you can take me. Push back. That's it," he coaxed, working his length into her.

She squirmed and panted until he was seated to the hilt. The pressure was exquisite. She'd never felt so full. There was pain, but not enough to make her want to stop.

Gabe pulled out and pushed back in. Lance pulled out. They built up a rhythm, one in, one out until her eyes lost focus. With the way her body lay, her clit brushed over Lance's belly, but it wasn't enough.

She groaned in frustration and suddenly a fingertip was there, covering her clit and rubbing in tiny little circles.

The three of them moved in accordance like they'd done this a million times. Gabe grunted one last time and slammed into her. Hot splashes of come drenched her colon a second before Lance's bombarded her womb. Yet the finger never stopped on her clit. She exploded around their cocks, milking them of the semen. The hair on Lance's chest abraded her nipples, heaping sensation to an already blinding climax.

Long minutes passed. No one spoke because they couldn't do anything but breathe and feel.

"You're going to be the death of us," Gabe muttered, pulling himself gently out of her ass.

"Nuh-uh," she disagreed. "You, me." Logical sentence structure was beyond her at the moment.

Lance lifted her face to his. "In case you didn't catch this part, we love you and want you to be part of our lives, no matter where we live. We can relocate to your home, wherever that is, you can come to our home in Florida, or we can build anywhere you want. As long as we're together."

The tears came again. Evan nodded, and knew she was smiling like a fool. She didn't care where they lived either. Hell, she hadn't even thought about them having a place somewhere beyond the island. She would have opted to stay here if it was the only way. Computers made it simple to work from just about anywhere. It didn't even matter to her how fast this all had happened, she only knew she couldn't live without them.

"Yes." She laughed, happier than she'd ever been in her whole life. "Yes."

His lips touched hers and then Gabe was there too and the three of them shared a kiss that bound them together forever.

About the Author

Between being a wife, mommy, cleaning woman, chauffer, coach and leader, there are a few minutes left to sneak in some writing time. Annmarie McKenna loves to hear from readers. You can visit her website at www.annmariemckenna.com or her blog at www.annmariemckenna.blogspot.com. Send an email to Annmarie at annmarmck@yahoo.com.

Look for these titles by
Annmarie McKenna

Now Available:

Blackmailed
Seeing Eye Mate
Checkmate
Two Sighted

Coming Soon:

The Strength of Three
Ultimatum
Look What Santa Brought
Mystified

Take Me

Mackenzie McKade

Dedication

To my wonderful critique partners: Jennifer Ray, Kendra Egert, Patti Duplantis and Cheyenne McCray. Thank you!

Chapter One

Cord Daily had only one Achilles' heel—Caitlyn Culver.

Ankles crossed, he leaned against a stack of hay, an alfalfa stem between his teeth. "Really? Cait's back in town." He pulled his black Stetson low over his eyes to hide the smile he fought to restrain.

His pulse hitched. He worked double-time to slow his breathing, even faking a long, drawn-out yawn of disinterest.

Thoughts of the tall brunette with eyes the color of the California sky made this boy's gut twist and his cock stir. For years he had dreamed of tasting her lips, stripping her naked and sampling what lay between those long, slender legs.

Stack Nelson stabbed the two curved metal hooks he held into a bale of hay and heaved it onto the back of his flatbed truck. The bale landed with a dull thud, sending dust and grass particles into the air.

"Yeah. Kendra said Cait called yesterday. She's home for the summer."

"Hmm..." Cord ran his fingers through his close-cropped, blond moustache and goatee.

For years he had lusted for the beauty, who was clearly out of his league. There was something about her. She was different from other women. She had a magnetic personality that drew him like a bug to light.

Yet Cord's—and his older cousin, Dolan's—playboy reputation had reached her daddy's ears in record time. Before Cord could make his move, George Culver had made his own.

How the bastard knew Cord's father's death had left the ranch in financial trouble Cord never discovered.

He had been young and dumb. The threat of destroying his cattle ranch had been enough to keep both him and Dolan away from Cait.

But not Cait from him.

The sweetheart of Culver Creek had set her sights on him. And everyone knew Cait got everything she wanted.

Well, almost everything.

In a surprise turn of events, her father whisked her off to Paris. She'd been gone for nearly two years. Two long years Cord had fought to get her out of his mind.

Stack cleared his throat, drawing Cord's attention. "Not interested?" The tall, lanky man dressed in boots, jeans and a denim shirt glanced at Cord from beneath his straw cowboy hat.

Cord shrugged, chewing nonchalantly on the piece of alfalfa, trying to focus on the sweet grassy flavor and not the woman who had held his attention since she was sixteen. "Maybe—maybe not."

Now at twenty to his twenty-four years, perhaps it was time he and Cait got reacquainted.

"Then you'd be the only cowboy this side of the Rockies not interested in the pride of Culver Creek." Stack drove the hay hooks into another bale and tossed it on the truck. "Hey, there's a bunch of us going to Norton's tonight. Why don't you come?"

Jester Norton opened his spacious basement home for a summer fling to welcome the warm, sultry nights. Just about everyone was invited for a weekend of poker, billiards, dancing, plenty of liquor and several unoccupied bedrooms for those seeking a little extracurricular activity.

Cord pushed away from the stack of hay and brushed leaves from his long-sleeve white shirt and blue jeans. "Maybe."

Stack climbed onto the flatbed and started rearranging the bales close to the cab of the truck. "Buy you a beer."

Cord shuffled his booted feet and pulled his keys out of his pocket. "Offer's sounding better."

"Shot of whiskey?" Stack coaxed with a grin.

"You talked me into it."

Stack pulled his glove off and shook Cord's hand. "Great. Later then."

"Yeah. Later." Cord headed toward his black Chevy dually and climbed in. Key in the ignition, he gave it a twist and the engine roared to life. The pungent scent of diesel filled the air as he jammed the truck into gear. With his elbow resting out the open window, the warm summer wind whipped through the cab, caressing his neck. He turned up the radio, tapping the tune to "Friends in Low Places" with his thumb against the steering wheel, and headed for home.

When Cord topped the hill, several of Culver Creek's red-tile roofs appeared like a beacon. Just the thought of seeing Cait again made his cock swell.

"Look away," he muttered to himself. His ranch's financial status was sound, but Culver was a powerful man.

It was good advice that Cord didn't heed. Instead, when the large wrought-iron archway announced Culver Creek Ranch, he guided his vehicle into the cobblestone driveway.

Jacaranda trees with rich green foliage and clusters of lavender flowers lined both sides of the half-mile long road. Straight ahead was the family's colonial-style home with tall white columns and large vaulted windows. Off to the left was a perfectly groomed racetrack, to the right was just one of four stables on the property.

"Turn around. Not a wise move." But before he could take his advice, Cait stepped out of the house.

His heart stuttered. He shook his head, whispering, "Red."

She looked so sexy in red—red T-shirt and dark blue jeans, red boots to match. A scarlet ribbon held her dark brown, shoulder-length hair into a ponytail that bounced as she crossed the yard and headed toward the stables. It was a huge white barn filled with thoroughbreds—race horses and other family stock.

Culver Creek was an impressive ranch with twenty-four individual corrals, eight small pastures, two ten-acre pastures and ten twenty-acre pastures with run-in sheds.

Unlike his cattle ranch that was half the size.

The pride of his ranch he'd acquired last night in a heated poker game. Cord had goaded Allen Claiborne, a leading horse racer out of Tennessee, into placing Mystery Walker's papers on the table—a two-year-old colt sired by Galaxy, last year's Belmont winner.

Claiborne was so drunk he hadn't known what hit him when Cord laid down a royal flush against his four aces.

Cord knew he should have felt guilty—but *nahhh...*

Not even the Culvers had a horse with this lineage. Cord could make a mint in racing or stud fees.

He gripped the steering wheel. Wise or not, he pulled his truck to a stop and watched Cait disappear behind the barn door.

If old man Culver caught him sniffing around his daughter, Cord was dead. Then again, perhaps he no longer gave a fuck whether or not Culver didn't want him around Cait. Cord wasn't a kid, and neither was Cait.

The truck door moaned as he opened it and stepped outside. He looked around, relieved to see no one about. Rubbing his sweaty palms on his jeans, he aimed for the stable.

As Cord entered, he heard Cait's smoky voice. "You're such a pretty thing." Cait's heart-shaped ass faced him as she hunched over looking into a stall.

What would Cait do if he sauntered up and pressed his hips to that precious little behind of hers?

The image of him unfastening her belt buckle and jeans, sliding them down to her ankles, while he cupped her breasts and drove into her sweet pussy, hard and fast, sent a quiver through him.

Best ditch those thoughts or he'd be saying, "Hi," with a raging hard-on. Inhaling a deep breath, he released it slowly, willing his cock to behave.

When Cord was mentally ready, he leaned against a stall and folded his arms across his chest. He crossed one foot in front of the other, resting the toe of his boot on the concrete floor.

"Nothing is as pretty as you, Miss Culver," he said with a low Southern drawl.

Cait nearly swallowed her tongue as she jerked away from the stall. Startled, her heart raced, only picking up speed when she saw who addressed her. Cord's deep, sexy voice and his soft laughter that followed sent chills up her spine.

In a last-ditch effort to steady her hands, she rested them on her hips. "If it isn't the bad boy of Santa Ysabel, California."

Palm over his heart, Cord cried, "Owww…"

One minute he sported a mournful expression, the next his eyelashes lowered and he narrowed his eyes on her. When he pushed away from the railing Cait knew she was in trouble.

Her breath caught on an inhale.

Breathe.

He approached with bold, arrogant strides, flashing a drop-dead sexy smile that melted her insides.

She had to remind herself that Cord might make her mushy on the inside, but she had to be hard as nails on the outside in dealing with this man. Haughtily, she swept her gaze up and down him, pausing deliberately at his groin, before they came eye to eye.

Two can play this game.

Cait had been barely nineteen when she left California. She wasn't the same girl now. Still little had changed when it came to her desires. She knew exactly what she wanted.

Cord Daily.

Rumors were his sexual antics ran wild. His taste for ménages had scared the living crap out of her. Not anymore. She'd take Cord any way she could have him.

Already she was imagining his lean, muscled physique pressed against hers, the feel of his slightly wavy blond hair between her fingers. The thought sent a twist of sensation in her belly and caused her heart to beat even faster.

The taut denim stretched low across his hips, outlining an impressive package—one she had every intention of unwrapping and soon, but not yet. The time had to be right or she'd lose him.

Slowly, he caressed her from head to toe, stripping her naked a piece of clothing at a time with just a look.

Little did he know that's how Cait wanted it—skin-to-skin. Night after night, she dreamed of Cord's hands roaming her body, heating her blood until she came apart at the seams.

Pulse pumping madly, she held her breath and prayed her aplomb wouldn't shatter. She managed not to flinch when he reached for the ribbon holding her hair and pulled, releasing her tresses to fall around her shoulders. She even contained a reaction when he used that ribbon to tickle her bare shoulder blades and tease the exposed swells of her breasts. But no amount of willpower could have restrained her gasp as he released the ribbon to slither down her T-shirt.

He was good—damn good.

Her knees weakened, while her chest rose and fell more rapidly than she would prefer. And that wasn't all that was going on with her body. The sting in her nipples twisted into an ache that shot straight for her pussy. She only prayed he couldn't scent her arousal.

Stay focused, Cait.

She knew this man. He liked the game—liked the hunt. But he had a little surprise coming.

She wasn't the prey—he was.

When she snagged the bad boy, she had plans to hold onto him, no matter what her father said. Who was he to determine Cord wasn't good enough just because he didn't offer anything to the family but cattle?

For Christsake, she was a woman and she'd damn well make her own choices.

Cord speared his fingers through her hair, jerking her to him, chest to chest, hips to hips. His lips were a breath away from hers, tempting—teasing.

Just another ploy to see if she'd close the gap between them—kiss him first—then he'd know he won.

Ain't gonna happen.

"Something you want, Cord?" When she spoke her mouth brushed across his. It was pure hell not to take what she wanted, especially with his trimmed goatee and mustache tickling and tantalizing her lips.

His eyes darkened, his voice lowered. "You, darlin'."

This was the opening she'd been waiting for—it was her move.

Cait's gaze peeled away from his as she smoothed her cheek along his. She felt the catch in his breathing as she brought her lips to his ear and blew lightly, before inhaling the rich scent of sandalwood.

"I want you too." She coaxed her tone to be soft, husky. "I've always wanted you."

If you only knew how much.

He tried to snake his arms around her, but she was quick in pressing her palm against his chest, holding him at bay. Slowly, she curled her fingernails so they bit into him.

His seductive mouth parted, drawing her attention.

God, how she wanted to taste him, knowing if she did there would be a power exchange and she would be lost. "*Uh-uh-uh.* Let's play first. You like to play games, don't you, Cord?"

"Darlin', right now I'd do anything you ask." He shifted his hips. "See what you do to me." He removed her hand from his chest, guiding it to his rock-hard groin.

Sinfully, he thrust his cock against her palm, working her hand up and down.

His intimate contact was more than she could have hoped for. The tightening of her grip rewarded her with deep growls that rumbled from his chest. The veins in his neck bulged. He leaned further into her touch and closed his eyes.

What next?

Her gaze darted around the barn. On a bench lay several strips of leather. Someone had been repairing a bridle. She released him and stepped away.

His heavy eyelids rose, his brow furrowing. "Where are you going?"

She gave him the most big-eyed, innocent expression she could muster. "I'm going to tie you up. That's what you like, isn't it?"

Cord's rich laughter caressed her. "Darlin', you've got that backward."

Her bottom lip protruded into a little pout. "Don't you want to play with me?"

He moved fast, his arm circling her waist, bringing her tight against his body. "Oh, yeah. I want to play with you."

She could live forever staring into his aqua eyes, more green than blue. But if she were too eager she'd be just another notch on his belt. She wanted more than that—much more.

The bad boy was going down.

She didn't have to feign the tremor of excitement in her fingers as she began to unbutton his shirt. "Then you'll let me tie you up?" She slid the material from his chest and arms to fall on the floor.

Gorgeous.

Muscles rippled beneath his deep, rich tan. She dipped her head, circling her tongue around his nipple, and felt it harden beneath her touch as she watched him.

His nostrils flared.

When his grip on her arms loosened, she could almost sense his surrender approaching.

Seducing Cord was easier than she would have imagined. Holding on to him would be the difficult part.

She clawed her fingernails down his chest, leaving a white path that turned pink as she followed the whisper of blond hair that trailed down his abdomen, swirling around his bellybutton before disappearing. Slowly, she raised her sultry gaze to meet his, and then she slipped her hand down his jeans.

Oh God!

He wore no boxers—no briefs.

Instead her fingers met the firm head of his cock. Stunned for only a moment, she circled the silky ridge, sliding her fingertip back and forth over the small slit now slick with pre-come.

"Please? Let me tie you up," she whispered.

His eyes darkened to a sea green. He clenched his jaw. "Darlin', do whatever you want." His words were tight and forced, his hips undulating against her hand.

"I'll be back," Cait promised, pressing her lips briefly to his as she extracted her hand. For a second she didn't think he would release her, but he did.

Cord's hot gaze followed her as she gathered the loose strands of leather off the bench. She stole a moment to compose herself. Her confidence almost took a nose dive when she saw that he'd undone the top button of his pants.

Just the whisper of a zipper and man-oh-man—

Focus.

Funny how difficult it was to walk when aroused. She'd swear she was weaving all over the place as she approached him. Snuggling against him, his arms surrounding her, she took small steps to maneuver him backward against a wooden ladder leading to the loft above.

With a soft smile on her face, Cait raised his arm so that it bent at the elbow. She'd been around livestock all her life and knew how to tie a knot, one even Cord couldn't bust free. As she finished the tie around his wrist, she swore his body had become a furnace; his heat burned through her clothing.

Focus.

When his other wrist was secured, she found the courage to kiss him—really kiss him for the first time.

She wrapped her arms around his neck like she had imagined so many times and pressed her mouth firmly to his. He tried to take control, but she pushed past his lips, plunging her tongue inside to taste and ravish.

Breathing elevated, he pulled against his restraints, the wood creaking. "Let me go, darlin'. Let me make you feel good." His sexy promise brought her back to reality. She stumbled back, tipsy from the euphoria.

Cait licked her lips, savoring Cord's masculine flavor. She inhaled deeply, knowing the next part of her plan sucked big time. Her body hummed with the need to strip the man naked and make a little yeehaw in the hay.

Instead, she tossed her hair over a shoulder, narrowed her eyes and said, "Try to get out of this one, Cord Daily."

Her plan was simple. Cord liked the chase. She had to arouse him to the point he couldn't think. Give a little—but leave him wanting. When she finally surrendered, loved him with all her heart, the man would be a goner.

Without another word she spun on the ball of her boots and hauled-ass out the door.

Chapter Two

"Cait!" Cord yelled her name, but she ignored him, the barn door closing with a bang behind her. In disbelief, he glared at the door.

The little vixen had tricked him. Suckered him into the position he now stood in. Bare chest, jeans scarcely covering his johnson, his wrists bound by leather straps to the loft's makeshift ladder.

And in her father's barn—of all the goddamned places he could be tied up in.

Perhaps that's what Cait wanted. His hide pinned above George Culver's fireplace as a trophy.

"What a dumbshit." Cord pulled against his bindings. No give. "Damn good knot." He stared at the door waiting for it to open and Cait to reappear. She was just fucking with him.

"She'll be back." A grin tugged at his mouth.

Gone was the shy girl he had known. The woman who fondled his cock in her hand, swirled her tongue around his nipple, knew what she was doing. For some reason that irked him and his smile turned into a scowl. The fact she was obviously experienced now made him madder than hell.

All the time he resisted taking her into his arms Cait was out learning about her sexuality with someone else. Of course, he'd been younger then and the threats her father had made to destroy him, ruin his business, had been the real reins holding him back from seeking what he desired.

Cait in his arms—his bed.

When she started coming on to him rational thought had taken a hike.

The word "dumbshit" once again popped into his mind.

Shifting his feet, Cord slid his ass against the wooden rung behind him. A sharp poke drove his hips forward as a splinter buried into his flesh, causing his jeans to slip further down his hips. Only his engorged cock wedged painfully beneath the waistline kept them from falling around his ankles.

He shook his head, thoroughly disgusted with himself.

What made him think he finally had a chance with Culver's little princess? Maybe this was her way of saying she wasn't interested anymore.

On a deep inhale he breathed in her feminine perfume, light and powdery, still lingering amongst the grassy scent of alfalfa and manure.

"*Moo...*" The occupant of the stall next to him stuck her head out and cried low and long. Etched on a gold nameplate tacked above one out of twenty or so stalls were the words "Bessie, the family cow".

Well hell.

Cord could swear the black and white beast batted her long eyelashes at him as she swished her tail back and forth invitingly. Good thing she was pinned. When she heaved her large body against the gate, the lock rattling, a hint of unease skittered up his back.

The thought of Culver's anger and the way Bessie was now staring at him wilted Cord's erection. His jeans slid down his legs to pool at his ankles.

"Fuck." He narrowed his gaze on his boots. "What the hell am I gonna do now?"

"Pray." His cousin's unexpected voice jerked Cord's head up. He came face-to-face with Dolan Crane, fellow carouser now turned veterinarian. "Couldn't stay away from her, could you?" His dark-haired kin chuckled as he touched the rim of his Stetson and nodded.

Cord shrugged. "Guess not."

Dolan had been the only person he'd ever confided in about his desire for Cait—at one time he had shared everything with him.

Cord pulled against his restraints. "How about a hand here?"

Dolan set down his medical case and pressed his palms together, clapping as his grin deepened.

"Funny." Cord shook his head, fighting the smile that played at the corner of his mouth. "I'm dead if Culver catches me like this."

Dolan stepped forward and began to untie Cord. "Exactly how did this happen?"

"Long story." His nudity around Dolan didn't bother him. He'd learned a lot from Dolan. His cousin and he had shared women. The last time was almost two years ago when Cait found the two of them in bed with her best friend, Tracy Reynolds.

He could still see the shock in Cait's blue eyes as she turned and fled. She'd left for Paris the next day. He hadn't seen her since, until today.

Reality was Caitlyn Culver was too good for him. Cord didn't need her father to remind him. The Culver's thoroughbred ranch was a far cry from the cattle ranch his father had left him. His mother had died in a car accident when Cord was only four. It had been the bachelor's life for him.

"Interesting story, I'm sure. Just so you know, Cait was guarding the door. Now I know why she was so happy to see me." Dolan released the final strap around Cord's wrist. "Still, you best remember Culver will have your balls if you mess with his daughter."

So she hadn't left him to rot. Wonder how long she would have waited to release him, if Dolan hadn't shown up?

Cord rubbed his wrists before bending to retrieve his jeans. "What'ya doing here?"

As he yanked the stiff cotton over his hips he remembered Cait's surprise when she discovered he wore no briefs. Her warm and sexy eyes had grown as big as saucers; her trembling touch had nearly undone him.

"Doc Zimmerman is on vacation. I'm standing in for him." Dolan cleared his throat, rubbing his thumb across his clean-shaved chin, then pulled at the tip of his dark mustache, giving Cord the look that said, "Boy, you're heading straight for trouble."

Cord pushed his fingers through his hair. "Hell, Dolan, she's been in Paris for almost two years. I just wanted to see her."

Truth?

Cait was like a lodestone drawing Cord with an invisible force. He had attempted over and over to stay clear of her, thinking that maybe the attraction was a conquest.

But it was more than that.

He'd tried to fight his growing feelings using other women, and although satisfying, there was always something missing. And that something was Cait. Her voice was smoky, sexy. Her body perfection.

What a sap.

Dolan moved toward the stall where a beautiful sorrel mare and her foal were housed. The colt stood on unsteady legs. He nudged his mother's teat.

"Well, you might as well make yourself useful. Grab that mare's halter and keep her calm while I examine the foal."

Cord put his shirt on before entering the stall. He steadied the mare as he stroked her neck. All he could think of was the fire he'd seen in Cait's eyes. She had been aroused, so what went wrong?

"Miss the old days?" he asked Dolan.

The foal tried to jerk out of Dolan's grip, but he held on tight. "Hell yeah. Been a little busy of late building my practice."

"Whad'ya say we rope us a filly tonight, tie her up, and see if we can make her moan?"

With a tip of his finger, Dolan nudged his hat up. A wicked grin spread across his face. "I'm game. Anyone particular in mind?"

"Oh yeah," Cord said.

ᘒᕽᘓᕽᘒ

Knock on the devil's door and he's bound to answer.

Cait knew Cord would be here tonight. Her earlier prank had ensured that. What she hadn't anticipated was that the dastardly duo had united.

Hell itself in the form of Dolan Crane stood next to Cord. Their broad shoulders, side by side, made an imposing sight in the spacious great room as they entered.

Where Cord was blond with smiling aqua eyes, Dolan had blue-black hair and blue eyes dark as the night. You'd never know they were related. They were both over six feet and muscular from hard work. Lifting hay and wrangling livestock tended to keep a man fit.

And they were dressed for seduction.

Black Stetson, jeans and boots—only the silk shirts they wore were different. Cord's was a vibrant blue caressing every muscle beneath it, while Dolan's was red, stroking his firm biceps as he shook hands with a man who approached him.

Seeing the pair together literally made Cait squirm and her body tighten in areas she'd rather ignore for the moment. She tugged at her short jean skirt and then the spaghetti strap of her white satin shirt, trying desperately to fade into the wall she leaned against.

It didn't work.

Even though the room was filled with thirty or more people, some dancing, some standing around talking, Cord found her in record time.

Their gazes met, locked.

Her pulse leaped before she forced a half-smile.

He simply raised an eyebrow, but that was enough to let her know she was in big trouble—and he'd brought reinforcements.

"Oh look! Someone let the cocks in the henhouse." Laughter broke out around the room as Kendra drew everyone's attention to the two men now shaking hands with their host, Jester Norton. The music started to play as Cord said something Cait couldn't hear and the robust Jester burst into hysterics.

Glad someone is having a great time.

Suddenly, Cait was so nervous she could almost hear the creak of time pass by. She had been prepared to take Cord on tonight, give him a run for his money.

But Dolan too?

Anxiety and excitement skittered across her skin.

Kitchen, living and dining room all meshing into one big play area made it difficult to plan an escape. She had three choices.

Bathroom? A woman darted in, removing that choice.

Downstairs? Hmm...pool table, bar and bedrooms. Dangerous.

Or she could stand and fight.

Her decision was made for her when Cord and Dolan finished their conversations, narrowed their gazes on her and made a beeline in her direction. Their confident, bold strides hit Cait like a jolt of lightning—trouble didn't accurately describe what she was in for tonight.

Reports from Kendra throughout the years were that Cord was up to his same old carousing, while Dolan had disappeared, apparently finishing his veterinary degree. Her father had expressed his displeasure in Dolan standing in for Doc Zimmerman, but in a pinch you took what you could get. Besides that, she had heard that Dolan was damn good.

Cait respected Dolan.

According to Kendra, he was ten when he lost both parents in an avalanche during a skiing trip. Cord's father had taken him in, raised him like a son, but when the man died he left everything to Cord. Dolan had accomplished a lot on his own. No daddy's money to pave the way.

Before Cord and Dolan reached her, they each stuck one of their hands in their pockets and extracted a strip of leather.

Eeek!

It appeared to be the same straps she had tied Cord up with in the barn, leaving her absolutely no doubt what was on their minds.

It was payback time.

Chills crawled beneath her skin the closer they got. She glanced around for Kendra, but she was wrapped in Stack's arms as he guided her around the makeshift dance floor of the living room. Laughter filled the air along with an array of perfumes, cigarette smoke and liquor.

Everyone was having a great time—everyone but Cait.

As she pushed away from the wall, two firm arms shot out before her. She ducked, but they were quick cutting her off and using their bodies to dash any hopes of escape. Like a damn fortress they surrounded her.

Cait threw a glance over their shoulders, stuck her hand in the air and wiggled her fingers. "Boys, I'd like to chat, but Kendra is calling me."

She wasn't fooling anyone. They didn't even look back to see who her wave was meant for.

Instead, Cord placed his palm against the wall above her head. "Liar. Kendra's dancing. Wouldn't be trying to avoid us, would ya, darlin'?" He brought his other hand up, twirling the piece of leather between his fingers.

With Cord standing so close, Cait forgot to breathe. She shifted her feet nervously. The scent of his cologne was driving her hormones wild. She wanted to fist her hands in his shirt and drag him to her lips. When rational thought resumed and air finally flooded her lungs she almost choked.

"Now that's just downright unfriendly." Dolan leaned forward and pressed his nose to her hair, inhaling deeply. "Good to see you again, Cait." His dark, sexy voice rippled across her skin like a warm summer breeze.

"Uh... So you're a vet." Her voice squeaked. How humiliating.

"Yeah, discovered I was good with my hands." Dolan held up his strap of leather. "Real good."

She eased away from him only to run into a solid wall of muscle on the other side of her. Cord gazed down at her with eyes that made her want to fall into his arms. Still, she pushed away, bumping into Dolan. They each took a step forward, trapping and sandwiching her between them.

Well crap. This was going to be harder than she thought. She became fully aware of the two firm cocks pressed against her body. Although apprehensive, she couldn't fight the excitement that filled her. She pictured the three of them naked and sprawled upon a bed, arms and legs intertwined. Her pussy grew hot and moist.

"All right, boys, you've had your fun. Let her go." Kendra to the rescue—or not.

She had to be only five-two, a small thing compared to Cait's five-seven, but she puffed up like a banty hen. With a jerk of her head, a flow of red hair went sailing over her shoulder.

Neither of the men stirred.

"We have some unfinished business," Cord grumbled.

Cait released a stream of uneasy laughter. "These two don't scare me." She snorted. "I can handle them." *Liar, liar, pants on fire.* But she had to play the game. She had to make Cord want her and the only way to do that was make winning her a challenge. "Besides, I don't know what Cord is talking about. I thought I made myself pretty clear earlier. I'm not interested."

Kendra tugged on Dolan's arm. "How 'bout you take me for a spin around the dance floor?"

Bless her friend for trying to even the numbers and give Cait a fighting chance.

Cord and Dolan shared a glance, unspoken words exchanged.

Dolan pressed his face to Cait's hair. She nearly jumped out of her skin, shattering her image of control as his wet, warm tongue circled the shell of her ear.

"Tonight you're ours," he whispered. Then he turned, taking Kendra into his arms, sashaying across the wood floor.

Before Cait could move, Cord pressed his body against hers, the wall at her back. The hard ridge beneath his zipper was tight against her abdomen. She fought the urge to squirm and position his erection at the place between her thighs that ached to feel him deep inside.

"That wasn't a very neighborly thing you did earlier." He pulled his soft Southern drawl over her like a warm blanket.

She tried to relax her shoulders, show him he didn't affect her.

But Lord knew he did.

"Neighborly? Do you screw all your neighbors?" She didn't even pause before saying, "Oh yeah. That's right. You do."

"Ahhh...darlin'."

"Save it, Cord. Your sweet-talk won't work on me." She didn't like the spark in his eyes. It gave her the feeling she had waved a red flag in front of a charging bull. Then again, that's exactly what she wanted.

"Really?" A tense silence grew between them. It seemed like forever before he said, "Close your eyes."

She frowned. "What?"

With his fingertips he drew her eyelids shut. Cord remained silent as a variety of sounds rushed to her brain. Shuffling. Boots across the floor. Clinking of glass against glass. A squeak and a bang. A door opening and closing. The jingle of coins in someone's pocket. It was amazing what she detected.

When Cord finally spoke she startled, straining to hear his ultra-low voice over the music. "Do you remember the first day we met?" Her hair tickled across one shoulder, the warmth of his hand followed, before cool air caressed her skin making her feel naked—vulnerable. "You wore two long braids, the tips brushing back and forth across your breasts."

Cait gasped. Did he run a finger across her nipple or was it just her imagination? Either way her nipples hardened painfully against her shirt.

Damn. She should have worn a bra. These warm summer nights caused her as well as everyone else to shun their clothes.

"Pink sweater, tight jeans." He trailed lips along her collarbone. "When you bent over..." He sucked in a deep breath. "It took everything I had not to touch you. You drove me wild."

When she realized her head lay to the side begging him to kiss her neck, her backbone went rigid. Her resistance lasted only a moment as his hand slipped beneath her shirt to the small of her back. His touch was like flames flickering across her skin as he teased the area with a finger.

"You were adorable. A pout on those pretty little lips when your daddy refused to let you take his truck while he inspected the horses at the racetrack." A calloused finger traced her bottom lip. Her mouth parted.

She noted a quiver in his breath as he inhaled before continuing.

"You wore some seriously sexy perfume." His deep, sexy voice caressed her ear. "Made me horny as hell." With a featherlight touch, he smoothed his fingertip down her shoulder to her elbow.

Shock filtered through her. She couldn't believe he remembered that day, so many details, even the fragrance of her perfume.

Cord's knuckles skimmed her cheek. "So beautiful." She felt his nose nuzzle hers softly. "You stole my breath away. I knew you were mine—that someday we'd be together."

Perhaps it was time to call bullshit, but Cait wanted to believe Cord. His words played on her heart like a bow upon a fiddle, each plucking the taut strings of her libido. She kept her eyes closed, refusing to wake from the dream she'd stumbled into.

Strong arms circled her, accentuating his powerful build. She couldn't have moved away if she had wanted to.

"From the second I saw you I've wanted you." He moaned, a coarse sound of desire. "To taste your lips." He captured her mouth tenderly, only to leave her hungry for more as he drew away. "To feel your silky skin...your body beneath mine." A growl rumbled in his throat. "I want you." His husky words were coming faster now. "Your long legs wrapped around my waist"—he ground his hips against hers—"as I bury my cock deep inside your hot, wet pussy while Dolan fucks that sweet ass of yours."

"Stop," she cried, unable to take any more. Her eyes sprang wide, but the picture he had painted still remained etched in her mind. Arms. Legs. Cocks. The pinch low in her belly twisted. Each breath was a desperate attempt to quench the flames blazing through her veins.

Cait almost died of embarrassment when she realized she was writhing against Cord wantonly. Thankfully, no one could see her. Both Cord and Dolan shielded her from prying eyes with their bodies.

When had Dolan returned? Had he stood there listening?

"Is she ready?" Dolan's deep voice and question only served to dampen her panties further.

Cord brushed back a tendril of hair from her eyes. "Cait?"

All she could do was nod.

Chapter Three

Cord raised the bedroom lights just enough so he could see Cait's beautiful face. Standing in the doorway, she startled as Dolan came up from behind and wrapped his arms around her waist. A twinge of jealousy twisted in Cord's gut when his cousin twirled her around and stole a heated kiss. But when their caress ended Cait's gaze snapped back to Cord's.

Mine.

He ached to possess her hard and fast, but he wanted the first time to be a memory she'd never forget. Dolan's presence would only heighten the moment. There was something about a woman's expression, her unrestrained cries when two men fucked her. It surpassed anything Cord had ever experienced.

Dolan ushered her inside and secured the door behind them.

Laughter, muffled music and the clash of balls across the billiard table were white noise. Dolan stroked his palms up and down Cait's arms, making her tremble. Cord's cock pressed painfully against his black jeans, a dull throb needing release.

Dolan turned her so that once again her back was pressed to his chest. From beneath his Stetson, he winked at Cord. His cousin's hands gripped the hem of Cait's white, spaghetti-strap satin shirt. "How 'bout we get rid of this?"

Even though lust brightened her eyes, she wet her lips and swallowed hard as color dotted her cheeks.

In a slow production meant for Cord, Dolan raised the material to reveal her bellybutton and taut abdomen. Cord almost groaned aloud when the swells of her breasts appeared, and then her rosy, extended nipples. Her arms rose as Dolan pulled the shirt over her head and tossed it aside.

Never once did she look away from Cord, or for that fact, pay much attention to Dolan as he reached beneath her denim skirt and slid her lacy panties down her legs and over her boots.

With a flick of his hand, Dolan tossed the sexy underwear to Cord. "For you, Cuz."

Cord caught the lingerie and brought it to his nose, inhaling her perfume and feminine musk. Blood shot to his groin. This time he did groan aloud. His hands trembled as he crammed the panties into his jean pocket, before he fought his belt buckle and button. A small amount of relief followed when he unzipped his jeans, releasing his engorged erection.

Cait's eyes widened when she saw he once again wore no underwear. She took a step forward, but was held back by a hand on her arm.

Dolan pressed his cheek to hers, his fingers plucking her nipples. "You want some of that, don't you, baby?"

"Yes," she hissed, her breasts rising and falling rapidly.

"Let's get your boots off." Dolan moved to kneel on one knee before her. The rim of his hat rose beneath her skirt, lifting it to tease Cord. When Dolan raised Cait's foot to remove her boot, he said, "Hmm... So moist, pink and swollen, begging to be tongued."

She whimpered as she grasped onto Dolan's shoulders to steady herself.

Cord's jeans and shirt felt like they shrank two sizes too small. He was suffocating.

Too many clothes.

His fingers were all thumbs as he fumbled with the buttons of his blue silk shirt. By the time he was bare-chested, Dolan had removed all of Cait's clothing.

Her beauty stole Cord's breath away. She was everything he'd expected and more, full breasts, a small tucked waist and shapely hips.

"Come here," he growled, needing to touch her.

There was no hesitancy in her approach. When she stood before him, she reached for his hat, ripped it off his head and threw it aside, stepping into his waiting arms.

Their skin touched. Time stilled.

Cord fought to restrain his excitement, slow the caress of his hands upon her body. He had waited so long—so very long.

"You're trembling," she murmured, gazing at him with an expression of wonder he couldn't comprehend.

Cord swallowed hard. He had to rein his emotions in.

Before he could gather his thoughts, she grasped his hand in hers and brought it to her lips. His chest squeezed, doing things to his heart he didn't want to admit.

There was something about Cait—

The spell between them was broken when a very naked Dolan stepped behind her and pressed his cock to her ass.

"Oh my," she squealed, releasing a tense giggle.

"Nice." Dolan rocked against her, driving her hips into Cord's.

Cord couldn't resist. He captured her mouth in an all-too-brief, fiery kiss. No tongue, no more than a taste, before Dolan whirled her around and did the same.

It wasn't enough. Not nearly enough. Cord reached for her, needing more, aching for more.

With a jerk, he pulled Cait out of Dolan's arms and back into his. Their mouths came together in a heated exchange. His tongue pushed between her lips, sinking into heaven. She tasted of spearmint—passion. He held on tightly, not willing to relinquish her to his cousin—not yet. Not until he drank his fill.

She met him hungrily, her fingernails biting into his shoulders. As he thoroughly kissed her, Dolan's hands moved over her body, stoking her arousal. Every once in a while Cord would feel the whisper of his cousin's touch. Yet it was Cait's soft, throaty cries that said she was theirs.

Their lips parted and Cait threw back her head. "Boys, I don't know how much longer I'll be able to hold out. I need you now."

"Nightstand," Cord groaned, remembering that Jester kept condoms and other essentials in the nightstand next to the king-size, wrought-iron bed. The scrape of wood against wood told Cord Dolan knew exactly what to do.

Cord was thankful for Cait's impatience. He couldn't wait any longer to take her—make her his.

With shuffled boot steps, Cord guided Cait backward. When their mouths parted they were both gasping for air.

Dolan had the bedding pulled back, his cock already sheathed. He stepped forward, pressing a small packet into Cord's palm as he took Cait's hand in his.

"Come here, little one." Dolan led her to the bed. From the nightstand he retrieved the strap of leather Cord had given him earlier and dangled it before her. "I believe this is yours."

Dolan's intentions had yet to seep into Cait's muddled brain. One thought consumed her. *Hot damn, Cord can kiss!* Her lips tingled, and sparks of desire burned across her skin. Eagerly, she watched him remove one boot and then the other before slipping off his socks.

Now the jeans. She held her breath. When they dropped to the floor, she silently said, *Oh yeah. That's what I'm talking about.* Long, hard and an impressive girth—the man was made for her.

As Dolan drew her wrists together all she could think about was Cord's cock thrusting in and out of her body. She squirmed, trying to ease the throb between her thighs. Her breasts felt heavy with the need to feel his hot, wet mouth upon them. It wasn't until she attempted to brush the hair from her eyes that she realized her hands were bound in front of her. Her gaze snapped to Dolan and then back to Cord.

A sliver of unease raced across her skin. "I don't know about this, boys."

Dolan looked dangerous—hip propped against the bed, his arms folded across his bare chest as he watched her every move. "Relax, baby."

Relax! She was naked, in a room with two men. Her body felt like a live wire strung tighter than a guitar string.

Cord didn't say a word, only ripped open the package he held and extracted a condom. She watched his strong hands slide the prophylactic down his cock. With his dark stare latched to hers, he took himself in hand and with long, leisurely strokes, began to masturbate as he approached. With each step closer, she felt her anxiety die a little. She wanted this man. Hell, for that matter she wanted Dolan too.

Instead of touching her like Cait anticipated, Cord walked past her and climbed on the bed to lie on his back. His eyelids lowered as he stretched out his hand. "Come here, darlin'."

Oh God! Cait couldn't breathe.

This was the moment she'd been waiting for. Her legs were like rubber, giving slightly when she placed a knee on the bed. With her wrists bound, she felt awkward, but Dolan helped her straddle Cord's hips, propping her palms on his chest.

The minute her moist slit made contact with the hard ridge of Cord's cock, she cried out.

Dolan chuckled. "I think we've got a screamer."

Embarrassment fanned hot across her face.

"I love a passionate woman." The wicked grin Cord flashed her eased her chagrin. He moved his hips so that his erection rubbed against her sensitive flesh teasingly, giving her a sample of what was yet to come.

Cupping her cheeks, he pressed his mouth to hers, his tongue seeking hers. Then he drew away. His strong hands gripped her waist and raised her as he shifted his hips to align himself with her sex.

Slowly, he began to enter her.

"*Ahhh...*" She stifled the cry midway as he stretched and filled her. Tears beat behind her eyelids. She had wanted this for so long. When he partially withdrew, she sobbed, "Please, Cord."

"Please what, darlin'?"

"Fuck me." She hated the plea in her voice, but that's exactly what it was—a plea. Cait had to have him—all of him—now.

When he thrust again, burying deep inside her, she tossed back her head and screamed his name. Her body clamped down on him.

"So tight," Cord groaned, desire flickering like flames in his eyes. "So friggin' tight."

There was something about his voice, sexy and deep—his husky manner of speech, especially when he was aroused, that thrilled her.

Pressed to her cradle, he rocked, pushing his cock hard against her womb, releasing starbursts of sensations. The tickle of his pubic hairs rasping against her swollen clit made her pussy clench over and over.

No. Not yet.

She panted, releasing quick breaths, wanting to ride the crest and needing to savor the moment. Each inhale/exhale stole moisture from her mouth, her lips. She wanted to kiss him, drink from his mouth to quench her desire, but her bound wrists were in the way. Yet being bound had its reward. It fucking turned her on. Her nipples were aching nubs, her breasts heavy with need. And she was wet—so very wet.

She had to think of something else, quiet the burn or she would lose it.

Relief filtered through her when Cord eased to a gentle sway, even as the muscles and tendons in his neck bulged and his fingertips tightened around her hips.

"Hurry," he snapped, his gaze darting to Dolan. Cord's nostrils flared as he inhaled a ragged breath.

Dolan chuckled, the bed shifting as he moved behind her. His strong hands smoothed across her breasts to pinch and tease her nipples. She arched into his touch, feeling another tightening low in her belly begin to build.

She tried to move her hips, but Cord held her steady. His gaze was so intense, he appeared angry instead of aroused. It was heady to know he walked the same tightrope she did, both wanting to fall into the abyss together.

Dolan's hands disappeared from her breasts and something cold nudged her ass. A small tip slipped inside her tight entrance and she nearly shot out of Cord's grasp as cold gel filled her cavity.

"Easy, baby," Dolan whispered against her ear at the same time Cord said, "Relax. Breathe with me."

Cait focused on Cord's perfect mouth, inhaled—exhaled, trying to prepare herself for what was to come. Still, she flinched when Dolan eased his finger inside, pushing past the first ring of muscle.

White-hot pain sliced through her. She struggled to breathe—to gather her composure.

Cord began an easy pace, moving her against his hips again, as Dolan cupped one of her breasts and tenderly rolled the nipple. Both men worked to draw her attention away from the spiraling burn.

While Cord focused on her other nipple, sucking and biting, Dolan nuzzled her neck, trailing kisses upward. He latched onto an earlobe, pulling it into his mouth as he inserted another finger deep into her ass.

The men were so in sync, stilling to allow her time to grow accustomed to the fullness. When she began to move her hips against Cord and pressing back into Dolan's hand, the men started to rock her between them.

Dolan scissored his digits, working them in and out. "Damn, Cord. She's tight."

"Mine," Cord growled, almost as if he was reminding Dolan. The raw possessiveness she saw in Cord's eyes turned pain into pleasure.

She wanted to be his—only his.

But there was no getting around the truth. It was incredible being with two men. Like a maelstrom, the beginning of her climax roared toward the surface. Taking deep breaths, she barely contained the rush of pleasure. When Dolan replaced his fingers with his cock, she held her breath. Little by little he pushed inside, his girth stretching her even wider until he slipped past any resistance.

"Fuck," Dolan roared.

Cord and Dolan began a gentle pace thrusting in and out of her body, while Dolan's hands smoothed over her abdomen and caressed her breasts. She felt every inch of them filling her pussy and ass. Jolts of electricity surged through her nipples.

Tender. She was so tender and sensitive.

Suddenly, their thrusts grew faster, harder, slamming into her at once. Deep—so deep.

A heat wave engulfed her, causing her to cry out.

Cord jerked her bound hands up and over his head; her chest thumped his, their lips coming together in a frenzy of tongues.

She couldn't breathe as fireballs of sensation exploded in her womb, blowing the head off any control she sought. Cord smothered her scream with a passionate kiss as her world splintered.

From the front and back, Cord and Dolan fucked her, holding her writhing body between them.

Colors burst behind her eyelids. She couldn't think past the throb echoing throughout her, a living pulse that threatened to consume her.

Hot. She was so hot.

Liquid heat rushed through her veins. She was only semi-aware of Dolan reaching his climax. He lunged once more and then stilled, releasing a groan that sounded like it came from somewhere deep in his chest. But it was the expression of ecstasy and the ardent cry that left Cord's mouth that stole her heart. The tightness in his face vanished. His eyes opened and the sated smile he gave her was so moving she snuggled into the warmth of his body.

The moment was surreal as Dolan collapsed atop her. Not only could she hear, but felt each of their heartbeats drumming so that they melded into one. It should have been awkward, naked between two men, their cocks buried deep inside her, but somehow it felt right.

Dolan moaned, pushing off the bed, his phallus slipping from her to leave her feeling strangely empty.

Cord on the other hand held her close and whispered, "I want you again."

Chapter Four

Cait lay atop Cord, her wrists bound and stretched over his head. His semi-hard cock stirred inside her as she gazed at him with sexy eyes, heavy and sated. "I want you too." The tender expression on her face made his chest tighten. He could lose himself to this woman and never regret it.

Hell, he was already lost.

In the adjoining bathroom, he heard Dolan turn the water on. Beyond the bedroom door Norton's party was in full swing, laughter, music, billiards and the occasional crash of a beer bottle striking the floor.

Never disengaging their bodies, he rolled her on her back, taking a moment to caress her lovely breasts with his gaze. He couldn't help himself. He bent his head and laved a nipple, feeling it harden against his tongue, as the other peak did the same between his fingers.

She made a soft needy sound that made him melt inside.

"I want to touch you," she whimpered. She squirmed to stress her need or to drive him out of his friggin' mind. Her floral scent and the sexual musk in the air made the tingle in his groin sharpen, firming his cock.

He was dying to feel her hands on his body, stroking and caressing. Throughout his lifetime he had discovered a lot about women. Their eyes conveyed their feelings. The way they touched a man revealed a lot about them too.

What would he discover in Cait's embrace?

The thought urged him to quickly untie her hands. When she brought her arms down she groaned. A moment of discomfort flashed on her face before her arms locked around his neck. She snuggled close and smiled. Cord knew this was where he belonged.

A loud crash against the bedroom door made them both startle and jerk their heads in that direction.

"What the fuck?" Dolan said, exiting the bathroom. "Sounds like it's getting rowdy."

"Maybe we should take this party to my place." Cord searched Cait's face for approval.

An intrigued smile tipped her lips. "Sounds good to me."

Norton's house rules were if you used the bed you changed the sheets. While Cait found her clothing and sashayed off to the bathroom, Dolan and Cord pulled on their jeans before beginning to strip the bed.

Dolan glanced at Cord. "Don't suppose you'd consider sharing her after tonight? Those little sounds she makes drive me crazy."

"Nope. After tonight, she's mine—all mine." Cord gathered the sheets in his arms.

Disappointment shone in Dolan's eyes. For a moment Cord thought he might argue the point—instead he turned and headed to the closet for clean bedding.

Bed made, they were finishing dressing when Cait exited the bathroom. She pulled nervously on the hem of her denim skirt. "I can't find my panties."

Dolan squared his Stetson on his head, then looked up from beneath the dark rim. "You won't need them. Besides, it'll make the ride to Cord's more interesting."

The flush of color across her face was adorable. Cord tossed Dolan the keys to his truck.

Cord gathered Cait in the crook of his arm and all three headed for the door.

Dolan went first, climbing the stairs and weaving through the crowd, putting distance between him and Cait and Cord so it wouldn't appear they were a threesome. No matter their attempts, Cord knew there would be talk tomorrow. With a little luck, it wouldn't reach George Culver's ears before Cord figured out how to respond to the man's wrath. His ranch wasn't the only thing in jeopardy; Dolan's career would suffer if Culver discovered the truth.

Cait must have sensed Cord's disquiet because she glanced up at him. "Are you okay?"

He looked into her worried eyes and all thoughts of her father disappeared. They were moving across the dance floor when he drew her to a stop. It felt right to take her in his arms, feet shifting to the slow music. More than once he had dreamed of dancing with her, their bodies pressed together, her lips so close he could taste them.

On a spin, he pulled her tight against him, wedging a leg between her thighs. She wore no panties. The memory made his cock swell and his pulse race. His fingertips skimmed down her back, slipping into the pocket of her jean skirt to rest on her ass.

Was she wet? Ready for him?

His answer came when she looked up at him, desire burning in her eyes. "Let's go," she whispered.

Hand in hand, they made it to the door. As they stepped outside, the sultry summer night folded around them. Stars twinkled above. The sweet scent of magnolias rose from the huge tree above that was dotted with big white flowers.

The lights of his truck blinked on, the roar of the engine sounded. Dolan sat behind the wheel. With an expression of male appreciation, he watched Cait crawl into the backseat, her skirt sliding up her legs flashing him a little of what hid beneath.

"How 'bout you drive?" he said to Cord.

"No way." Cord had plans for the drive home. And he was starting with a kiss.

Before she could fasten her seatbelt, he pulled her into his embrace. Her lips were soft against his. He moved his mouth lightly across hers, little nudges, as he stared into eyes that captivated him.

A nibble here.

A nibble there.

She tasted so good.

The night and dark, tinted windows hid them from sight. Cord didn't think twice of ridding her of her satin shirt. Her nipples reacted to the cool air, growing taut before his heated gaze. He captured an extended peak in his hot mouth.

"Fuck," Dolan growled, his glare simmering in the rearview mirror. "I need some of that." Momentarily, his hands left the steering wheel. He cursed again. Sounds of him fighting his belt buckle were followed by a curse as he quickly grabbed the wheel to straighten the truck when it veered to the right. A sudden jerk of the vehicle, and then he went back to work on his belt. Metal scraped metal, the hiss of his zipper followed by a deep sigh of relief. "Wonder what that tight pussy tastes like?"

Funny, but Cord was wondering the exact same thing.

Tugging her hips, Cord laid Cait on the seat. He positioned her so that Dolan could see her in the rearview mirror. Her legs were warm as Cord smoothed his hands up them beneath her skirt to raise the denim around her waist. She didn't speak, just watched him. Her full breasts rose and fell rapidly. On her own accord she parted her thighs so that she was spread wide.

"Damn you, Cord," Dolan grumbled, one hand on the wheel. His body shook and his breathing was labored. Not to mention, the truck swayed time to time over the "idiot bumps" in the road, making a riveting sound and bouncing the vehicle to let Dolan know he'd crossed the line.

Cord buried his head between Cait's legs and inhaled her womanly fragrance. When his tongue touched her clit, she came off the seat moaning. He grasped her hips, holding her in place as he flattened his tongue along her slit, then licked along the sweet folds several times, before flicking it over her now swelling bud.

The truck jerked to the right and then the left.

Cord prayed the man kept the damn truck on the road. Still he couldn't help teasing his cousin. "Hmmm... She tastes sweet."

"Fuck, I knew it," Dolan choked as the truck accelerated.

Cord grinned against her moist flesh, his tongue parting her, thrusting inside to mimic what his cock had in mind.

Cait tore off his cowboy hat, tossing it to the floorboard as her fingers threaded through his hair, pulling him closer. "Yes," she moaned. Her back arched off the seat, her thighs spreading wider.

Cord lived to please, especially Cait. He shoved his hands beneath her ass, raising her hips for deeper penetration, sucking, licking and biting until she writhed uncontrollably.

The grip she had on his hair tightened, creating a sharp burn across his scalp. "Feels. So. Good," she gasped, her hips meeting each thrust.

Add to that the sounds his mouth made against her heated flesh, Cord's groin throbbed painfully. He needed to be inside her. Instead, he crammed two fingers deep within her as he drew her clit between his lips.

"Cord!" Cait screamed his name, shattering in his arms. She bucked, twisting and turning as he continued to wring out every sensation from her quivering body. Her pussy clenched and released around his fingers. Blood filled her clit so it pulsated against his tongue.

Cord couldn't recall ever seeing anything as beautiful as Cait in the throes of passion. She whimpered, small cries of ecstasy. When she finally lay quiet, her eyes closed, her breathing steady, he knew he'd never let her go.

Cait's eyelids rose to find a tender expression on Cord's face as he watched her.

What was he thinking? Or for that matter, what was Dolan thinking? His dark gaze darted to the rearview mirror and then back to the road.

Cait couldn't remember when she'd felt so sated, so thoroughly fucked. She started to stretch when the leather seat stuck to her bare back. "Owww!" The sudden pain increased as she moved her ass to sit up. "I hate leather seats." Her grumble met laughter from both men. "Ha ha."

"Come here, darlin'." With a devilish grin Cord coaxed her to his side.

She took his face into her hands. A lump caught in her throat. She wanted this man so much. Not for just one night—but forever. However, she wasn't an idiot. All she had to do was

115

mention the word love and he'd be down the road faster than she could say it.

The truck slowed and came to a stop in front of Cord's ranch-style home. She'd never been inside, though she and Tracy had passed by it more times than she cared to admit.

Tracy.

Her friend's—make that ex-friend's—betrayal still stuck in Cait's craw. She had confided in Tracy how much Cord meant to her. With a little help from her friend, Cait's nineteenth birthday present to herself had blown up in her face.

Cait lifted her arms and allowed Cord to slip her shirt over her head to cover her. She pulled down the skirt wadded around her waist, while memories continued to churn in her head.

It had been a perfect plan for her to meet Cord at Norton's and reveal her feelings. Everything was going as arranged that night, except for the part where she walked into the bedroom she'd scheduled and found Tracy in bed with Cord and Dolan.

The truck door squeaked as Cord opened it and helped her out.

Before Cait pushed the ugly memory out of her mind, she had one laugh on Tracy. According to Kendra, talk was Cord had never touched Tracy again.

Cord snaked his arm around her shoulder, while Dolan held her by the waist as they headed for the door.

She glanced from one handsome man to the next. This was what Cait had been missing.

After that fateful night at Norton's, Cait had been shipped off to Paris. A surprise birthday present from her father. It was just supposed to be a visit with her estranged mother—a visit that had lasted almost two long years. The truth was he'd caught wind of her feelings for Cord and for some reason George Culver would do anything to keep them apart.

Of course, her father's horses came first—his daughter second. Her mother hadn't even made it on his radar screen. She'd hung on as long as she could, but when Cait was fourteen her mother had left to join her family in Paris. She hadn't even bothered to fight for Cait—her father held all the money, all the power.

Cord eased away the furrows on her forehead with his finger. "You're thinking too hard." He unlocked the front door and everyone stepped inside.

Dolan flashed a roguish grin. "I know how to cure that." Dolan pulled her into his arms and pressed his lips to hers.

The kiss was hungry, demanding, lacking the playfulness Cord's caress usually contained. His mustache tickled her lips, his tongue tangling with hers.

Before she knew it he had her stripped of her shirt once again. With one palm he kneaded her breasts—one and then the other—pulling and pinching her nipples until they tingled. She didn't have time to even look around the room before Cord moved beside Dolan and in unison they bent, taking a hard peak into their mouths.

The rims of their Stetsons overlapped, and rubbed against her collarbone as they licked and sucked. She removed both hats and cast them upon the tile floor. Then she pushed her fingers through their hair, holding them to her.

Cord and Dolan shared a glance, releasing her, before Dolan began to unbutton his red silk shirt and unzip his jeans.

Cord walked away, returning with a cushion off a brown leather couch positioned before a big screen television. A fireplace was cattycorner from the TV. He placed the cushion on the floor before her. He looked a little hesitant, and then he said, "Kneel."

When she did, Dolan stepped before her. He ran his fingers through her hair. His dark blue eyes appeared almost pitch black. "I'm dying to feel your beautiful mouth wrapped around my cock." He crammed his hand in his pocket, retrieving a condom, and handed it to her as he slid his jeans to his knees.

Cord stood off to the side. His expression was hard to read.

Cait directed her attention back to the man who stood before her. She could smell his musky arousal, making her hands tremble as she tore open the packet and extracted the rubber. Her fingers circled his shaft, pumping from base to tip several times. She leaned forward, swiping her tongue around the large head, winning a sharp intake of air from Dolan. She carefully sheathed him and took him into her mouth.

"Oh yeah..." Dolan groaned, deep and long.

Cait could have sworn Cord growled. From the corner of her eye, she saw him step closer, before moving behind her.

With a slow, steady rhythm Dolan fucked her mouth. His fists curled into her hair, his hips swaying back and forth.

Excitement burned in her belly causing moisture to build between her thighs. She slid her tongue along the bulging vein, flicked it across his sensitive tip, wanting to taste his salty essence, instead receiving the bitterness of latex.

Her mouth watered. Each time she swallowed, Dolan cried out.

She wanted to crow, "Look who's screaming now." Instead she cradled his balls in her palms, gently kneading, pinching his scrotum and pulling the loose skin away from his body.

"*Ahhh...*" Dolan moaned on a strangled breath.

When Cait felt her skirt rise, her bare ass exposed, she couldn't help her teeth scraping across Dolan's sensitive skin. Even that appeared to thrill the man as he tossed back his head, eyes closed, and cried, "Fuck yeah."

Perched on pins and needles, she waited impatiently to see what Cord would do next. When his naked torso nestled to her back, Cait sighed around Dolan's cock.

"Suck him good, darlin'," Cord's warm Southern drawl hummed against her ear. "I'm next."

His hard shaft was wedged between her thighs, pressing against her slit. With long, smooth strokes, he tormented her swollen folds, intensifying the throb that already existed.

Just the thought of Cord deep in her mouth made her pace quicken. She released her hold on Dolan's balls and smoothed her palms along his hips to cup his ass. Breathing through her nose, she easily took him to the back of her throat and swallowed.

"Sonofabitch," Dolan hollered.

She grinned around her mouthful and swallowed again.

"Yeah." He sucked in a sharp breath. "Just like th—"

He froze.

The hold he had on her hair tightened, sending a tingle across her scalp.

Dolan's climax exploded. His cock jerked against her throat. She felt the shiver that raced through him as she continued to milk him.

"Whoa, baby." His body convulsed.

Palm to her forehead, he tried to break the suction she had on him. She drew her tongue over his sensitive head once more before releasing him. He stumbled backward; his legs appeared to be unsteady.

"Cord—" That's all Dolan said, as if too weak to even finish his sentence.

Cord had waited long enough. He pushed to his feet, making quick use of a condom, before moving to face Cait. With lust-ridden eyes, she gazed at him. Slowly, her sweet mouth formed a perfect "O" that made his cock throb.

"You want some of this, darlin'?" Just the thought of how her lips would feel wrapped around his dick made a shudder race through him.

She reached for him. "Yes." Her soft hands trembled against his skin as she circled her fingers around his firm erection.

The burn tingling at the base of his balls flared into a white-hot conflagration when she wasted no time slipping him between her lips.

"Tight. Hot." He had to breathe through his mouth to get the oxygen he needed.

With her forefinger and thumb she gripped him tight at the base, moving her hand with each pump of her mouth. On upstrokes she twisted her fingers one way. On the downstroke she changed directions, alternating the pressure. Blood slammed into his balls making them hard and tender. It was enough to blow his control straight to hell.

She continued to manipulate him with her hand as she sucked, nibbled and licked.

Her eyes dilated. Her nostrils flared.

Then in a surprise move she released him and pushed to her feet, bracing her palm to his chest. She drove him against the nearest wall. "F-fuck me. Now."

From the corner of his eye, he could see Dolan lounging in an overstuffed chair, a smirk on his face.

She didn't take off her little short skirt or her boots before grasping his neck and pulling herself up to lock her legs around his waist.

Cord spun on a heel, changing their positions so that her back was against the wall. He positioned his hips and with one thrust drove deep inside her.

"Yes," she cried out. "Hard." The word came out on a growl.

He slammed his hips into her cradle, his cock bouncing against the walls of her cervix.

She buried her face into his neck and bit him.

It hurt so good.

The ache between his thighs became painful, causing sparks of electricity to splinter in his groin. He held his breath, hoping to prolong the inevitable.

With long licks she laved the wounded area with her tongue, taking turns to suck his flesh deep into her mouth and bite again. Her fingernails raked across his back while she rode him hard, fast. Her breaths were audible, shallow and raspy, her hot gaze hungry and wild.

Her inner muscles clamped down on him. She threw back her head and released a loud cry. As her orgasm washed over her, his thrusts intensified, ripping another groan from her trembling lips.

Suddenly, his body tensed.

Stars burst behind his eyelids as liquid fire shot down his cock. The earth-shattering climax tore through him leaving no place untouched. He pressed his forehead to the bend of her neck and shoulder and allowed himself to savor the moment.

The squeak of the chair as Dolan rose was the first sound to break through the dream state he was lost in.

"Unbelievable. She's fuckin' hot." Lust simmered in the depths of Dolan's eyes. "More. Gotta have more." He took a stiff step forward. The hungry expression on his face worried Cord.

Not looking good.

If Cait affected Dolan as she did Cord, then his cousin might not be willing to walk away come tomorrow. And that was unacceptable.

Mine—all mine, echoed in Cord's head. The woman had haunted his dreams for years. No way would he allow Dolan to take what he knew was his.

Cord released her, letting her body slide down his. "Cait, spend the night with us?" He was caught between wanting to wake in her arms and needing to put some distance between her and Dolan. His self-confidence had never wavered like it did at that moment.

Would she want only him or now that she'd had the taste of two men would she want more? Of course, there was a second that he wondered if this could simply be a one-night stand for Cait.

She smiled prettily. "Love to. I told Dad I was staying at Kendra's tonight."

He took her hand in his, leading her down the hall to the bedrooms. Whatever tomorrow brought, they were going to have a helluva night judging by the sexy look on her face.

Chapter Five

Bundled up in blankets that smelled of sandalwood, spice and sex, Cait squinted against the ray of light filtering through the parted curtains.

She was alone.

Not quite how she had pictured awaking this morning. Disappointment swamped her. As she attempted to move, pain greeted her at every turn. "Ow." She smiled, remembering her decadent night with Cord and Dolan.

"So this is what is meant by being ridden hard and put up wet." Her giggle sounded girlish. The two men had turned her every which way but loose, and she had loved every minute of it.

As her eyes adjusted to the light of day, she noted that her clothes and boots lay on a padded bench in the corner. No panties again.

She hadn't seen much of Cord's home last night, but what she'd seen was decorated in Western décor. Wood and leather, bulky furniture and Western art hung on the walls. His large bed was cut from pine, as well as the dresser off to the right. To the left was an adjoining bathroom she had discovered after their last heated session. Then she had fallen asleep wrapped in two men's arms.

It was a fantasy straight out of a wet dream. But the best part was the tender moments when Cord had touched her like she was a piece of china.

She pushed a sated sigh from her lips and rose. With a stretch, Cait tried to work the soreness from her muscles and the sensitive areas of her body.

Where are the boys?

"Duh? Ranch," she said aloud as she headed toward her clothing.

Cord worked his own ranch with several hands. Of course he would be out feeding stock and taking care of business.

After dressing, she opened the door and entered into the hallway.

It was like a shrine.

Pictures of Cord from the time he was a baby to adulthood lined the walls. There were several pictures of his mother and father, one that tightened her chest. A beautiful blonde woman smiled proudly at Cord as a toddler, with his chubby cheeks and flyaway hair. He hugged her like she meant the world to him.

His mother.

Cait had heard stories of the horrific car accident that had stolen Cord's mother from him. His father had never remarried, mourning her passing until his own.

A love like that was what every woman wanted, including Cait. And she wanted her other half to be Cord. Bad boy or not, she knew once he settled down he'd be just like his father.

She moved quickly through the house wanting to see Cord. Needing to know that what they shared last night wasn't just a dream and praying it meant as much to him as it had her.

The screen door whined as she released it and let it slam shut. In the distance, Cord stood talking to a man. Dolan was nowhere in sight. She didn't know whether to bother Cord and the man. Just before she decided to go back into the house, Cord turned. He was frowning, his features tight. He shot her a look of warning, but before she could step into the house the other man turned around.

Cait's heart skipped a beat. Her feet froze.

It was her father.

By the blush of heat that raced up his throat and spread across his face, he didn't look happy.

Who cares? I'm an adult. Still her knees threatened to buckle with her first step, while her stomach did a flip-flop. Cait squared her shoulders. Time to face the music or more likely the shit hitting the fan.

By the time she reached the two men, the color in her father's face had faded. He smiled, giving her the feeling of the calm before the storm. "Caitlyn, I didn't expect you here so soon."

What?

Cord gave her a puzzled look that echoed her own confusion.

She cleared her throat. "Father."

Where was the yelling? The fireworks? The threats?

Cord draped his arm around her shoulder, drawing her to his side. The possessive action made her visualize a kid poking a stick at a rattlesnake. Any minute her father would strike.

Instead, he winked at her.

Now this is just freaky.

Cord must have thought so too, because he shot her a suspicious glance.

From the corner of her eye movement caught her attention. A remarkable bay colt kicked up his heels as the gentle breeze blew newspaper into his corral.

So this was why her father was here. Of course, it didn't explain his odd behavior, especially toward Cord and the fact she'd spent the night with him.

"Beautiful conformation." Cait had an eye for horses and this one was a winner with long, strong legs. "Who owns him?"

Her father slapped Cord on the back. "Well that's what Daily and I were discussing."

"A perfect match for Misty Dawn and Taylor Tweeds," she spoke her thoughts aloud. The mares were just a couple of Cait's personal horses.

"Exactly," her father agreed. His eyes sparkled.

Cord frowned; his arm slipped from her shoulder to his side.

The colt held his black tail high in the air as he galloped across the pasture. "Look at him," she breathed. "I'd love to have him."

Her father pulled out his checkbook and pen. "How much do you want for him?"

This amazing creature belonged to Cord?

"He's not for sale." Cord watched her intently.

"Ridiculous. This is a cattle ranch, no place for a thoroughbred. Tell him, Cait."

Cord's face hardened. He narrowed his eyes.

"Uh... Well... You need equipment, a trainer, a racetrack." Cait knew the expense alone would break most people. Did Cord have the financial wherewithal for a high-powered animal?

"Without the proper training you'll ruin the colt," her father added.

126

Cord fisted his hands, then realizing what he was doing he relaxed them. But it was clear—he was upset.

Her father was an intelligent man. He knew how to play the waiting game. "No hurry." He tucked his checkbook away. "Dinner tonight? You, Cait and me at the house. Maybe you could join us at the track tomorrow. Bring Mystery Walker, use one of our jockeys and see how he takes to the track."

An invitation to the ranch?

Cait nearly swallowed her tongue. Any minute she expected the music to *The Twilight Zone* to play. She couldn't believe what she was hearing. But then maybe it wasn't so surprising. Horses had always come first with George Culver. He clearly meant to have this colt. Even at the expense of losing his daughter to the one man he had been hell-bent on keeping her away from for years.

What was wrong with her? This was exactly what Cait had wanted, so why did it sting so badly?

Cord glared at her. "So last night was about Mystery Walker?" She flinched at the accusation in his voice. But it was his ominous burst of laughter that chilled her. "You're good, darlin'. Culver peddling his daughter for a horse. Who would have guessed?"

What?

A moment of confusion was washed away by shock that ripped her hand from her side to land with a smack against Cord's cheek. The impact was so great his head snapped to the side. As she swung again, he caught her wrist.

Fire raged between them. The air filled with electricity.

The stabbing pain to her heart was quickly replaced by red-hot anger sweeping across her face like a brushfire. "You sonofabitch." She jerked out of his grasp, fighting the tears that burned her eyes.

Her father moved toward her. "Caitlyn! Apologize to Daily."

"What?" Cait's gaze shot to his. Did she hear him correctly?

"Apologize to Daily," he repeated.

This isn't happening.

Cord pretty much called her a whore. "You want *me* to apologize?" She propped her hands on her hips and glared up at him. "Fuck you. In fact, why don't the both of you go straight to hell?"

Cait spun around and took off, heading for the road. Her booted feet pounded the ground. Each step made her madder and madder.

She was such an idiot. Her arms swung wildly by her sides.

What had she ever seen in Cord? And why did it take so long before she saw the truth?

A tear betrayed her, rolling down her cheek. Another followed. Soon her vision blurred. She heard a truck come up behind her, but she stared blindly ahead.

"Caitlyn, get in." It was a demand issued by her father. But she didn't take orders from him anymore. Instead she ignored him. "Dammit, Caitlyn. I need your help here. The colt is sired by Galaxy and I want him."

Cait jerked to a stop. "Fuck you!" She stared disbelievingly into her father's gray eyes. "You arrogant prick. Cord isn't good enough for me, unless you can get something of value from him. Well, *Daddy*"—she'd never called him daddy—"it looks like you've lost it all." She started to laugh, the tight explosive sound bordering on hysteria. "My ass isn't for sale and you're not getting what you want for once."

His mouth clamped shut. Fury raged in his eyes. Tires squealed, spitting gravel as he tore off down the street leaving her standing there—alone.

Not bad for a day's work.

Cait had lost the only man she had ever loved and her father too.

Cord felt numb, except for the burn on his cheek. Cait had a helluva slap—nearly tore his head off. He watched Mystery Walker prance along the fence line. "All this because of you." He shook his head, refusing to believe he had spent the best night of his life with the woman of his dreams all because Culver had sought his horse.

What was worse was Cord had played right into Cait's hands.

And to think he had flown through his chores this morning wanting to get back to bed before she woke up.

Around five o'clock Dolan had received an emergency call from the Tucker's. One of their prize mares was having difficulty foaling. That meant Cait was all Cord's, but then her father had arrived, the bastard friendly and wanting to chat.

Cord huffed at his stupidity. All he could think of was protecting Cait.

Angrily, he pushed away from the fence. A gentle breeze swept around his neck, cooling his heated skin.

His blood had turned to ice when Cait stepped from the house. He knew when Culver saw his daughter, put two and two together, the man would be livid.

"Fool," Cord grumbled and then laughed. He had been trying to warn her to go back into the house, and all the time she knew exactly what was going on.

"It appears I'm back to dumbshit again." He squared his Stetson on his head. His boots struck the soft ground, stirring dust into the air. "What an idiot."

Still he had to hand it to her. Cait was quite the little actress. She had looked genuinely surprised, and then hurt when he insinuated she had seduced him for a horse.

Culver was a sonofabitch to use his daughter in such a way.

Cord's stride slowed as Cait's wounded expression flashed before his eyes. He rubbed his sore cheek. Her slap held enough rage to feel real—smarted like hell.

In fact, she had appeared furious with her father. He had never heard her speak like that to Culver. Then she had stormed off on foot. Her father probably picked her up down the road.

Still the whole thing needled him. Something wasn't right.

Had Cord acted too quickly in accusing Cait of being in cahoots with Culver?

"*Ya think?*" his subconscious ridiculed. "*She held you like she cared.*"

No one could be that good at pretending.

Everything he knew about women said Cait was falling for him. It was in the way she'd held him, stroked his body, and the way she looked at him. Cord would have bet his life on it.

Or was he trying to hold onto something that wasn't there?

No. He jerked to a stop. *Dammit! The night wasn't a lie.* No woman had ever duped him like that, or was that the reason he refused to accept what stared him in the face?

He rubbed his fingers over his mustache and goatee as he shook his head. It had been he and Dolan who had gone after her, not the other way around. Hell, she'd tied him up—left him.

God, this was fucked-up.

His gut churned.

Memories of her touch, her kiss, the heat of her body against his collided with thoughts of her deception.

Had he been wrong?

Bowing his head, he pinched the bridge of his nose. "What the hell have I done?" Footsteps made him look up.

"By the way Cait was storming down the street I'd say you screwed the pooch." Dolan frowned accusingly. "What happened?" His cousin looked as if he'd showered. He was wearing clean jeans, a T-shirt and his hat.

Cord sucked in his breath. "I think I fucked up bad."

Quietly, Dolan listened to the events of the morning. Then his expression hardened. "You're a goddamn putz."

So much for the buddy support system.

Apparently, his cousin wasn't through.

"That woman's in love with you. I've never seen anyone so desperate to please a man." Dolan shifted his feet, then his face hardened. "If you let her go"—he paused for only a moment— "don't expect me to step aside. A woman like her comes around only once in a lifetime."

Cord's anger rose like a tidal wave, calming just as fast.

Dolan was right.

Shit.

Cord headed toward his truck. "I better go after her."

Dolan snorted, following close behind. "If she wouldn't talk to me, she sure as hell won't talk to you. She's a mess right now. Anything you say will only be fuel to the flame."

Cord spun around to face Dolan. "Dammit, I love her."

Dolan eased to a stop. "I know." The tendons and muscles in his neck slowly thickened. Cord got the feeling there was something more Dolan wanted to say. It felt like a blow to his stomach when his cousin finished his thought. "If you can't patch this thing up—she's mine."

The truth gleamed in Dolan's eyes.

Cord had to move fast.

Chapter Six

Enough is enough.

It was the third time Cait had reapplied her makeup after her bath.

Like it did any good.

Puffy, red eyes stared back at her from the mirror above her dresser in between yanking lingerie and other clothing from one drawer and then the next. Every time she thought of Cord and his cruel words she burst into tears. But she was through with crying, through with thinking about him, and she was through with her father and California.

"Sonofabitch," she snarled.

Before she had washed Cord and Dolan's scent from her body, her father had stormed into her bedroom trying once more to get her cooperation in obtaining Mystery Walker. When that didn't work he had threatened to take her allowance away.

The idiot.

In a couple of months she'd be twenty-one and come into her inheritance left by her grandfather. For the moment she had plenty of money.

Then he threw down his cards. "I'll ruin him, Caitlyn. By the time I'm through with him, he'll have nothing, including Mystery Walker. Do you want that?"

Why hadn't she seen how devious her father could be? And why did it hurt so much when she turned her back on him and walked into the bathroom without a word? She shouldn't care what happened to Cord. Should she?

Returning to Paris was sounding better by the minute.

Two suitcases sat by the door. She dumped the armful of clothes she held into the bag laying on her bed before running her sweaty palms down her jeans. Her blue cotton T-shirt stuck to her chest, while the damp braid down her back left a wet spot where it lay.

It was summer, too warm for a fire. Still one burned in her marble fireplace. After speaking with her father she had been chilled to the bone, requesting Lawrence, their butler, to start a fire hoping to chase away the cold.

It hadn't worked.

Cait released a heavy sigh. Footsore and mentally drained, she had walked miles before Stack had driven by offering her a ride home. Instead, she had him drop her off at Kendra's where Cait's car was parked. Stack had ridden the way in silence.

Smart man. He asked no questions—she said nothing.

One more look around her bedroom of pinks and yellows. The ensemble she wore last night was thrown in a pile next to her big sleigh bed. She picked the skirt and shirt up, crossed the room and tossed them into the hearth. Sparks flew, popping as smoke spiraled, its heavy scent filling her nose. Blindly, she stared into the flames, watching the fire engulf her clothes to consume them.

If she could she'd burn every memory of last night.

Another shuddering sigh shook her from head to toe, jolting her into action. She walked across the marble floor to her bed, quickly zipped the bag and picked up the house telephone to dial the butler.

"Lawrence, can you please take my bags to my car?"

"Yes, ma'am."

The telephone clicked. As she set the receiver into the cradle, Cait slowly sat on her fluffy, pink comforter.

She felt empty—alone.

Yet self-pity was a waste of time. Things happened for a reason.

Disheartened, Cait rose to her feet. Kendra had offered her a place to stay until she decided where she wanted to go.

Maybe she needed a vacation in the Bahamas, maybe a cruise. All she knew was she had to get away from here.

 C8ഉ0ഔ

Evening rolled in along with a wave of anxiety that made Cord's skin prickle. His knee bounced up and down as he waited impatiently, staring at the telephone. Stetson atop his head, keys in his hands, he was ready to go the minute Stack called to say the coast was clear.

After Cait had left the ranch this morning, Cord had parked down the road from her house trying to find the words to apologize. Instead, he watched her 2007, red convertible Corvette zoom by piled high with suitcases.

She was leaving.

The knowledge did two things: One, it confirmed she wasn't in league with her father and, two, scared the living shit out of him. He couldn't bear the thought of never seeing her again.

A moment of panic struck replaced by relief as he discreetly followed her to Kendra's house. Again parking out of sight, he had called Stack and waited until his friend spoke to Kendra, confirming that Cait wasn't leaving town—not yet.

Stack had sounded a little stressed. Kendra wasn't giving up much information, but she agreed to go with him to Norton's tonight. He had asked if Cait would be attending and Kendra said, "No."

Cord thrummed his fingers against the bulky leather chair he sat in. "Come on, Stack."

When the telephone rang Cord lunged for the receiver, wasting no time to press it to his ear. "Stack?"

"Yeah, it's me." Loud music played in the background. "We're at Norton's. Cait's alone at Kendra's."

"Good." A combination of dread and excitement hummed through Cord's body. "Now where did you leave the key?"

Stack released a frustrated breath. "Kendra's gonna kill me."

Cord was so close. Stack couldn't cop out on him now. Cait would never answer the door if she knew it was him. "Please."

"I left it in the milk can next to her front door. Buddy, you owe me."

"I know." Cord slammed the receiver into its cradle, pushed to his feet and started for the front door.

He wasted no time climbing into his truck and heading down the road. Telephone poles, trees and houses were a blur as he sped by.

When he entered Kendra's subdivision, he sucked in a breath and squared his shoulders. He had no doubt that convincing Cait to give him another chance would not be easy, but it would be worth it.

Kendra's porch light burned brightly. He steered the truck into the driveway, cut the engine and opened the door, then closed it quietly behind him. With determined footsteps, he aimed for the milk can. The key was right where Stack said it would be.

A deafening silence lingered as he entered the darkened house, pocketing the key. He'd been there a time or two, but hadn't paid much attention to the layout. It wasn't a large home, so it shouldn't be difficult finding Cait. In fact, the glow of a light beneath one of the doors led his way. He turned the knob, thankful it wasn't locked.

"Forget something?" Cait called over her shoulder. Her gaze was pinned to the computer before her, a colorful picture of palm trees and the ocean on the screen. She pushed away from the desk, her chair rolling across the wood floor.

The moment she saw him her expression became pinched and then blank. Without a word she turned her back to him, scooted up to the desk and let her fingers fly across the keyboard.

For a moment, he listened to the *click-click-click* of her fingernails striking the keys. He stepped closer and inhaled the clean scent of soap and floral shampoo that surrounded her. She was dressed for bed in a red silky camisole and matching short-shorts.

God, he wanted to touch her. His cock hardened with just the thought. He shut and locked the office door before moving deeper into the room. "We need to talk."

More silence greeted him.

"Cait, I'm sorry. I—"

She rose from the chair and started to walk past him, but he grabbed her arm.

Her gaze snapped to his hand. "Get the fuck away from me."

Their eyes met, hers filled with rancor.

Still he didn't release her. "Please, just listen to me?"

With a chill in her voice, she growled, "I'm not interested in anything you have to say."

"Cait."

An icy glare of indifference stared back at him.

"What I said— It was just— Dammit, Cait. What did you expect me to think?" This wasn't going as he had planned.

Her eyes widened. She stiffened. "Well, let's see. How about giving me the benefit of the doubt?" Before he could say anything, she continued, "No. That's right. You played the whore card, didn't you?" Sarcastic laughter burst from her lips. "Remember, you came looking for me." This time she did yank her arm from his grasp and headed for the door, but not before spinning around and saying, "By the way, my father's plans are to ruin you. Steal your ranch, your horse, your life. Might think about making it easy on yourself and just give him the horse."

Cait unlocked the door, but he placed a palm against it barring her escape. She was slipping away from him. He had to do something, fast. "I love you."

Her hand fell from the doorknob to her side. When she turned so that her back was against the door and she faced him, there were tears in her eyes.

"Now who's the whore?" She swallowed hard.

He tried to brush his hand across her cheek, but she jerked her head away. "Cait."

She refused to look at him. "Forget it. It doesn't matter."

He pinched her chin, forcing her gaze to meet his. "I love you." A huff of disbelief met his vow.

"Man, you'd say anything to get what you want." She yanked her chin from his hand.

Cord had to make her understand. "It's not like that, Cait."

Her brows pulled together in an expression of pain. "Then how is it, Cord? Would you marry me to save your ranch—your horse?"

"What? Yes—no, I mean—" This was definitely not turning out how he planned.

She snorted. "That's what I thought."

His hand slid beneath her hair to cup the nape of her neck. He drew her closer so that their noses touched. "No. It isn't what you think. I'd give up everything I own for you."

"Stop it," she demanded, struggling to break his hold.

"Everything—for you." He brushed his lips softly across hers.

A tear ran down her cheek. "I can't believe how cruel you are." Sorrow rimmed her eyes. "Do you have any idea what you meant to me? What I would have done—did do just to have one night with you? Shit." She released an exasperated breath. "Just let me go and leave me the hell alone."

She did care. Now all he had to do was get her to believe him.

He gave her a firm shake. "Listen to me."

"Give it up, Cord."

"Hell, yes, I'll marry you," he yelled.

Her eyes widened with what appeared to be shock and disbelief.

"I'd get in my truck and drive to Las Vegas this very minute, but not to save my ranch or some damn horse." Emotion caught in his throat. His voice softened. "Woman, you make me crazy." He shook her again. "I can't think when you're around." He pressed his body to hers, forcing her to feel his arousal. "Cait, I want you. Not for one night, but forever. If your father wants Mystery Walker, he can have him. It would be worth it if I walked away with you."

Another tear raced down her face. She inhaled a shuddering breath. "Stop it. No more lies."

"Let me prove it to you. Marry me?" Cord slipped his hands beneath her camisole, smoothing his palms over her warm, silky skin.

"No. Stop." She slapped his hand.

"Ahhh...darlin'." His fingertips drifted past the elastic of her shorts, stroking the cheeks of her ass.

She whimpered, trying to pull away, but he held on tight.

"Say yes." His kissed the corner of her mouth, slid his tongue across her bottom lip coaxing her lips to part.

"N-no," she insisted, but this time she went limp in his arms.

He pushed her shorts down to her thighs and the satin material fell to her ankles.

"Cord—" His name was a desperate cry muffled at the last second.

"Say yes." He drew her camisole over her head so she stood before him naked, vulnerable.

She shook her head, frowning. He could almost see her internal struggle to resist him, even as her body warmed to his touch.

With his fingertip, he drew small circles around her nipples, watching them tighten to hard peaks. He bent, taking one into his mouth, laving it with his tongue.

She gasped, arching into his touch. Her hands fisted in his hair.

With half-raised eyelids, he glanced at her. "Yes?" He blew on her wet nipple and goose bumps skittered across her skin.

She closed her eyes, as if the mere action would erase him from her presence.

One kiss and then another, he covered her breasts, moving down her abdomen to dip his tongue in her bellybutton, before he dropped to his knees.

He scented her arousal, a musky aroma that increased the throb between his thighs. Wedging her legs apart, he dipped his head to taste. He lapped at her pussy, sucked her swollen clit between his lips, then plunged his tongue into her channel.

Her eyes sprang open. "Oh God." Her knees buckled, giving slightly.

Cord could sense her surrender. He moved back from her, a smile tilting his lips. "Yes?"

"Yes," she hissed. "Yes-yes-yes."

Chapter Seven

Cord stood, moving quickly to undress, but it wasn't fast enough. Small, lightning-tinged explosions rocked Cait's body, the ache between her thighs becoming more intense.

Her breathing was labored as she used the cool door in Kendra's office to keep her naked body upright.

She needed him—needed him now, almost desperately.

He had broken her will when his tongue thrust inside her, licking the sensitive walls of her pussy.

No. That wasn't true.

It was the soft expression on his face as he said, "Woman, you make me crazy." She knew that feeling, because she lost it every time she was around him.

When Cord was unclothed, he retrieved a cushion from the chair where she had sat in front of the computer. He knelt, resting his haunches on the pillow. His engorged cock sprang from the nest of curly hair, making her mouth water. Eyes dark with desire, he extended his hand to her.

Cait folded her fingers around his. He guided her down to straddle his thighs, lowering her so his shaft parted her swollen folds, stretching and driving inside. The position spread her unbelievably wide, allowing him to go deeper than she had ever felt him.

Instinctively, her muscles clenched and released around his thick erection.

"Tight," he groaned. "So fucking tight and hot."

He folded his arms around her back, holding her close. With shallow strokes, he began to make love to her. He pressed his cheek to hers. His tenderness was heartbreaking. She clung to him. Each caress carried her nearer to Heaven's door.

The flutter of sensation in her belly and the small explosions in her pussy signaled her oncoming climax. As he continued to thrust in and out, the heat—the throb built until she couldn't hold on. It burst, vibrating along her body, from her vagina, her clit, her very womb. Before she could catch her breath, another soft flare of pleasure rose, spreading throughout to leave her moaning, long and low.

Cord released a muffled cry against her shoulder. She felt his unsheathed cock pump once, twice, and then again as her mind whirled. Too late to do anything about protection.

The intimacy made the moment surreal as they stayed locked in each other's embrace.

"Darlin', I do love you," he whispered the reassurance against her ear.

She released him so that she could gaze into his eyes. "I love you too. I always have, Cord."

His eyes sparkled with a happiness that made her chest taut with emotion. He gave her a big bear hug. "Let's leave for Vegas right now." He moved her off his lap, stood, and then helped her to her feet.

"Really?" The thought of being Mrs. Cord Daily made her grin ear to ear.

He brushed back her hair and kissed her softly on the lips. "I want you as my wife before the sun rises."

Cait cuddled up close to Cord, seeking his warmth. George Culver was in for a rude awakening. His little plan was just about to backfire even more. There was absolutely no way he would have let Cait and Cord get to this point without intervening. She couldn't wait to see her father's face when they came to call as husband and wife.

Cord popped her playfully on the ass. "Get dressed."

In record time they were clothed, in the truck and heading down the road. Cait hated the console that separated them. She wanted to touch him so badly her breasts were heavy, her nipples rasping painfully against the light summer dress she wore.

Cord's gaze darted toward her and then back to the road. "Cait, what about Mystery Walker?" he asked with an air of caution.

She wasn't a fool. A colt out of Galaxy was every man's dream horse. She knew it would kill him to give him up, especially to her father.

"If you've a mind, we can build our own stables." Cait leaned over the console to stroke his arm, wishing he didn't wear a shirt so she could feel skin and muscle beneath her palm. "You know I have connections. A horse with his lines can be a goldmine. I've learned a lot being the daughter of George Culver." She wouldn't tell Cord about the money she would inherit. With it they would be able to build stalls, a racetrack, even buy more stock. The thought was exciting. She couldn't wait to get started.

Cord changed lanes, then glanced at her again. "I don't want that animal to come between us." Even in the darkness, she saw the truth in his eyes. Unlike her father, with Cord she came first. That made her love him even more.

"Nothing or no one is ever going to come between us." She frowned, the edge of the console nudging her ribs. "Well, except for this damn console. What happened to bench seats?"

His easy laughter swept over her. "Do you want me to pull over, darlin'?" He grinned, steering the truck over to the side of the road.

"Sounds good to me. Backseat?"

He cut the engine, opening the door at the same time she did. They both laughed as they climbed out of the truck and scrambled into the backseat.

When they came together again, Cait knew that from this day forward she would never want another man. She had found her own slice of heaven in the arms of Cord Daily.

About the Author

A taste of the erotic, a measure of daring and a hint of laughter describe Mackenzie McKade's novels. She sizzles the pages with scorching sex, fantasy and deep emotion that will touch you and keep you immersed until the end. Whether her stories are contemporaries, futuristics or fantasies, this Arizona native thrives on giving you the ultimate erotic adventure.

When not traveling through her vivid imagination, she's spending time with three beautiful daughters, two devilishly handsome grandsons, and the man of her dreams. She loves to write, enjoys reading, and can't wait 'til summer. Boating and jet skiing are top on her list of activities. Add to that laughter and if mischief is in order—Mackenzie's your gal!

To learn more about Mackenzie, please visit www.mackenziemckade.com. Send an email to Mackenzie at mackenzie@mackenziemckade.com or sign onto her Yahoo! group to join in the fun with other readers and authors as well as Mackenzie!

http://groups.yahoo.com/group/wicked_writers/

Look for these titles by
Mackenzie McKade

Now Available

Six Feet Under
Fallon's Revenge
A Warrior's Witch
Bound for the Holidays
Lisa's Gift
Lost But Not Forgotten
Second Chance Christmas

Coming Soon:

Bound By The Holiday
Take Me Again
Merry Christmas Paige

A Scorching Seduction

Marie Harte

Chapter One

The Pacifica Resort, Planet Ermu

Fia af' Nicos—agent and spy for Racor, the Fyresh System's military headquarters—grumbled under her breath and prayed the damned cloth barely covering her breasts would hold. How any woman could be expected to work around this place in scraps of silk was beyond her. Granted, sheer cloth was much cooler than heavy *lurpa*, and the burning summer suns on Ermu had turned her skin from white to honey brown in just two months, but the staff might have been given actual clothing to work in instead of these tiny bits of material.

She glanced down at the lavender two-piece clinging to her sweaty body. Two small triangles hid her nipples, and an equally small triangle of silk covered her mons—provided she shaved—held in place by a thin strip of silk around her waist and between her cheeks. Lovely. Like most of the other women waiting tables, Fia was supposed to haul drinks and small meals, catering to the Pacifica's clients. The food and drink were superb, and the waitstaff was expected to be as pretty and as tantalizing. She'd only just managed to avoid sex in her short stay, foisting off her many admirers on her nympho roommate, Clea.

"Fia," a deep voice rumbled, sending unwelcome ripples of lust through her body. "The senator at table four has been asking for you."

She nodded, giving the giant male a quick smile, and found the senator poolside, lounging next to his inebriated wife. With her attention divided between the senator's lackluster flattery and the hot summer suns, she had a hard time focusing on her quarry—the reason for her cover in this "paradise".

Glancing at the giant and his partner out of the corner of her eye, Fia recognized Racor's war heroes with little difficulty, despite their island garb. Both Trace N'Tre and Vaan C'Vail stood heads above most guests, hunky security guards who easily blended with the beautiful people paying through the nose to enjoy this resort.

Vaan, Racor's greatest assassin, wore only low-riding, cropped trou that ended at midthigh, showcasing his muscular legs, washboard stomach and broad, tanned chest. His hair had been bleached almost white, but the expanse of tan skin turned darker by the suns only made his ice blue eyes stand out that much more.

Not to be outdone, the giant, Lieutenant Colonel Trace N'Tre, stood beside him wearing a frown and similar garb. Trace was an inch or two taller than Vaan with more muscle on his body. The high commander of covert operations in Racor's TAC Army, Trace led the best by being the best. He had strength in spades, agility and a quickness of mind respected by his men and envied by his enemies.

And at the moment, his displeasure seemed centered on her. *Shit.* She quickly gave the senator all of her attention, mentally gritting her teeth when his hands reached up and rubbed her breasts, squeezing her nipples with rasping grunts for her to move closer. Glancing at his wife, Fia saw her slumberous gaze admiring as well and realized the couple meant for her to be a third, a popular trend at the Pacifica.

Known for its hedonistic approach to vacation, and with a reputation for delivering whatever and whomever its clients wanted, the Pacifica made more currency than any other resort on this small pleasure planet. Had it not been in the middle of the harsh summer, Fia might have surrendered to temptation a time or two, relieving her sexual desire to better focus on her mission. But she knew better than to succumb in this heat.

A native Vendon, Fia had grown up under an orange star. Accustomed to a certain amount of radiation, the Vendons had developed unique skills living in the Cyoc System. There, they had once been able to blend, camouflaging themselves in any environment, merging with the sun's rays to alter visible perceptions. However, when the planet's core threatened mass destruction, a mass exodus of Vendons spilled into the Fyresh System, solving most of their problems, while causing others.

The transition hadn't been too hard, except that they'd had to adjust to living under the light of two suns. It wasn't so much a problem on Racor, the moon where she'd been raised. But here on Ermu, the brilliance of the summer suns played havoc on her body. She could no longer vanish in the shadows. She could still, however, slightly alter her body to look different enough not to be recognizable—shorten her stature, elongate her face, bulk up her chest—all of which she'd done for this particular job.

The twin suns presented other problems. Under too much exposure, a Vendon could lose all sense, mindlessly vulnerable to everyone and everything. And then there were the sexual side effects.

Fia forced a smile at the senator and bent lower to hear his whispered proposition. *Ugh.* Unfortunately, her mind and body weren't in tune. Thanks to the suns' rays, her body began to tingle, and she knew she had to leave the heat until she cooled enough to regain control. Thankfully, the senator thought her shivering a product of his touch. She stared down at his fat fingers, at his squinty eyes more interested in her breasts than his constituents starving in Lermot. She inwardly cursed while smiling pleasantly, fanning her overheating body with a vigorous wave of her large tray.

Had this mission occurred during any other season, she'd no doubt have been finished by now. But with the harsh suns beating down on her, her body played tricks she didn't find funny, *in the slightest.* God forbid she have a heated orgasm in front of these two idiots.

The senator's wife ran a hand up the inside of Fia's thigh, and Fia hurriedly made an excuse to bring them both more Ner wine. The dissipated senator was bad enough, but his wife made her skin crawl. Even Clea had refused the witch, and Clea would bed a four-handed Richet for the right price.

Intent on finding a cooler spot in which to hide, Fia ran smack into Trace.

"Easy, Fia." His body felt as hard as stone, his chest gleaming like diamonds in the heat. Like Vaan, his body was hairless but for his thick, shoulder-length black hair, and she felt an irresistible urge to pet him. "Feeling all right?"

"The senator didn't harm you, did he?" Vaan approached silently, his voice like ice.

She chanced a glance at him, conscious to remain shy in keeping with her persona at the club. To avoid a lot of hassle, she'd pretended to be a quiet sex sharer who commanded in the bedroom. Her incredible reputation as a lover was such that once she'd posed her cover, offers from all over the planet and half the System had funneled in. She'd received the job at the

Pacifica with recommendations from several wealthy benefactors—real men and women she used as sources—and with no governmental ties to Racor.

Both Vaan and Trace were sharp enough to spot an obvious plant, which was why both men hadn't been caught by Racor officials in over a year. Just a few months ago the government had learned that their traitors had fled to Ermu, but the planet's unique purpose in the System granted Ermu control when it came to denying the System's military, which made Vaan and Trace's ability to enter the world quite extraordinary. Fia still didn't know how they'd received sanctuary on the pleasure planet—two warriors on the run from the System's militia.

"Fia?" Vaan's voice softened, and he lifted her chin, meeting her artificially brown eyes with his own.

She stared, unable to help it, knowing she had to reach the shade, and quickly. By the moons, his eyes looked like ice, so cold, so soothing. And the feel of his hand on her face, the texture of calloused fingers gently caressing her flesh...

Heat built in her womb, and her limbs felt shaky. She clutched the tray in her hands for dear life and forced a wobbly smile. "I'm fine. It's just this heat."

Trace nodded. "Grab some water and take a short break. Reba can handle the senator and his wife." He motioned a voluptuous redhead to take the table, and the senator happily welcomed the topless woman.

Moving even as he said it, Fia found refuge in a shaded cubby, secure from prying eyes. A burst of heat burned through her and she gasped, caught on the edge of a powerful orgasm. Those damned suns were majorly screwing with her hormones, and she just barely avoided climaxing before the guests. She couldn't help a small groan and knew she had to cool down before rejoining the group by the pool. Shaking, she headed for her small quarters and a cold, cold shower, grateful for the Pacifica's generous water bounty.

CʒʒʘɞƆ

Trace watched Fia walk away with a frown on his face. "I'm telling you there's something seriously wrong about that woman."

"What's that? The fact that she didn't throw herself at you within the first five minutes of meeting you?" Vaan drawled. "Or is it that she's so eminently fuckable, and you're too hardheaded to make a move?"

"Funny. You thought the same when she first came here."

"Yeah, but it's been two months. She works hard, is discreet about her trysts, and looks so damned good it's hard not to like her."

"She has been pretty discreet." Trace rubbed his chin, aware he'd been in the suns too long. His dick felt on fire, and shy little Fia hadn't helped matters. Mastering his body, he forced his blood to cool, conscious of Vaan's probing gaze. *Shit.* Sometimes he really didn't like being Vendon. Though he could change his appearance at will, doing so took more energy than he wanted to expend if he wanted to keep alert and alive against Racor's best. Hell, his body had a mind of its own that had nearly gotten him killed more times than he could count. That he was still alive shocked the hell out of him.

"Looks like you have a problem." Vaan grinned, staring at Trace's tenting trou.

"Shut up." He closed his eyes, trying hard not to inhale Vaan's surprisingly alluring scent. Sweat and determination. Sheer, unadulterated sexuality. "Back up, dammit."

Vaan chuckled and gave him some space.

Trace blinked into knowing blue eyes. "I'll tell you again, I'm not interested."

"Sure." Vaan had the audacity to ignore his heating temper. "Look, let's go back to my room. I have a few thoughts about how to get back to Racor and put Joanen the hell out of commission. And let's face it, you need a break."

Managing to will his erection down, if not away, Trace put Dron in charge and left the damned heat, sighing with relief under the cooling fans in the Pacifica's employee corridor. "Have I thanked your cousin enough for letting us stay here?"

Vaan shrugged. "Considering she's working us for no pay, we're probably even."

"Hardly. You know as well as I do they're still after us. Until we can prove Joanen guilty, we're walking dead men."

Vaan scowled. "You're a real downer, you know that? Between you and me, we can survive anything. Even your dumbass cock. Shit, Trace, just get laid. You'll feel better."

It's not as if Trace didn't want sex, or even need it. But he'd had a bad feeling for weeks, constantly looking around him for the eyes he could feel, but couldn't see. Everyone was suspect, from the new chef, to his fellow security guards, to pretty little Fia.

"How much do we really know about Fia?" he asked, palming his door scanner for entry.

Vaan sighed. "I said let's go to my room, but okay." He joined Trace inside and reset the security. "She checks out, like every other new hire since we've been here. It's not as if Racor would have posted the militia here *in case* we found the planet. Hell, they were still chasing their tails six months ago before Jeret found us. Lucky for us, he hates Joanen and his cronies as much as we do. Those extra months he gave us to cement our cover here was a blessing. And if damned Rinold hadn't found us, Jeret would have given us more time. But he had to tell them something or they'd have guessed where his loyalties really lie."

Trace lay back on his bed and took a deep breath, his body finally relaxing. "I know. I don't blame Jeret for giving up our locale. I'm just pissed Joanen is still in office, the fucking *Exec.* At this rate, he'll make Prime before we can stop him." He growled. "We should have killed him when we had the chance."

"Right. And then *we'd* be hanging, having killed the Exec with no evidence of *his* treason."

"But at least he'd be dead."

"True. But the lies he planted were too deeply embedded to dig free, at least they were back then. Between our sources in the barracks and in the fleet, our time is coming."

"Yeah, sure. So tell me how we're going to return to Racor. I can't believe I'm saying this, but I'm tired of all the naked women, the floorshow sex and constant laziness around this place." He sat up and flexed his arms, feeling the need to crush, to pound something. "I need to train again."

"So let's." Vaan yanked his friend from the bed in a blur of speed, sending Trace to the floor on his ass.

"Fine, asshole. But not in my room." Trace grinned, seeing the answering response in Vaan's eyes that lightened to a white blue. "Let's use Vela's gym."

They prodded and taunted each other along the route to Vela's—Vaan's cousin's—private gym.

"Shouldn't you knock?" Trace asked as Vaan pushed through the unsecured doorway.

"Why should I? She didn't lock it."

They entered into a narrow hallway which led into a small bedchamber, where Vela normally took her bedsport, but which, thankfully, remained empty today. Beyond the bedchamber was a solarium, filled with green grasses, red trees, pink flowers and blue light, bathing the area with a soft, cool glow. It gave the quarters an exotic feel, and the scents from the varied plants made one think of sex, hot and cloying.

Like Vaan, Vela upheld the morals of the Orads. They believed in mutual pleasure, limitless sex and rarely let bygones go unpunished. Not vindictive so much as just, the Orads had created Orad, a planet full of those desiring order, and Racor, a moon to enforce the laws and combat chaos. Whatever aided in the pleasure of such a society was welcome, which explained Vaan's cousin's connection to the pleasure planet, Ermu. And Trace had to admit that Vaan seemed a better fit in Ermu than Racor. Which completely flew in the face of Vaan's incredible success record as an assassin, a record which still astounded Trace.

Friends since university, the two had joined the TAC Army together, and been selected for covert ops off the bat. But there they'd ventured in different directions. Vaan had mastered the skills of the death squad, while Trace found a knack for leadership, understandable considering his penchant for discipline, brute strength and the need for absolute victory.

Hiding his Vendon ancestry, not wanting to give his competitors any hint of weakness, he'd made it to the top of the unit, the youngest lieutenant colonel ever promoted within the TAC Army. And within two years, he'd brought Racor's select teams to greater and greater success, tamping down rebellions and ensuring peace and prosperity throughout the System. Occasionally he'd run into Vaan, and on their downtime they'd partied together, even shared a woman or two between them. All had been right with the universe. Until he'd accidentally stumbled upon the Prime's right-hand man, the Exec, Joanen Fen'Wal, plotting to kill the Prime.

And he'd planned on using Vaan to do it, in a convoluted scheme that still made Trace's head hurt thinking about it.

A sudden noise alerted him that they weren't alone.

"Vaan, Vela's not going to appreciate us invading her space. I told you we should have knocked—" The rest of Trace's words were cut off as they rounded the corner of the solarium and spotted Vela sexing it up on the thick gym mats. She played with two people, a dark-skinned man and a lushly figured woman. Vela had her mouth over the man's cock while she rode his mouth, all the while another woman licked Vela's ass. Vela's partner had dark hair and a slim yet busty build, and Trace immediately thought of Fia, his cock stiffening in response. A closer look showed the woman to be Clea, one of the staff, and he stared, unable to stop watching the trio getting it on. Grunts and groans filled the small gym as the bodies on the floor writhed in pleasure, in culminating need.

"*Shit.*" Trace's earlier calm might never have been. Thoughts of the enigmatic Fia, and the sight of the three fucking each other scored his cock with desire, especially knowing Vaan saw the same, making him more than uncomfortable as his shaft rubbed against his trou.

"Now that, my friend, is how you do things in the Pacifica." Vaan's gaze grew sly as he noted Trace's problem. "Well, let's make use of the area in the corner. Vela won't mind. I'll even let you attack first since you're handicapped with a third leg."

"Fuck off," Trace growled and, wanting to be rid of his condition, tried to turn his lust into aggression, a feat which had worked before. Ignoring his "problem", he followed Vaan to the corner of the gym and lunged.

Vaan, however, had lightning-quick reflexes. Even on the run for more than a year, the System's fiercest assassin kept in shape, and his ability to continue to evade Trace made Trace grin. Vaan's next stunt, however, had Trace scowling.

Ever since they'd been on the run, his feelings for his friend had been more than confusing, and Vaan, damn him, encouraged the craziness. A look here, a touch there. Sexual teasing that more than stoked Trace's confusing lust. And what the hell did that mean?

By no accident, Vaan slid his hand over Trace's cock before diving low, rolling to his feet on Trace's left. "It's only a matter of time, you know."

"Vaan," Trace warned, and managed to knock the assassin on his ass. *Arrogant fucker. How do you like that?*

Vaan laughed. "I love it when you get that look in your eye, the one that says, 'I'm going to seriously make you pay.'" Apparently, he did, because Trace noted Vaan's impressive erection straining his dark blue trou. Not helping the sexual tension in the slightest, Vela and her cohorts were crying and gasping, and he looked over in time to see them grinding on one another as they came. Then both Vela and the male turned on Clea, sucking, biting and licking her everywhere.

"Yeah, that's it. Good, hmm?" Vaan's voice came from behind him as he pressed the length of his cock against Trace's ass.

Startled, not to mention unnerved, Trace immediately countered with a Vendon handclasp, allowing his body to flow like water as his joints realigned. He caught Vaan behind his back and yanked the struggling male before him with what looked like boneless arms.

"Fuck. That freaks me out, Trace," Vaan said, gasping.

"Oh, and sporting a hard-on for your good buddy doesn't freak me out?" Trace held Vaan away from him, conscious of how much he really wanted to pull him closer. *Which made no sense.* Trace had never in his life desired a man, never looked twice, and loved pussy in all shapes and sizes. But Vaan stirred something within him that he couldn't explain.

Vaan winked, and Trace threw him into the wall, which wasn't padded.

"If it wasn't the summer, I wouldn't be having this problem," Trace growled.

"Ah, but we're in the shade here, my monstrously large friend. Now what's your excuse?"

"It's hot."

"So it is," Vaan said, licking his lips as he stared at Trace.

Trace narrowed his gaze and would have spoken when Vela interrupted.

"That was so good," she murmured and stretched. "You boys don't strain yourselves. And try not to break anything, hmm? We'll be at my private pool."

She and her friends left, laughing amongst themselves, and Trace heard the secure chimes lock as she exited the chamber.

"Did she mean don't break anything as in the frou-frou furniture or as in our bones?" Trace asked.

"Probably the furniture." Vaan trod on the balls of his feet, his gaze glued to Trace. "So what do you think about hitching a ride out of here next week?" He feinted and kicked out at Trace's ankles.

Trace nimbly dodged the attack and shot forward, knocking into Vaan's midsection and taking him down to the mat. As Trace used the advantage of his heavier weight to pin Vaan down, he grinned, pleased at having subdued his tormenter. "Sounds good to me. I need off this hellish planet."

Vaan pushed up, trying to free himself, only to have Trace bear down, his forearm across his friend's neck, his torso planted on top of Vaan's. Unfortunately, the feel of their sweaty, naked chests meshing tore at his control.

"Why's that?" Vaan panted, catching hold of Trace's nipple. "The suns getting to you?"

"Ow. That's cheap, Vaan." Trace grimaced when his friend pinched his flesh, uncomfortably aroused. "Keep it up and I'm going to—"

"Come in those tight-fitting trou?" Vaan ended in a thick voice. "You know you need to let go, or that sexual fire is going to combust the next time you bake outside."

Trace suddenly realized how hard he was pressing down, how firmly his cock pushed against Vaan's straining shaft. Cursing, he moved to rise when Vaan tweaked his nipple with a painfully pleasurable grip. His cock stiffened into steel.

"What the fuck?"

"Come here," Vaan whispered, the sober look on his face contrary to the sensual hold on Trace's body. That alone made Trace relent, and he leaned closer to hear. "There's someone watching us, someone uninvited. Play along."

Trace forced his body to relax, when he really wanted to find their spy. "Fine," he whispered back, his lips so close he brushed Vaan's ear. He felt disturbingly pleased at his friend's gasp. "But don't think you can take advantage of this."

"I wouldn't think of it," Vaan murmured, sliding his hands across Trace's bare chest, stirring the blaze in Trace's body to a full-out fire. "Just follow my lead and I'll take you right to our visitor."

Marie Harte

Groaning, Trace knew this wouldn't be easy. And when Vaan rocked into his cock, it was all he could do not to blow. "You'll pay for this."

"I hope so, Trace. I really do. Now follow me." And with a wicked smile, he ran his hand down Trace's front and gripped his cock, hard.

Chapter Two

Fia stared, wide-eyed, at the men grappling on the floor. By the suns, the stars and the black dust in space, she'd never imagined to see *those two* going at it. Both so incredibly masculine, so appealing and taken with anything in a skirt, Trace and Vaan had never once hinted they might prefer a man over a woman. Hell, in the brief time she'd been here she'd seen Vaan with at least a dozen female companions, and Clea praised him as the best lay she'd ever had, which was really saying something.

Trace, she knew by reputation. He had his share of women in Racor, and even on Orad, Racor's home planet.

But the sight of so many muscles interlocked, of hard thighs straining against one another, of two such sexually charged men rubbing against each other...she felt so wet she could just scream. She'd washed up after her bout in the suns, but had foregone a shower when she'd heard Vaan and Trace taunting one another in the hallway outside her room.

Not wanting to waste a valuable opportunity, she'd heard more than she expected to out of her quarry. They had doubts about her, *good*. They were as perceptive as she'd thought. And Jeret was an accomplice, as Exec Joanen had suspected. That wasn't so good. She liked Jeret, a quiet, disciplined warrior who'd filled in for Trace quite well. He'd already squelched mutiny among the covert ops folks, a mutiny Joanen knew nothing about. But Fia kept an eye on everything and everyone, determined to put the pieces of this puzzle together.

Why the hell would two of Racor's most famous heroes, two men who had given their lives to the service of the System, suddenly plot to kill the Prime, whom they'd saved again and again and received just praise and reward for it? Looking into both men's backgrounds had presented nothing to corroborate Joanen's allegations. Contrary to her specific orders from the Prime himself to keep out of it, she'd deliberately gone against protocol. But Micha, her older brother, the head of Racor security, needed answers. Like her, he didn't trust the Exec, and Trace and Vaan were two of his best and favorite warriors. Hence she'd disobeyed the Prime and left Micha in the dark, so as not to implicate him should things go wrong.

But really, she'd hit a wall. *That damned summer heat.* She needed to return to Racor, where the mountains and elliptical pattern of the moon's orbit kept her far enough away from the suns. Yet she'd spent so much time at the Pacifica, invested so much already. She'd spent two freaking months in a doll get-up, being groped, hit on, and kissed by all manner of creatures. The heat made her burn, in more ways than one, and while she suffered in silence, these two, the objects of her mission, were sexing it up with enough heat to stimulate her to another orgasm.

Taking a deep breath, she decided to step out of the room. Vela's display had been arousing but not extreme. But watching Vaan and Trace was way more than she could handle. Which would explain why she remained rooted to the floor when the men rose to their feet, astounded by the vision of the two of them together.

Vaan had his large hand wrapped around Trace's cock through his trou, and he pumped with sure strokes, urging

Trace to move harder and faster against him. Trace cursed and groaned, his mouth curling against Vaan's neck, making the blond gasp his name as they thrust against one another. When Trace's hands gripped Vaan's ass, she thought he might actually have climaxed. But instead, they stumbled closer to her hiding place.

Not good. Instead of ogling the pair, she should have made her escape.

Vaan pushed Trace against the wall right next to the tree behind which she hid, locking his mouth to Trace's. She thought she heard Trace groan, saw him put his hand over Vaan's chest, flicking at the man's nipples. Vaan growled low in his throat before shoving Trace's trou to his feet.

Awed, Fia could only stare at the huge cock glistening with arousal. She caught a brief glimpse of a plum-colored crown, of a thickly veined shaft totally devoid of any hair, and then Vaan's fist obscured her view, allowing her brief peeks of the seeping cock begging for release. Trace stood with his head back and his eyes closed, the cords of his neck prominent.

"Vaan," he rasped angrily, confusing her.

"Take it," Vaan ordered, and did something with his hand, causing Trace to cry out as he shot, semen splattering against Vaan's golden, tightly packed abs. "That's it, Trace. Come hard." After a moment, Trace stilled, breathing heavily. "Now we can finish this."

Finish this? Excitement swelled within her, her clit throbbing, her nipples hard, as she imagined Trace returning Vaan's favor. Or better yet, leaning low to take Vaan in his mouth, the way she'd dreamed of doing since she'd begun this chase...

"Well, hello," Vaan drawled, suddenly yanking her out from behind the tree. "Little Fia. Did you enjoy the show?"

Fia stared, still trying to function through the lust swamping her.

"I think she liked it," Trace rumbled, yanking his trou back up his frame. "And you owe me big for this."

"I can't wait." Vaan sounded amused, but the cold look in his eyes warned her to tread warily. "So tell us, Fia, what were you hoping to find here?"

She swallowed, rubbing her thighs together to ease the ache in her sex. Glancing from an icy Vaan to an angry Trace, she didn't have to pretend too much fear as she quivered and dropped her gaze.

"I'm so sorry." She spoke timidly, trying to work herself into tears. "I didn't mean to spy on you. I just...I wanted to talk to Vela and she always says to come in and make myself at home. And then I saw you two." She lifted her face, making sure both men caught the tears forming in her eyes. "You were so beautiful, so sensual." Her voice vibrated with longing she didn't need to feign. "I couldn't intrude, and I'm sorry if I saw something I wasn't supposed to. I swear I won't tell anyone."

Vaan pulled her closer, positioning her between him and Trace against the wall. Hiding her eyes again, she couldn't help staring at the sticky mess on his belly. Her body felt a wave of heat, and she sucked in a breath. Hell. She'd never been so horny in her life, and in front of her most dangerous suspects to date. She must be losing her mind.

Blaming it on the heat, which—even in here—penetrated the hazy coolness with its thin blanket of humidity, she glanced over her shoulder up at Trace, unprepared for his hungry gaze.

"You think she's lying, Vaan? You're better at this than I am."

"I don't know. Are you lying, Fia?" Vaan's voice softened, and her lust mingled with caution. She clenched her fists, prepared to defend herself. As a spy, she'd been trained alongside the best. And though she knew she could never beat Trace or Vaan, either separately or together, maybe she could distract one of them enough to make a run for it.

"I'm sorry," she said again, allowing tears to spill. "Honestly, you were so perfect together that I couldn't look away. I never meant to alarm you."

"I bet you didn't," Trace murmured, staring down at her with puzzlement in his eyes.

Vaan shocked her by shoving a hand between her legs. "Hmm, she's wet. And her nipples are definitely hard. You can see the arousal in her dilated pupils." He glared. "You just liked watching, is that it?" He tugged the thong down her legs and threw it aside, then began rubbing her clit, making her arch into him despite her resolve to remain strong, ready to leave should she need to.

"Test her." Trace's voice was menacing, and so damned erotic she moaned again. "Fuck her. She's here to wait on the clients, let's let her wait on the staff, see if she's as good as everyone claims."

Damn it. She'd never been forced into sex before, and she didn't intend to start now. But as much as she wished she could deny it, she wanted these two, wanted Vaan to sink inside her. Wanted Trace to join in after he watched a bit. Hell, her fantasies shot her mission all to hell. How could these two criminals make her feel this much passion if they were indeed guilty of their accused crimes? It made no sense.

Then Vaan's fingers slid up into her, and she gasped his name.

"Good idea, Trace." Vaan's eyes were shuttered. "Turn around, Fia, and bend over."

Without giving her a chance to say no, Vaan spun her to face Trace.

"Don't worry, Fia. I've got you." Trace's lips curled, but the hardness in his gaze slowly melted. "Fuck her, Vaan. Let her take you to the bliss so many others have raved about."

That bliss *Clea* had wondrously provided, pretending to be Fia. He would know when he took her that she wasn't who she claimed to be. She was too tight for a sex sharer, and too unskilled compared to the experts in the sex field. Her thoughts soon scattered as Vaan's thick cock filled her.

"The others were right." Vaan groaned and pulled out, only to shove back in harder. "She's tight, and so damned hot. This won't last long, not after what you did to me."

Trace frowned. "What I did to you?" He broke off as Fia moaned, and she saw him staring at her as he licked his lips. "Fuck, I'm hard again. I want this."

Vaan must have mouthed something over her head, for Trace nodded. Vaan pulled out and clamped a palm over her shoulder, pushing her down.

"On your hands and knees, Fia," Trace directed.

Quivering because she understood what he wanted, she couldn't help herself. The Vendon within her responded to the heat around them, needing both men on another level altogether. But more than the heat, more than this case, Fia wanted them.

Trace sank to his knees and peeled back his trou, exposing his long cock. "Suck it while he fucks you, Fia," he breathed, his hand steady as he stroked himself.

What the hell am I doing? Fia asked herself even as she accepted his shaft. He groaned as she took him deep, her desire spiraling out of control as Vaan rode her hard. Trace was large, his shaft smooth and deliciously warm. And his taste was addicting, making her wetter and desperate to come.

"That's it, baby. Open wider. Balls deep, Fia. Oh, yeah." Trace began moving, lightly at first, then harder, almost matching Vaan's thrusts. Filled and yet frustrated, she needed to come so badly. But she still wasn't prepared for Vaan's questing fingers reaching her clit.

The pressure over her sensitive bud forced her to moan, and her tightening lips on Trace's cock had him groaning her name. Vaan's balls slapped her thighs as he pounded into her, his tip slamming into her G-spot with unerring accuracy until she couldn't hold back any longer.

Vaan shuddered suddenly, coming hard, and stimulated Fia into a mind-blowing climax. She clenched him tight, her womb aching to be filled, and was rewarded by his hoarse shout and Trace's burst as he shot honeyed cream down her throat.

She swallowed his every drop, licking him clean before letting him fall from her mouth. Vaguely aware of Vaan pulling free, she made no protest when both men helped her to her feet. Dazed yet sated, she felt like a baby lear cat after consuming a bowl of cream.

"She's definitely worthy of that reputation," Vaan said with a sigh as he righted his trou. "But I still don't understand something."

"What's that?" Trace asked.

Shit. What had she missed? Shaking her head, she tried to clear her mind.

"Why didn't Vela say anything to her before she left? Much as she likes an open-door policy, she'd never leave Fia in here by herself. I distinctly heard the security chime sound when she left." Vaan stared down at her, his eyes clouded with satisfaction, but no less suspicious. "So how did you manage to sneak in here?"

Great question. The truth, that she'd used Vela's stolen personal security code and snuck in undetected, wouldn't work. She'd have to boldly lie, ruining her cover for sure. Her alibi had a great big hole in it, since one conversation with Vela would prove her a liar. "Vela gave me her codes."

"Bullshit."

Vaan obviously didn't believe her. And Trace didn't flinch, crossing those huge arms over his broad chest. Mother of Racor, but their forcefulness made her hot. She wanted them both again. Instead, she put her thong back on, drenching the thin material and flushing at the discomfort of wet panties, if one could call a line of silk and a miniscule triangle "panties".

Fia cleared her throat delicately. "I, ah, Vela and I have an intimate relationship, much like the one she shares with Clea."

"What, so you're her sex slave?" Trace asked, looking more than interested. "That I'd like to see."

"And so would I." Vaan smiled, the expression, unfortunately, not meeting his eyes. "Why don't we find Vela and verify your story."

She nodded right away, and could tell she'd taken them both aback. "Please let's. Once she tells you I spoke the truth, you'll forgive me for being in here, won't you? I'm really very sorry." *Hell no, I'm not sorry.* After that more than satisfying orgasm, her body once again felt like her own. And she'd learned some valuable information that Micha and the Prime would want to know.

Trace stared at her from head to toe as they left the gymnasium for the hallway. "Where are you from, Fia?"

"Nowhere, really. I was orphaned when I was three and grew up shuttled between Jergin and Aptor. That's where most foundlings are raised." She noted the softening in Trace's, if not Vaan's, face. Vaan, the assassin, remained wary. Yet Trace, Racor's legendary assault commander, was a sucker for a woman with a sob story. "I had a very loving childhood, though. And when I reached my majority at fifteen, I decided to become a sex sharer. It's respectable work and pays very well."

Vaan lifted a brow at Trace, who scowled but said nothing.

"That's what I've always told my friend here. Sex is to be treasured, explored, not deemed dirty or wrong." Vaan stared smugly at Trace.

Fia frowned, enjoying her role. "But if you feel that way, Trace, then why are you here?"

"Good question," he muttered, and Vaan chuckled.

"Don't mind Trace. He's just upset that I got the better of him in our entanglement."

"Shut up, Vaan." Trace's gaze narrowed, and Fia encouraged his small temper, knowing it would aid her as a distraction.

"But you both seemed so wrapped in each other," she said earnestly. "Trace, your climax was so beautiful, Vaan's hands so giving." To her delight, Trace flushed and Vaan grinned widely.

"I told you I knew what you needed," Vaan murmured.

"And I told you I'd make you pay for that." Trace kept Fia between them while his attention fixated on Vaan.

"Um, I hate to interrupt," Fia said meekly. "But would it be okay if I cleaned up in my chambers before we met Vela?" She blushed, staring at her bare feet. "I want to maintain a good impression, and I feel a trifle, ah, used."

Vaan glanced from Trace to her, his eyes gleaming. "I don't think I've ever seen you look better, Fia. You're practically glowing." Damn. Now Trace looked speculative as he stared at her. "But all right. Take us to your room."

Within minutes, they stood in her spartan quarters. Unlike Clea's side of the room, Fia's had little adornment. Only a silken bedsheet and a blooming *orvid* marked the room as hers. While they checked the security of her windowless room, she worked on appearing shy, demure. A difficult task with a bed so near the objects of her desire. "Um, I don't suppose you'd let me change in private?" She forced another blush. "I'm not used to dressing in front of others."

Vaan's eyebrows rose. "What? You're just used to *undressing* in front of others? You are a sex sharer, aren't you?"

She called on some tears and forced a flush.

Trace shot Vaan a sharp look and the light-haired assassin sighed. "We'll be right outside, Fia. And don't even think about running away or there'll be hell to pay." His eyes burned as they lingered over her breasts.

The minute they left, she jammed the security box by the door, buying her a little time. She'd been more than pleased to share Clea's room, partial to the hidden chamber directly behind the armoire, a secret meeting place Clea and Vela liked to use when Vela felt naughty.

Moving with a sense of urgency, Fia threw a few sets of clothing and a pair of sandals, her communicator—which didn't work except in one small area deeper into the island—a knife and a map into a small bag and passed into Clea's secret chamber. From there, she squeezed through a narrow window leading to the central garden and inner courtyard. She quickly weaved through guests and curious staff alike, nodding pleasantly while gauging how much distance she'd put between herself and the men trained to hunt down their prey until found.

She could only hope she'd given herself enough time.

CRELED

"She's been way too quiet for way too long," Trace said grimly. He banged on the door and, not hearing anything, nodded to Vaan.

Unfortunately, her door failed to open with the security codes.

"I can't believe she's stalling. What does she think will happen when we open the door?" Trace shook his head.

Vaan scowled. Cursing to himself, he finally overrode her block and opened the door. As he'd suspected, the little liar had run. Before leaving her alone to change, they'd searched her room. Apparently, they hadn't searched well enough. Though irritated, Vaan couldn't help admiring the alluring young woman.

Long black hair, deep brown eyes and a body that made him hard just from thinking about it, Fia had been a temptation he'd done his best to ignore since her arrival two months ago. Fighting his sweltering attraction to Trace was bad enough, but the timid sex sharer had stirred protective instincts within him he'd been hard-pressed to face. He didn't like feeling such an animal attraction for such a shy, malleable female. And despite a face and body made for sex, something about her had seemed...off.

Like Trace, he'd been suspicious. But after two months of nothing but her stellar service, as well as reports of her amazing fellatio and sweet little pussy, he'd been more than inclined to relax his vigil, at least as far as Fia was concerned.

Now, however, he felt like a fool. And the feeling didn't sit well at all.

"Trace, find her. I'm going to talk to Vela, and do some research into our missing girl."

Trace nodded as he left.

Vaan found Vela lazing about in her private pool with Clea rubbing her shoulders.

"Hey, Cuz."

Vaan shot her a frown, glancing at Clea, but Vela shrugged.

"Honey, Clea knows more about me and this place than the Racor army. So tell me, what has you all hot and bothered?"

"Did you give Fia your security codes?"

Vela sat up straighter. "No, why?"

"Because she used them to break into your quarters, and she somehow vanished from her room without using the front door."

Clea grinned. "That's because she probably went through the armoire to our private room."

Vaan gritted his teeth as he glared at Vela. To her credit, she flinched under his gaze. "Why wasn't I informed of that particular passage? And how many more are there in the compound, that as your head of security, I should know about?" Damn it all to hell. This place could have been crawling with the TAC and they'd never have known it until the shackles fell.

"Come on, Vaan. I can't share all of my secrets, now can I?"

"Vela..."

"Oh, all right. That particular passage connects with the central garden. If you're small enough to fit through the window, you could conceivably find yourself in the inner courtyard. From there it's a few more steps before you reach the compound perimeter. But don't worry. Even if she's after you, she couldn't let anyone know you're right here."

"Unless she has a communicator, and she knows just where on the island her signals will pass."

"Oh," Clea said, biting her lip. "I gave her a map of the island a month ago, and I mentioned that little spot near the mirror pool." At Vela and Vaan's frowns, she sighed. "She seemed homesick. How was I to know she was after you?"

"So until this conversation, nothing seemed strange about her? Her side of the room is completely devoid of character. That doesn't strike you as odd?"

Clea shook her head. "No, I asked her about that. But she said she was an orphan, and I thought she might have been down on her luck. She didn't do the clients, and seemed kind of out of place here. But she begged me not to say anything. Poor kid. She really needs this job."

"So if she didn't service the customers, who did?" Studying Clea, he had his answer. "You did. You both have roughly the same build, the same coloring except for the eyes and lips, and the same proportions."

"Maybe we should invite Fia back for a third." Vela grinned, and Clea chuckled, running her hands over Vela's shoulders to her breasts.

Vaan rolled his eyes. He'd learned all he needed from these two. "I'll see you later. Vela, Trace and I'll be out of touch for the next few days, I'm sure. Have Jakes take over the watch."

She nodded, obviously distracted by Clea's tongue in her ear.

Quickly leaving, he found Trace pacing at the edge of the compound bordering the tropical jungle covering the rest of the island. He could see the summer heat taking its toll on his friend, but had no time for pity.

"She entered here, not so long ago. We need to find her."

"Yes, we do." Vaan relayed his information, and Trace's eyes darkened steadily until they were burning with anger. "But not you, not now. I'll track her. I need you to head for the mirror pool here," he said, handing Trace a map. "It's mostly through thick vegetation, so you should be sheltered from the suns. I located it once a few months ago. Use this and your nav guide to reach the pool. That's where she's eventually got to be headed for a withdrawal. There's nowhere closer to communicate from, and since she knows we're on to her, she'll want a quick extraction, pronto."

"Right. I'll grab some supplies and meet you at the pool. But if I don't see you there by third moon, I'm coming after you. When you find her, don't let her go, Vaan. You know what's at stake."

Trace handed Vaan a dagger, and Vaan took it and moved out. He surged into the jungle, uncaring of what beasts might lie in wait. He had a new objective to handle, and a burst of excitement spiked his blood. Vaan lived for the chase, for the thrill of the hunt. And now he had new prey and a new thirst for vengeance to quench.

Chapter Three

Fia sighed and leaned against the tree, willing her legs to stop shaking. Between the dreadful suns, the summer heat and the oppressive humidity in this tropical paradise, she wanted to lie down and rest until winter. She'd run as far as she could, until the suns had set and a cool breeze filtered through the overgrown trees.

Soft sounds, muted cries of feathered friends, hisses of large but not poisonous snakes and grumbling lear cats filled the air. The scent of sweet *ahmin* and *orvid* tickled her nose, making her long for a real vacation, one in which she wasn't being chased by alleged traitors bent on killing her brother-by-marriage, Phillip—the Prime.

Damn. As if she needed that reminder. Her sister would be furious when she learned Fia had assigned herself to this case. Despite Phillip and Susia's protests, Fia knew if anyone could find and bring the traitors to heel, it was her. She'd constantly been successful in her missions, lulling the enemy with her looks and feigned timidity. Rarely did the opposition look beyond her heaving breasts and deep, if artificial, brown eyes. Which reminded her...

She carefully removed the false lenses, blinking into the night with pleasure. Because her eye color was so unusual, she often wore fake lenses to mask her identity. Everyone on Racor knew that the Prime's wife possessed deep purple eyes, as did her lesser-known sisters. Little did anyone suspect that Racor's top spy, the infamous Myst, was in fact Fia af' Nicos, sister-by-marriage to the Prime. She answered only to her brother Micha, Director of the Racor Covert Ops, and as such, had virtual anonymity.

In fact, it was as much to soothe Micha's state of mind as it was to save the Prime's life that she'd taken on this mission. Claims that Phillip's life was in danger constantly floated around the military. But this time she'd heard some speculation that the Exec, Joanen, was involved. And low and behold, soon after the Joanen rumors, the Exec wanted Micha's best men, Trace and Vaan, found, butchered and brought to the Prime with their heads on a platter. Covering up for his misdeeds, apparently. But how had Joanen persuaded Trace and Vaan to set fire to Phillip's houseboat? She wished she knew the answers. Because the deeper she dug, the more questions appeared.

Rising to her feet, she groaned and began trekking toward the pool again. In another hour she'd be there. And yet...she stopped and stared toward the ocean beyond the trees, the warm, blue water glinting in the moonlight.

"Screw it. They have no idea where I am. In fact, they're probably expecting me to hit the mirror pool, since it's the only place where I can use the comm unit."

She cursed at the realization and knew finding the pool would have to wait until she had a better plan.

Dropping her bag and her nasty clothing to the sandy ground, she actually thanked her maker that she'd run during the summer. The evening temperatures were warm rather than overly hot, allowing her body some respite. And if and when she did happen to overheat, she could take refuge in the undeniable beauty of Ermu's ocean. Letting go of the stretch on her skin, she let the Vendon blood flow through her, growing taller, slimmer and less bosomy while allowing her face to resume its normal heart shape. As she did so, she studied the area around her.

The stretch of beach to the left and right of her seemed endless, even as it trailed off into the curves of the island. Seeing and hearing no one near, she walked across the sand, sighing at the feel of silk under her toes. She stepped into the water and sank deep, needing the soft caress of water over her heat-sensitized skin. Though her trek had been made through the shadowy jungle, she'd felt the brutal warmth of the suns. And memories of what Trace and Vaan had done to her never quite left her mind.

She groaned and slicked back her hair, still not sure whether she'd dreamed it or if she had actually had sex with both arrogant males. Such beauty, such strength, and they'd been all hers for one glorious bout of sexual play. Her clit pulsed and she fought the urge to touch herself. Much as she could have used the added release, she needed to keep a clear head. And if she gave herself over to bliss, she'd no doubt succumb to the temptation of sleep.

Floating, she instead returned to her favorite pastime—wondering about Trace and Vaan. Seeing them together this afternoon had explained some of what she felt when she watched them. She'd always sensed a curious draw between the two, but had never pegged it as sexual. Seeing them today, however, had shed a clearer light. Yet when they'd taken her, they'd moved in harmony, in unison, and she'd unexpectedly felt a part of that unit. Not only had she bonded physically, but emotionally as well. The feeling had been both unexpected and strangely welcomed.

Due to the nature of her job, Fia had no close emotional ties. Oh, she loved her brother and sisters and Phillip too, but those relationships felt almost unreal. She constantly guarded herself around others, not wanting her secrets to be let loose. The loneliness should have made her want to leave the agency. But instead, it only made her crave the action more. Anything to fill that void.

She swam a bit, shaking off her maudlin thoughts, and couldn't help wondering what Vaan would taste like, what Trace might feel like inside of her. Both men aroused her, made her want, and she couldn't understand it.

Sighing at her strange libido, she walked out of the ocean like a sleepwalker and fell to her knees in the sand, her hair hanging half in her face, her chest heaving while she tried to regain her energy.

Which is how Vaan saw her as he stepped out of the tree line.

Crap, crap, and double crap. Vaan looked more than angry as he spied her on her knees. Quickly regaining her feet, she knew she had no chance of defeating this warrior with anything other than trickery. Crouched and ready, on the balls of her feet, she waited, prepared to defend herself.

But Vaan just stopped a few feet from her and stared, making her more than aware of her nudity.

"The absence of that miniscule clothing changes you quite a bit," he said quietly, his voice husky. "I like the new you. I truly do." He palmed his cock and watched her, licking his lips.

Caught by his seduction, she barely avoided the kick aimed at her knees. Narrowing her gaze, she considered the fact he'd moved to incapacitate and not kill her. He danced out of reach and tried again, almost tripping her. For several minutes she blocked and evaded his attempts to throw her off balance and off her feet.

Tired of his games, she crouched low, inviting an attack. When he granted her wish, she flung a handful of sand at his eyes and punched him in the gut, aiming for the sensitive spot just below his left rib. Instead, she grazed his rock-hard belly and bounced off.

"Not that shy, are you, Fia?" he grunted and stood, grinning like a devil.

"Screw you." Damn it. He didn't even seem winded.

"Only if you ask nicely. But, Fia, there's so much more we haven't discovered about each other. So much more about you I want to know. And I promise you, I'll find those answers. I took aces in interrogation at the agency." He dove for her and she rolled away, then came to her feet and raced back into the jungle, needing to escape before he made good on his threats. Her heart hammering, she could hear him breaking through the thick ferns and *yarva* bushes as he narrowed her lead.

She zigged and zagged, jumped over a gnarled tree root that the moonlight thankfully illuminated, and suddenly stopped to hide behind the large tree to her left. She heard him run by and she doubled back, needing the items in her bag. But when she finally made her way back, she found her bag missing.

"Shit." She fisted her hands on her hips, never sensing the blow to her neck that shot her into complete and utter darkness.

Cßஇஐ

Trace stared with appreciation as Vaan walked into the pool's clearing with a naked and bound woman over his shoulder. He gently set her down and stood, stretching.

"She looks light, but she has a good bit of muscle. I'm not sure how I missed this before, but the woman's solid. And tall. And a lot heavier than she looks." He frowned. "And the moonlight may be playing tricks, but I'd swear her eyes were purple, not brown."

"Our little Fia, or should I say not-so-little Fia, is just full of surprises." Trace studied the woman and felt lust spear through him like a drug. "What the hell?" He leaned closer and took a good whiff. "She's Vendon," he rasped, unconsciously rubbing his crotch.

"*What?*"

"I can smell it on her. No shit. This woman's Vendon, Vaan. That would explain these subtle body and facial changes. And damned if she isn't hotter in her natural form. Look at those breasts." He caught himself stroking his cock with sure measure and stopped before he came. Fuck, a female Vendon. No wonder he hadn't wanted to sex it up with anyone at the Pacifica. With one of his own kind near, he'd never go to another woman before bedding a female from his homeworld. "Why the hell is she here? And what do you think she really knows?"

Vaan crouched down and looked at Trace, and Trace felt again that surging desire, now held for two people. Vaan smiled slowly and touched Trace's thigh in light, butterfly strokes that made Trace uncomfortably hard. "I know a hell of a lot of ways to ferret out information, Trace. And I daresay you'll like what I can do. Let's get her ready before she wakes."

While Vaan washed the sand and grime off Fia in the mirror pool, Trace laid out the huge blanket he'd brought, just one of the many supplies he'd packed to meet any emergency, and set pleasure rods into the ground, used normally to tie up people in domination games at the Pacifica. Vaan placed Fia in the middle of the blanket, then bound her hands and ankles to the four rods placed above her head and below her legs. From Trace's bag, he also procured some fruit and bites of meat, and a bottle of Ner wine.

"You going to fuck her into answering you?" Trace joked, wondering if he could stand watching Vaan do it without joining them. Fia's naked body was stirring him past his control. And every damned time Vaan put something soft and wet between his lips, Trace wanted to replace that food with his cock.

Vaan simply smiled and shook his head. "We're going to do a hell of a lot more than fuck, Trace. Fia's no ordinary plant. She's been trained in covert tactics, and her communicator is top of the line—Racor issue. And I recognized some of her moves. She's been Micha-trained, dammit." He leaned over and ran a strand of her black hair over his fingers, then eased his hand down to the juncture between her thighs. "Yeah, tonight we're going to feast. And one way or the other, she's going to tell us what we want to know."

Trace swallowed loudly, more than ready to begin the interrogation. He was too eager, he thought, and stood, looking away, wishing again that the damned summer heat would fade. The suns had since set, yes. But he had a feeling the moonlight was affecting him to some degree as well.

He heard Vaan approach.

"So are you really pissed about this afternoon? Are you angry because it happened, or because someone else saw it happen?" Vaan asked quietly from behind him.

"I'm not pissed. Just confused."

Vaan sighed. "It's just sex, Trace."

"It's not just sex," Trace said angrily, knowing it to be true. *Shit.* "Just forget about it, okay?"

Vaan said nothing, and when Trace turned to see his reaction, he caught an expression so soft he had to blink, wondering where his hard-assed friend had gone. But Vaan's mischievous smile returned in a heartbeat and he winked. "Consider it forgotten. But that doesn't mean it won't happen again."

Trace groaned. The jerk wouldn't let it go.

"Tell me you don't wonder what my mouth would feel like over your cock. And don't lie. I know lies when I hear them."

Trace gritted his teeth, just the thought of Vaan's mouth over him made him want to thrust into something. "Let's focus on this mission."

"Fine." Vaan shook his head. "Jeret arrives in a week. He'll have the files we need. Then all we have to do is find the Prime and show him what we've got."

Trace stared, incredulous. "'All we have to do?' Are you out of your mind? Joanen won't let us get within three feet of the Prime. And how exactly do you plan on us leaving the planet? Much as I want to, we can't trust Jeret. Hell, Vaan. The only thing keeping us safe from the TAC right now is the stranglehold Ermu has on the System. Luckily for us, your cousin wields considerable weight with the Racor-Thim Council."

Vaan smiled, his lips both sensual and cruel. "Then it's a good thing we have Fia to aid us, isn't it? I'm sure with her help, defeating the TAC will be a piece of cake. After all, she's the first and only Racor agent I know of—besides us, of course—to successfully breach the planet's security."

Fia groaned, and Vaan and Trace stared at one another.

Vaan stroked a finger over her cheek. "It's time."

ભજી

Fia woke with an incredible headache, an aching *frethia* nerve and her arms and legs spread-eagled.

"What the hell?"

"Welcome back, Fia," Vaan said in a pleasant voice.

She could make out his features thanks to the streaming moonlight caressing her bound skin. *Shit.* "What are you doing, Vaan?"

"The question, I think, is what have you been doing, you naughty, naughty woman?" Vaan knelt beside her, Trace taking the opposite side. And she found herself the unwilling prey between two hungry, vengeful warriors.

"I don't understand. I ran because you scared me." She began to cry. "I'm just a pleasure worker. Please don't hurt me."

They stared at her, both men silent.

And then Vaan began to clap. "You're very good, but the communicator, not to mention your defensive tactics, gave you away."

Damn Micha and his mandatory training. She'd told him he needed to expand. Racor fighting was effective, but too identifiable.

Studying the dangerous glints in their gazes, she decided to try honesty. It might buy her some time before she could escape. And Vaan wouldn't be expecting such a move.

"Why?" she asked quietly, making both men pause. "Why would you forfeit your hard-won reputations? Why would you plot to kill a man who's brought only peace and justice to the System? What could you possibly have to gain?" She tried to see their expressions, but shadows darkened their faces.

Vaan cupped her breast, squeezing almost playfully. And though she hated her body's natural response, she couldn't help it. Her nipples peaked and her loins flooded with moisture. "There we are," he said coolly. "You like my touch, much as you wish you didn't. Now we can make this easy, or we can make this hard."

"It's already hard," Trace muttered, then quieted at a stern look from Vaan.

"But you're going to answer my questions, one way or another."

Knowing how skilled Vaan was at interrogation, she knew she had to answer. But how much to tell him? He might be good, but she was better. No one could outmaneuver Myst in a battle of verbal skills.

"Fine. Ask away."

"Good girl." Vaan leaned down and took her nipple in his mouth, sucking deep.

She gasped, arching up, and realized she'd have to work against his skill and her sensual nature. A challenge she found herself looking forward to.

While she waited for his question, Trace dragged his large hand down her body, playing with her folds. She darted a glare in his direction and saw his lips part, his gaze seemingly centered on her sex.

"Why are you here?" Vaan asked.

Trace slid a finger along her cleft, stroking the soft flesh of her clitoris.

"To find you two," she answered without missing a beat. But her heart wanted to thump out of her chest.

"For whom?"

"For the good of Racor, who else?"

Trace pushed his finger into her vagina, slowly, deeply, until he touched the heart of her womb. She couldn't help the gasp that left her, and tried to pull back from the intense feelings. But he wouldn't let her. Instead, he added a second finger, stretching her slightly, before stilling inside her.

"Try again," Trace growled.

Vaan leaned down and suckled her breasts, his teeth beading her nipples into pearls of desire. And when he licked her taut buds, she moaned and shook her head, trying to deny the erotic sensations.

"Fia?" Trace prodded.

"For the Prime, that's who I'm here for."

Vaan stared into her eyes, and the moonlight shifted, showing the surprise on his face. "The Prime sent you here?"

"No. I came here on behalf of the Prime. Too many things don't add up in this case."

Trace pulled his fingers out and thrust them deeper. "Keep talking."

"Or what? You'll fingerfuck me to death?" she snapped, incredibly frustrated.

"Ah, that's the Fia I like." Vaan chuckled. "I never cared for that shy routine. This Fia is much more attractive."

"Fuck you." Not smart, but it felt good to have the last word. Of course, bound and helpless before two larger-than-life criminals, death would be the best she might hope for. But at least she'd go out strong.

"That's it, Vaan. You can ask her more once I'm done."

Vaan opened his mouth, then sighed. "Go ahead. Those damned Vendon hormones."

Fia blinked, shocked, from Vaan to Trace. "Did he say Vendon?"

"That's right," Trace said, a hard smile on his lips as he shed his boots, trou and thin shirt. "And you know what, Fia? I can smell the Vendon in you as if you had it tattooed to your forehead. And now we're going to fuck, so I can put out this fire in my cock."

"Damn, Trace, you really know how to finesse them," Vaan teased, but she could feel his hungry gaze as he watched them both.

Before she could speak, Trace dropped between her thighs and began to feast. His mouth shot her to heaven in an instant, the shock of Vendon hormones, secreted by his tongue over her clit, igniting her orgasm. Her release made him groan, and he consumed her as if devouring a midsummer banquet.

Without cease, his tongue slid around and over her clit, plumping it into another rise toward bliss. The feel of his smooth face against her thighs increased the sensation growing in her loins, and she writhed in sensual torture, wanting more while needing respite from the intensity of feeling.

He added to the sweet torment by touching her everywhere. His calloused palms were rough, tantalizingly erotic over her sensitized skin. Long fingers plucked her breasts, squeezing the nipples Vaan had so recently kissed.

On and on the pleasure continued, two more blisteringly hard orgasms, and still Trace wouldn't budge.

"Please." She twisted under his hard hold, begging Vaan's help. But the man sat, enraptured. He'd pushed his trou far enough down to expose his cock, and he sat with his legs splayed, his massive shaft in his hand as he fondled himself.

The look he shot her told her to expect as much, if not more, when he took a turn.

Trace suddenly stopped and glanced at Vaan.

Vaan's hand quickened over his cock, and he stared at the two of them as he came, milky white fluid spurting over his fingers. As the assassin climaxed with a groan, Trace finally shuddered and left the vee of her thighs. Licking his lips, he pressed them to hers and plunged his tongue into her mouth.

Without further warning, he thrust his cock deep. The minute his flesh filled her empty channel, he levered up on his elbows, giving him full view of her face.

Fia could only stare, helplessly ensnared by the Vendon male so thoroughly claiming her.

Trace said nothing, but he gazed into her eyes as he pounded into her slick heat. He paused only to suck her breasts, to tease her nipples into stiff points. He varied the angle of his thrusts, riding her clit while he fucked her deeper and harder, until she couldn't take any more.

"That's it, Fia," Trace breathed, prodding her G-spot with every push. "Come around me. Suck me deep."

She could do no less, and felt him shudder as he clenched her hips, coming inside her. He thrust again and again, groaning, and finally stilled.

"Better now?" Vaan asked quietly, his voice hoarse.

"Oh yeah." Trace withdrew and flopped next to Fia. "I came really, really hard."

"Yeah, you did," Fia whispered, trying to catch her breath.

Trace leaned up on an elbow and stared down in concern. "I didn't hurt you, did I?"

"No."

"Look, this isn't a date," Vaan said irritably. "We're trying to get some answers."

"Relax, Vaan." Trace grinned, running a finger over her breasts. "She's not going anywhere."

Fia stared up at him, a sudden awareness penetrating.

How could she have missed it all this time? For two months she'd watched these two joking with each other, working hard for Vela, taking care of her girls. They hadn't done anything but their jobs, to the *nth* degree. And from what she had read of their military records, heard from firsthand accounts from their men *and* knew from her brother, none of their criminal behavior ran true to form.

"You didn't do any of it, did you?" she asked Vaan, intent on his answer. "The bomb, the murders, the rapes?"

"What?" Trace's eyes grew round. "Arson and murder weren't enough? Now that asshole's adding trumped-up charges of rape? I'm going to fucking kill that bastard when I see him again."

"Who?"

"Joanen, who else?" he snarled and stormed to his feet, leaving the area.

Vaan stared at her, then shook his head. "Nice. You must be very successful at what you do."

"The best," she said through a smile, relief making her lightheaded. No, Trace definitely hadn't raped anyone. Nor, did she believe, had he tried to murder the Prime.

"The best, hmm?" Vaan slowly shed his clothing and joined her on the blanket. "So now you suddenly believe we're innocent, and I'm supposed to let you go so you can help us regain our reputations."

"No." She grinned. "But you can keep me tied up and have your wicked way with me. Come on, Vaan." She felt free to say what she'd been wanting to ever since she'd laid eyes on him. "I'm helpless. Yours for the taking."

Vaan's eyes narrowed. "This is no game, Fia."

"I know," she said softly. "This is your life, Trace's life and mine, in case you hadn't noticed. I work for the Prime too, on a level Joanen would not find assuring if he knew."

Vaan stared into her eyes, his look thoughtful. "Funny, but if I'd seen you in Racor before, I'd know you. I know everyone there, every assassin, every covert warrior, every spy. But there are rumors of a very special person, a spy for the Prime no one has ever seen. He, or *she*, brings him news that's allowed him to stave off rebellions, to save worlds and even to bring the hardest criminals to justice. They call *her* Myst."

"Really?"

He licked his lips, glancing at hers. "Really. There but not there, real but not real." He kissed the corner of her mouth, then tugged at her bottom lip with his teeth. "Are you real, Fia? Or are you an illusion of whom I'd like you to be?"

Fia kissed him back, feeling the sensation all the way to her toes. "What do you think, Vaan?"

"I think at this point I don't really care. I want you, badly."

"Seeing Trace made you hard, hmm?" she teased.

"Trace and you. I've been lusting after you for months. But that shy thing, it really put me off. I don't like needy women."

"Yeah, well I'm not into blonds."

He laughed and rubbed his cock over her moist mound. "Liar. I can always tell the lies from truth. Tell you what. If you really believe in our innocence, prove it."

"How? In case you missed it, I'm tied up at the moment."

"Find us a neutral source who can put us back on Racor, and find us a way to see the Prime without the Exec's knowledge."

"I can do that. But do you really expect the Prime to believe you based on your say-so?" She frowned. "The Exec's gathered a lot of evidence against you two."

"So then why do you believe us?"

"Because I can't stand the Exec," she said bluntly, earning Vaan's smile. "And I just can't believe that two men, two hardened warriors who've spent their lives acting with valor, to be anything but the heroes you are." She paused. "Besides, a good friend of mine believes in your innocence. And it would mean a lot to him if I brought back his two best warriors."

Vaan's eyes narrowed. "*His warriors?* You're not talking about Micha af' Nicos, are you?" He palmed her breast, his excitement palpable. "Who the hell are you, Fia?"

"I'm the person you need to please, right now." She squirmed under his touch. "Make it hot, and I'll even put in a good word with the Prime."

Vaan laughed. "Okay, now you've lost me. But my cock has other ideas. Too much talking, I think," he murmured and sat up, straddling her belly. "Now why don't I prove my innocence another way?"

Chapter Four

Vaan quickly removed her restraints, still wary enough to keep her under close watch, but needing too much to do anything except take her. By the moons, but he had a feeling she really believed in their innocence. And the thought made him want to hug her, hug her and rattle her for putting herself in such danger. Siding with them against the Exec could land her in a world of hurt, no matter who she said she knew.

Freeing her ankles and her wrists, he turned back to mount her but found himself pushed to his back.

"I'll do you if you do me," she teased, and turned around, straddling his face with her pussy as her lips engulfed his cock.

He lunged up, unable to keep from groaning her name, and began to eat her with great licks and rasps of his tongue. She tasted so good, a mixture of her sweet come and Trace's salty seed. And her mouth. Shit, but she had him near to coming already. No wonder Trace hadn't lasted long earlier in the day. Fia could have made a fortune in oral sex sharing.

She laved his crown, her tongue pressing the most sensitive portion of his shaft, making him harder. Her hands caressed his balls, rubbing his sac into pressured knots needing to spew. Up and down, her hands, her tongue and mouth sucked him into oblivion.

He came suddenly, with such force he saw stars. He felt as if he jetted forever, and she swallowed every drop. As he caught his breath, he again became aware of the flavor on his tongue. Trace, Fia. Together. Images and thoughts collided, and he stiffened again as she continued to suckle him. Determined to have more, he resumed licking her pussy.

"Wait," Trace said from behind them. "I want some of that."

Vaan stared, bemused, at Trace staring down at them. Lust and affection glazed his brown eyes.

"Come on, Vaan, share."

Vaan sat up and turned Fia in his arms. "You want to do her together?"

Trace nodded, stroking his hard cock. "You want pussy or ass?"

"Mmm," Fia gasped. "You guys are making me horny again. What is it about you two?"

"With him, it's probably the Vendon calling. But with me, it's pure sexiness," Vaan answered.

"Asshole," Trace muttered with a grin.

"Yes, speaking of assholes." Vaan reached around Fia's ass and stroked her puckered hole. "Want some of that, Trace?"

Trace nodded, his expression one of intent.

"I'll be on the bottom. I want a piece of that pussy again. You use her come and lube up. Relax, Fia." Vaan prodded her ass, gently testing. "It'll be good. Trust us?"

Staring down at him and glancing back at Trace, she nodded.

He lay down and pointed to Trace. "Take it."

Trace reached between her legs and slid her cream into her ass, stretching her with his fingers until he widened the hole that hadn't seen any action for more than a year. But the pain soon blended into pleasure, and she found herself riding Trace's hand, pushing back onto him, feeling an alien fullness that made her want to come.

Vaan grabbed her from Trace and pulled her over him, shoving into her and laying her on top. Then Trace sandwiched her, gently prodding his cock into her tight hole.

"Fuck me, this is good." Trace gritted his teeth as he pushed past her sphincter and seated himself fully.

Fia couldn't breathe. Ecstatic to feel both men inside her, she remained still, growing accustomed to the sensation.

"Move, Trace, you have to move so I can," Vaan panted. "I can feel you through her, your cock sliding against mine."

"Oh yeah," Trace said and began moving slowly, trying to find a rhythm with Vaan. One pulled out while the other pushed in, and gradually, then more quickly, they began taking her to new heights.

Vaan found her clit and began playing with her, reaching around her every now and then to stroke Trace's ass. Trace alternately groaned hers and Vaan's names as he pistoned faster and faster. And then Vaan was tensing, his cock feeling like steel as she felt herself impaled.

"I'm coming," Trace groaned.

"Me too," Vaan said and shot deep. The friction of his hand and penis, of Trace's thrusting and his heavy body, pushed her into an explosion of passion. She cried out and came, gushing over them. On and on she clenched, unable to do more than feel. Minutes or hours might have passed as she held onto their bodies tightly, not wanting to let go. Eventually, gentle hands put her between them on the blanket, and with a racing heart, she said what was on her mind.

"We're going to kick Joanen's ass. You're coming back to Racor with me. And after that, fellas, it's me, you two, and a date with a bed."

Trace and Vaan smiled, reached across her and linked hands.

෨෫෨෧

The ride from Ermu to Racor had been without incident. In Vela's priceless smuggler's shuttle, a perfectly nondescript airbus that could have come from any planet in the System, they'd exited the planet's atmosphere. Thanks to Jeret's heads-up, they'd left the planet by way of Ermu's third moon. Most of Racor's ships were stationed between the first and second of Ermu's moons, since going by way of the third moon meant also bypassing a mean asteroid field.

Fia's—or rather, Myst's—piloting abilities made short work of the aimless rocks. And after exiting the field, they'd used Jeret's distraction—an exploding garbage hauler—to blend into the other pleasure planet traffic, one more nondescript shuttle among hundreds of others hoping for entrance to a planet of untold pleasures.

Leaving Ermu's orbit, they'd spent the next few days plotting and planning while Fia fed her brother information through a coded transmission. Even intercepted, it would make no sense to anyone but Micha. Electronic garbage floating in space until read by the right person—Racor's head of security.

The tricky part had been taking Jeret on board without alerting the myriad spies and agents hampering his every move. Apparently, Joanen had begun to suspect Jeret, who made no pretense about dodging his commander's every order.

But Myst could do anything, and with the help of some of hers and Vaan's contacts, they'd finally smuggled Jeret and those damning documents and vidstills off his ship into the shuttle.

Jeret joined them by the controls, having awakened from a short nap in the small, solitary berthing quarters near the rear of the vessel. Between the four of them, space was tight. Fia had a hard time controlling her blushes when Jeret gave her an amused look. Though she and her lovers always used the berthing quarters for their sexual escapades, it wasn't as if Trace and Vaan were trying to hide the fact that they fucked her together and apart, or that she loved every minute of it, as attested to by her loud cries of satisfaction.

Trace, when not fucking her into oblivion, had spent the past few days trying to figure her out. He asked her endless questions about her personal life, and she answered as honestly as she could without telling him anything about her identity as Myst, or as sister-by-marriage to the Prime. Vaan, that cagey assassin, merely listened, probably hearing and observing every nuance she didn't want him to note.

It wasn't that she didn't trust him and Trace, but if their mission to seek justice didn't pan out, she wanted nothing of her past to shadow guilt on either of them. Myst's successes, though legendary, had never been truly accepted by Joanen. The man had never liked her, and constantly badgered Micha for information about Racor's most mysterious spy. But Micha, Racor love him, gave Joanen nothing.

The same way she'd given Trace nothing.

The comparison didn't sit well with her, and she knew she needed to tell him and Vaan the truth soon. But they didn't need another stress on top of the allegations against them at this point. Or so she told herself.

Just then, Trace looked up from the files he was reading, his expression clearly one of awe. "Damn, Fia. Where the hell did you get this file? Who did you say you worked for?"

"She didn't," Vaan said dryly. "But she will."

"You going to make me?" she teased, aware of the joy coursing through her blood, a feeling that shouldn't have been present considering the danger they faced. But with Trace and Vaan by her side, she felt she could accomplish anything. She only hoped their relationship, tenuous as it was, might last.

"Baby, I'll do more than make you. I'll have you begging to tell me everything you know. That's if this oaf can keep his hands to himself. He fucks like a stallion, but hell, the way he treats you, you'd think you were made of glass."

She blushed and glanced at Jeret, who stared at the three of them with a smirk on his face.

Trace frowned. "I'm not into hurting women. I'm a warrior, not a torturer."

"Oh?" Vaan's voice grew quiet, his eyes hardening as he stared at Trace with a coolness Fia found incredibly sexy. "You're saying I get off on torturing women?"

She cleared her throat. "Vaan, why don't you pin him down later. Right now, we need to get you two in to see the Prime, while Jeret distracts the Exec. Can you do that, Jeret? I realize you've done a lot for us already, but nothing can stick to you...yet. You're taking a chance trusting me, but I can promise you that you'll be cleared of these conspiracy charges the moment I talk to some folks higher up."

Jeret pursed his lips and, after a few moments, nodded. He looked at the Smuggler's Pod, a small, one-man craft adjoined to the ship via a pressurized sealant lock. Once entered, he'd have no chance of going back. The pod was exit only, a smuggler's last chance at escape. Vaan had programmed it to take Jeret back to Racor, to the palace where he'd be immediately swarmed by Joanen's guards.

Jeret reached for the helmet near the pod's door. "Just so you know, Trace, my position was never anything more than temporary." He grimaced. "All that posturing to keep the governmental idiots off our backs is way too much for me. Hell, I'm a soldier, not a bureaucrat."

"Good luck, Jeret." Trace stood and shook Jeret's hand.

Vaan slapped him on the back, but Fia hugged him goodbye. He took her by surprise with a very thorough kiss, but laughed off the growls from the proprietary males by her side.

"Hey, this might be the last kiss I ever have. Give me something to remember, would you?"

Trace and Vaan cursed him with smiles on their faces, and after a final wave goodbye, Jeret left them alone.

"What did Jeret say about posturing? That sounds political to me." Vaan shook his head.

"It's not that political," Trace explained with a smirk. "Not really. Basically I tell them all to kiss my ass and I do what I want."

Fia stared up at his giant frame, taking in the size of his arms and chest beneath his military uniform, a one-piece black jumpsuit that emphasized the cut of his build. "I can see that."

Just then, a chime sounded, reminding her of how close they were to her appointment.

"Wait, Fia." Trace grabbed her by the arm, and Vaan closed the space between them. "Shit, you say it, Vaan. You know I'll just screw it up."

Vaan smiled. "True. Fia, Trace and I wanted you to know that no matter how this turns out, we appreciate all you've done for us."

"I'm just sorry it took me so long to see the truth."

"You did, and we're thankful," Vaan added.

Thankful? That's all they felt?

Trace shook his head and grunted. "What C'Vail is trying to say is that we're keeping you once this is through."

"*What?*" She could only stare. She'd been hoping for more fun together. But he sounded like he wanted them to be...permanent. So why didn't the thought frighten her?

Vaan scowled. "Didn't you just tell me to do the talking? Hell, Trace. You're going to scare her off. Don't listen to him, honey. We come through this alive, and we'll keep dating, hanging out. Maybe even have a real vacation. You'll be our third."

"Our *permanent* third." Trace growled. "Both of you. I'm keeping both of you. And if I have to drag you both by the hair to Ermu to make if official, I will."

For the first time since she'd met him, she saw Vaan speechless.

"Don't speak, Vaan. You'll just complicate everything. I want you, you want me. We both want Fia, and she's so used to our massive cocks that no normal male will ever do it for her again."

Vaan choked, and Fia couldn't help laughing.

"Just say yes, Vaan," Trace ordered, his voice softer than she'd ever heard it spoken. "You know it's only a matter of time."

Vaan flushed, then kissed the breath out of Fia and the amusement from Trace's stunned face. "Okay. Now that the distant future seems to be taken care of, what say we save ourselves from the more imminent threat of death?"

CREAR

Fia met with her brother in the secrecy of the family palace. It had taken her twice the normal amount she usually paid in bribes to skulk about the palace, and she had a definite bone to pick with Micha about how he was royally screwing up her network. A good spy always had an avenue for remaining invisible from the blasted head of security. She learned more about the kingdom from the palace servants and military men when they spoke to each other without fear of being overheard. Trust her brother to sway her sources just when she needed them.

"So you're going to bring Phillip to the wardroom in ten minutes?"

Micha sighed. "I just said I would. What's with you? You're pacing like a recovering addict."

"Sorry. I'm just concerned that two innocent men are about to be beheaded for crimes they didn't commit," she snapped. "They're in there right now with Joanen badgering them. He's already arrested Jeret, you know."

"Relax, Fia. I told Phillip and Susia about what's been really going on. And despite your wonder-spy abilities, I've had Joanen on full-time watch since you left. Trust me, even without your damning evidence, the Exec is going down. And if you think I'm bad, wait until you watch Phillip nail him."

"I know we have Joanen. I just don't want Trace and Vaan caught in the crossfire."

"Trace and Vaan, now, is it?"

She scowled. She so did not need this, especially now. "They're good men."

"The best."

"I believe in them."

"So do I."

She glared. "Are you in love with them too?" Realizing what she'd just said, she stammered, trying to correct her words, but her brother gave her a sharp look before leaving the room. "Crap."

Taking a deep breath, she used the hidden passage in Micha's room to travel toward the wardroom. She exited into a small closet and carefully entered the wardroom to see everyone's attention centered on the giants standing in the middle.

Seeing Trace and Vaan bound in chains infuriated her, and she took a step forward before someone grabbed her by the arm.

"Not now," Susia, her sister and wife of the Prime, whispered as the crowd quieted. "Phillip wants you out of sight. We'll wait back here with Berent." Eyeing the largest man she'd ever seen, Fia sighed and waited.

"Attention," Joanen cried in that weaselly voice that made her head throb. She saw Trace and Vaan exchange angry looks. "Once again, Myst has pulled through. Thanks to our great agent, two traitors to the empire have been tried and found guilty."

"Guilty?" Fia whispered furiously. "When the hell did they receive a fair trial?"

The grumbling in the crowd drowned out her words. *Good. Trace and Vaan are as well liked here as they are out in the fleet.*

"Silence," Phillip, the Prime, said as he entered the room behind Micha. "I have come to bear witness in the testimony against Vaan C'Vail and Trace N'Tre. My assassin and my commander. What say you, gentlemen?" he asked of Vaan and Trace. "Are you guilty of treason?"

"No, Prime, we are not," they answered in unison.

"Well, then, we have a problem here," Phillip said, his black eyes twinkling as he sought Susia. He acknowledged both Susia and Fia with a subtle nod. "Either my loyal men are traitors, or my Exec is lying to me."

"My Prime," Joanen gasped. "There is only one course here. To behead the guilty, to preserve the empire and the Prime Line."

"Prime Line?" Phillip scoffed and the crowd of nobles and military leaders murmured low. "Joanen, I dissolved the Prime Line directive years ago. No leader should be appointed due to birthright, but because he, or she, earned it. Now you say my men are disloyal, but you show me no proof. Those mandates and pictures from a year ago have since been proven false. What more have you to malign these men?"

Fia could see the amazement and the hope shining in her lovers' eyes. Could it be so easy?

"I-I-I, my Prime, please," Joanen began.

"I have something, Prime," Micha said clearly and stepped forward. "Your loyal Commander Jeret, who for some reason is now in police custody, sent it to me just yesterday. I've had the documents verified, of course, and all is in order."

He handed Phillip the folder, which was broadcast on a large vid screen taking up half the southern wall. Pictures of Joanen attacking a young man, of him sodomizing a barely conscious woman, and more littered the wall. Incredulous grumblings devolved into cries for justice as the crowd swelled.

"*Silence.*" Phillip held out one hand, and the crowd stilled. "Here I have two loyal men accused of crimes they didn't commit. And I have one man who abused his power, hurt the innocent and falsely imprisoned loyal supporters. I hereby sentence Joanen Fen'Wal to death by combat. Tomorrow morning at dawn, *Colonel* Trace N'Tre will fight Joanen Fen'Wal to the death." Amidst the cheers of the room, Phillip spoke again. "I'm sorry, C'Vail, but if I let you have him, this would be over too quickly. A poisoned dagger can't compete with a long sword."

Vaan grinned. "Understood, my Prime."

Micha cleared his throat. "Then by the order of Prime, year 3054 day eight aught six, we order all charges against Colonel Trace N'Tre and Lord Vaan C'Vail dropped. To Joanen Fen'Wal, we order death in the most painful manner possible. Trial ended. Please clear the room."

The doors opened amid cheering and hollering, and it took some time before all but Phillip and his guards, Micha, Susia, Fia and her lovers remained. Fia tried to step forward, but Susia shushed her and kept her hidden behind Berent.

"You're both probably wondering why you're still in chains," Phillip said softly, instantly alerting Fia, Trace and Vaan.

"Yes, Prime." Trace stood with his legs braced, his arms crossed belligerently across his chest.

"I have more questions I couldn't ask in front of the others. Questions pertaining to those who helped you get this far."

Trace and Vaan exchanged a look.

"Others, Prime?" Vaan shook his head. "There were no others."

"Really?" Phillip glanced at Micha. "Because my brother tells me he sent a spy to bring you both back. To incarcerate you, were her orders. And yet when questioned, she says nothing."

Trace tried to step forward, but his chains held him back. Vaan quickly spoke. "You have an innocent woman under question, my Prime. Another of Joanen's victims."

"Not so," Micha stepped in.

"What the hell are they doing?" Fia muttered.

"Shh. Just wait. Trust me, you'll love this." Susia watched as if entertained by characters on a stage.

"Bring the woman to me," Phillip ordered.

Micha nodded and left, only to grab Fia moments later and drag her through another secret door behind Berent.

"Micha, you jerk—"

"Shut up or I'll gag you. Just let this play out and I'll let them go. Jeret's already a free man. And I put in promotions for Trace and Vaan, didn't I?"

She nodded and reluctantly joined him again, this time in cuffs, in the wardroom. Seeing the fear in Trace and Vaan's eyes, she wanted to reassure them, but a poke from Micha kept her silent.

Unfortunately, Trace saw that poke, and he glared. "You touch her again like that and you'll answer to me."

Micha stared, one brow raised. "My Prime, have I just been threatened with witnesses present?"

"You have, *brother.*" Phillip took a step closer to Vaan. "What say you, Lord C'Vail? Is this the woman who helped you? The woman who turned on her Prime, on her vows of loyalty when she helped you?"

Phillip's anger was in fact real, and she knew she'd catch an earful later, not so much for acting disloyal, but for putting herself in danger by confronting an assassin and the commander of his elite army.

Seeing their Prime's anger should have made both men tremble, but Trace and Vaan scowled at Phillip.

"I do not know this woman," Vaan lied.

"Nor do I," Trace added. But of course, he couldn't keep his big trap shut. "And if you put so much as a mark on her, Prime or not, I'll sever your head from your royal body."

Everyone gasped, except for Vaan and Fia, who groaned.

Phillip, however, quickly recovered. "Another threat against the royal family?"

Micha choked and Susia grinned.

"Hell," Vaan sighed. "My Prime, the woman is innocent. I would hate to see any member of the royal family dead for having harmed such a lovely creature. Surely the *Colonel* spoke out of a sense of duty to your directive—to protect the innocent."

"Oh?" Phillip stared hard at Vaan.

"Yes, my Prime. A woman like this one would surely have friends, family, even lovers determined to keep her safe. She might even have a special friend, a man who takes offense at the way she's being treated. A man who might see fit to enter your royal chambers, or those of your offending family, and take vengeance when you least suspect it."

Phillip literally goggled and Fia groaned. Great, now Vaan had made an even bigger threat than Trace. Had to be the heat. Damned summer suns.

"Micha?" Phillip nodded, and his brother let Fia go. Fia, in turn, quickly released both men with Micha's key.

She tried to push them behind her, but Trace took the opportunity to kiss her before shielding her with his body, and Vaan covered her flank, glaring holes into Berent, who stepped closer.

Phillip's lips twisted into a grin. "Your loyalty to the line is unquestioned. As is your love of my sister."

"Your sister?" Trace and Vaan said as one.

Susia joined her husband, and when she did, Fia found herself under an intense comparison.

"When we get out of here, I am going to seriously spank your ass," Trace growled under his breath.

"As am I, *Myst*," Vaan murmured in her ear.

"I thank you both for your loyalty." Phillip's smile grew wide. "And for taking such good care of my biggest headache. With you two protecting Fia, Micha's life should be much calmer."

"Ah, Phillip?" Micha cleared his throat. "You do recall promoting me to Exec, right? That's not exactly an easy job."

"No, but with Vaan's help you'll be fine. Vaan, you'll be taking Micha's position as head of security, but more specifically to handle covert ops. Except, of course, during those instances where we need your special talents. And Trace? Once you've easily dispatched Joanen, I need you to oversee the extensive training here in Racor, as well as assisting Vaan with any tactical issues developing. That won't be a problem will it?"

Both men grinned, while Fia glared at Phillip. "And what about me, oh great Prime?"

Phillip buffed his nails against his plush robe, and she knew he had something up his royal sleeve. "With the way those two are looking at you, I have no doubt you'll be needed more in a nursery than overseeing the System, little sister. But until then, Vaan will be issuing your orders."

She stared, her mouth agape, at her new boss. "*Him?*"

"Unless that's a problem?" Phillip asked with a smirk.

"No," she said slowly, wondering how to make it all work. Then again, she normally gave Micha her own marching orders, only needing his stamp of approval to do her job. Between her contacts and informants, Myst did the rest.

"Good. Now get out of here." Phillip waved her away, and she left in a daze, trying to figure out how to deal with the exciting new changes forthcoming.

She walked through the secret passage, dragging Trace and Vaan behind her, past Micha's room, toward her chambers. They entered quietly. The room smelled musty, but the bed had been freshly made, the linens clean and soft.

"Now, about that spanking, *Princess Prime*," Vaan growled and tossed her on the bed.

"Vaan," she tried, and looked to Trace when Vaan continued to approach. "Trace?"

"Uh-uh. Not after that scare you just gave us."

"Not my fault! Micha did that. The worm."

"There may be a way you can get out of this," Vaan said thoughtfully, his eyes sparkling.

"I say we spank her." Trace began removing his clothes.

Fia sighed, unable to prevent a laugh. "What do you want, Vaan?"

"Aside from that tasty pussy, you mean? I still haven't heard you agree to permanent status with Trace and me."

"I did too."

"When?" Trace asked, nearly naked.

She noted Vaan removing his clothing as well. "I must have."

"You didn't." Vaan stood nude, glaring down at her, his erection massive and impossible to miss.

"Okay, I agree to permanence with you two. God help us all." She glanced from Trace to Vaan and added slyly, "I'll make the bond permanent just as soon as Trace gives you what you deserve."

"Oh?" Vaan looked confused, until he saw where Trace was staring. "*Oh.*"

Trace licked his lips. "I'm not sure about this, Vaan. But for you, I'd do anything. For either of you."

Fia smiled, pleased Trace was finally unbending enough to commit fully to Vaan as well.

"You don't have to," Vaan began before Trace tackled him to the bed next to Fia.

"Just shut up and enjoy," he grumbled, and went straight for Vaan's cock.

Fia kissed Vaan's nipples, his mouth, his neck, adding to his pleasure while Trace groaned his desire.

"That's so fucking good, Trace," Vaan gasped, unable to keep from moving. "I need to come."

"I bet you do, too," Fia said to Trace, and reached for him. She pumped him, watching her men as they sought release. Vaan came first, blowing into Trace's mouth with force. Trace, bless him, swallowed it all as he came over Fia's hands.

After catching their breath, they turned to her. She grinned. "I love watching you two go at it. So sexy." They stared, still dazed. "You know I love you both, right? And I know you love me. Not everyone threatens the Prime and means it, or lives to tell the tale.

"And speaking of living..." She winked at Trace. "How long do you plan to toy with Joanen tomorrow?" Trace stood two heads taller than the elder statesman, and could wield a blade in his off hand with more skill than Joanen might learn in a lifetime.

"I had planned to torture him a bit, but I don't want to waste any more time away from your luscious body."

Vaan chuckled. "How could we not love you, Fia?" He leaned down to press an encouraging kiss to her belly.

Trace palmed her mound. "Of course we love you," he teased, glancing at Vaan. "It was only a matter of time."

About the Author

Marie Harte is an avid reader who loves all things paranormal and futuristic. Reading romances since she was twelve, she fell in love with the warmth of first passion and knew writing was her calling. Twenty years later, the Marine Corps, a foray through Information Technology, a husband and four kids, and her dream came true. Marie lives in Georgia with her family and loves hearing from readers.

To learn more about Marie Harte, please visit www.marieharte.com and http://marieharte.blogspot.com. Send an email to Marie Harte at marie_harte@yahoo.com or join her Yahoo! Newsletter group at

http://groups.yahoo.com/group/M_Hgroup.

Look for these titles by
Marie Harte

Now Available:

Ethereal Foes: The Dragons' Demon
Enjoying the Show

Coming Soon:

Rachel's Totem

Honeymoon Castaways

Dawn Halliday

Dedication

For L. You know why.

Chapter One

June 16—Saturday

Air whooshed past the windows of the small plane, an eerie, gentle sound compared to the normal roar of the engine and propeller.

"We're going down," Andreas Bailey said in a matter-of-fact voice.

Every muscle in Catalina Robinson's body tensed. She reached for her husband. David took her hand, but scowled at Andreas, who sat in front of her in the pilot's seat.

"Not today." Dave spoke into the microphone of his headset. "We're off-limits to practical jokes. It's our wedding day, man."

Cat breathed a sigh of relief. Andreas always tried to scare them when he took them flying—stalling, steep turns—once he had taken the plane into a harrowing spin. She hadn't spoken to him for a month after that. He'd had to woo her back into friendship with a dozen red roses and dinner at China Grill.

Andreas kept the plane level, but the vast ocean below loomed larger with every second, betraying the swiftness of their descent. He repeatedly turned the ignition, but the engine did not even attempt to turn over.

"This is no joke." Andreas kept one hand firmly on the stick, the other adjusting various instruments. "We're going down."

Cat stared at Andreas's broad shoulders, the chocolate-colored skin of his shaved head over the top of the seat. Since she sat directly behind him, she could not read his facial expression, but the tone of his voice sent a shiver of dread down her spine. She turned to Dave. As she watched, the blood drained from his face.

"What's wrong?" Dave asked through thin, tight lips.

"Engine's frozen." Andreas leaned across the empty passenger seat beside him to turn the knob of a control. "Oil leak, maybe."

"What can we do? How can we get it started again?" Dave was almost shouting.

"Oh my God," Cat whispered into her headset. Terror overcame her. She couldn't move. The wind whistled. The plane plummeted towards the earth. She couldn't look out the window, but she knew what was down there. Miles upon miles of nothing but the vast, deep Caribbean ocean. There was no way they'd survive a crash on the open sea.

Cat looked down at her legs. Beneath the white satin skirt of her wedding dress, her knees knocked together in a steady rhythm, an uncontrollable reaction to her fear. *Bump. Bump. Bump.*

Andreas's even voice broke through her panic. "Calm down. The engine is not going to start. I'm going to try to land without killing us."

Cat riveted her gaze to the altimeter. They were at two thousand feet, descending fast.

The airplane banked, and she clutched Dave, pursing her lips so she wouldn't scream. Andreas continued calmly. "I'm
218

going to try to find a place to land on that island. Just sit tight. Make sure your shoulder harnesses are on securely."

Cat wrenched her head to look out the window. A tiny macaroni-shaped blob shimmered green and brown in the middle of the sea. She saw no evidence of human life—no buildings, no roads. No runways.

Please let there be somewhere to land, she prayed.

She squeezed her eyes shut. Through her headset, she heard Dave's harsh breaths. He held her hand in a bone-crushing grip.

When she gathered the courage to open her eyes, the island looked larger. She could see trees now, a scruffy jungle. Waves crashing on a coral reef. The vast ocean beyond.

They were close.

She forced herself to look at Dave. He was so gorgeous. She always thought she'd eventually marry someone of Latin descent, like herself, but when she'd met Dave, she had instantly known he was the one. Sexy, intelligent and assertive, he was the perfect all-American man for her. She fell in love with him on their first date. She had married him that morning in a big, Catholic wedding in Miami, attended by two hundred of her extended Puerto Rican family, most of whom she had never seen before, all of whom loved her tremendously. Thirty of Dave's friends and family had come. He didn't seem to mind the imbalance.

Tonight was her wedding night. She and Dave had special plans for it.

Blinking back tears, she brushed a strand of dark blond hair out of his eyes. God, she wanted to live.

He cupped her face in his hands. His eyes were the color of the ocean outside the window, but much more calming. "We're going to be okay."

She took her headset off. "I love you."

"I love you too, babe." He tossed his headset away and curved his hand around her neck.

Andreas was making a mayday call. "Mayday, mayday, mayday, this is Cherokee two-five-seven-one delta..."

The voice faded to the background as Cat pressed her lips against Dave's. Pulling her in closer, he crushed his mouth to hers, thrusting his tongue inside, curling it and sweeping through. He had never kissed her with such urgency before. She threw her arms around him and tried to think only of Dave, of their love for one another. As if that would keep them alive.

"Hang on!" Andreas shouted. "Here we go."

She clung to Dave. She wanted to reach for Andreas, to hold him as well, but he was wrangling with the controls. She brushed his shoulder, running her fingers over the crisply starched shirt of his best man's tuxedo. Despite her righteous anger over the spin incident, she knew he was a good pilot. She trusted him. If anyone could save them, he could.

All she could see out the window beyond Dave's shoulder was blue, blue ocean.

She closed her eyes, too afraid to watch.

They hit the ground with a hard bang and a bounce. The airplane flew for two or three seconds, and then touched down again. The impact flung Cat away from Dave and slammed her into the opposite window.

Crashing noises. The bone-chilling screech of twisting metal. Cat could not see. The motions of the plane flung her around as if she was weightless. It seemed like everything turned upside down beneath her.

She saw a tangle of limbs, black and white, Dave's tux pants and her wedding dress. She'd refused to take her gown off for the trip, knowing today was the only day in her life she'd get to wear it. Then she smashed into the back of Andreas's chair and everything faded.

CSSO80

"Cat, you okay? Are you okay, babe?"

Cat opened her eyes and blinked through the fog. "Dave?"

She straightened, rubbed her eyes and looked around as he released her seatbelt. Things were settling, the body of the airplane still vibrating from the impact. The crash must have knocked her out for a few seconds.

Dave's fingers ran over her head. Searching for a concussion, she supposed. Not like he'd be able to do anything about it—he was in finance, not medicine.

"I'm okay," she said, pressing the back of her hand over her eyes. She felt banged-up, bruised, but she couldn't be seriously injured. "Andreas?"

"I don't know."

They looked at the slumped form in the front seat.

"Oh no," she whispered. Her eyes blurred with panicked tears.

Dave climbed beside Andreas and shook him gently. "Hey, Andreas? You with me, man? Wake up."

Cat watched helplessly. Her whole body trembled. The tears welled over and streamed down her face.

Dave frowned. "He's pretty bloody. I can't tell where he's hurt. You have anything to help clean him up?"

"Is he...is he alive?"

"He's breathing."

Thank God.

She searched around frantically, but found nothing. Then she remembered her dress. Her beautiful, expensive, designer wedding dress. It was a fitting end for it. Most wedding gowns didn't end up being useful at all. If this could help their friend, then it was worth a hundred times what they had paid for it. Taking one of the seams of her skirt between her shaking hands, she yanked as hard as she could. A big piece of satin tore off, and she handed it to Dave.

Andreas groaned and jolted upright. Cat clasped his muscled shoulders as Dave carefully removed his headset. "It's all right," she murmured, leaning over the seatback. He swiveled his neck to look at her, blinking his dark, almond-shaped eyes. A thick band of blood striped one side of his face.

"Cat. You're crying." Andreas reached up to cup her cheek. "Are you okay?"

She covered his hand with her own. "Yeah, I'm fine. I'm not—it's nothing... You?"

"Yeah." He laughed shakily. "What, did I pass out?"

"You did," Dave said. "Where does it hurt? Any broken bones?"

Andreas rolled his shoulders. "Nah. Don't think so."

"Well, you've got a hell of a gash on your head." Dave handed him the balled-up piece of satin.

The plane swayed. Cat bit back a scream and clutched Andreas's hand. Now that the sand and spray had settled, they sat right at the edge of the encroaching waves, on the verge of being dragged out to sea.

Andreas squeezed her hand reassuringly. "Thought it would be a smoother landing on the wet sand...but it wasn't that smooth, was it? Let's get out of here."

Cat kicked off her satin pumps and clambered out on Dave's side in her pantyhose. She jumped off the low wing and splashed into knee-deep water. Churning waves tugged on the hem of her dress.

The plane looked like it had collided with a Mack truck, with one wing crumpled and the propeller bent every which way. But if the tide swept it away, they would lose everything.

She took a position behind one of the wings and Dave stood behind the other, in deeper water. Andreas went to the nose. On the count of three, they pushed, pulled and heaved, rolling it to higher ground.

"This island looks uninhabited," Andreas said over the surf. "It's small—maybe about a mile across. No signs of civilization. Got your cell phones? Mine doesn't have a signal out here."

He paused, straining to work the plane over a small hill of sand.

Cat hadn't even brought her cell phone, but Dave had. It was his work phone, and he wasn't sure of its range. Once they pushed the plane past the line of the tide, they opened the baggage compartment, sifted through their luggage, found Dave's phone and turned it on.

No signal.

Cat never thought she'd experience such horror in reaction to that flat little bar. She wrapped her arms around her body, shivering, though it must be at least ninety degrees out. "Does that mean we're stuck here?"

"It's okay. I made calls, I squawked seventy-seven hundred, so any plane within radar or radio range would see or hear us. The transponder and radio shut down during the crash, but the ELT should be working. I switched it on when we were going down." Andreas looked at their questioning faces, then explained, "The ELT transmits a radio distress signal. Pilots monitor the radio frequency in flight. It'll keep transmitting until I turn it off. We just need to wait—we'll probably be rescued in a couple of hours." He flashed them a dimpled grin. "You'll just get a late start on the wedding night."

Dave squeezed his shoulder. "I'm sorry about your plane."

Andreas shrugged. "Did what she was supposed to do. Kept us alive." He slung one arm around Dave's shoulders, and the other around Cat's. "I'm just glad we're all still here."

They walked up the beach together in silent companionship. Andreas rarely touched Cat, but his heavy arm on her shoulder comforted her. She leaned into him and surveyed their surroundings.

The sun beat down on crystalline white sand, unmarred by footprints, but speckled with bird prints, rocks and shells. Hills, like miniature sand dunes, rolled from one end of the beach to the other, the cause of their rough landing. Cliff-like walls of rock bordered the length of the beach, an easy climb for a rugged sort of person, which Cat was not. A dense forest of twisted stubby trees and weeds loomed beyond.

The ocean was sandy-bottomed, and appeared shallow for quite a distance offshore. The afternoon wind covered the surface with choppy waves and whitecaps. Bigger waves began to curl far offshore, and then journeyed into the long, rounded cove where they'd landed. In the distance, Cat could see the dark shadows of submerged coral.

She glanced up at Andreas. Blood trickled down the side of his face and over the white collar of his tux shirt, congealing in the heat of the day. He was a mess. She motioned to one of the flat rocks. "Sit down. I'll clean your cut."

He sat, giving her a bemused look.

"While you do that, I'm going to take a look around." At her terse nod, Dave wandered off towards the tree line.

Andreas watched him go, and turned to Cat. "I'm okay."

"You are not okay—your face is a disaster. You look like you've been in a battle. Hold on a minute." Lifting her sodden skirt, she trudged back to the plane and found some water and a roll of paper towels.

She rotated the water bottle in her hands. As far as she knew, Andreas only carried a gallon or two in his plane. What would they drink here? Dying of thirst on a desert island was not the way she wanted to go.

Biting her lip, she debated whether to use seawater to cleanse the wound.

No. She'd heard that bacteria lived in seawater. Better to be safe than sorry. Anyway, even if they didn't find any water here, Andreas said help was on its way. They'd have to survive with what they had until they were rescued.

Cat went back to Andreas and knelt beside him, squirted some of the precious water on the paper towel and brushed it over his skin.

He closed his eyes.

Wiping the blood away revealed his cut—a big gash on his temple. "Oh, Andreas. You need stitches. This is so wide."

He made a harsh sound in his throat. "It's small, considering—"

"—what could have happened," she finished. They had come close today. If the plane had been any lower, if the landing had been harder, if they had been anywhere else—they probably wouldn't have made it. She dug her stockinged toes into the sand.

"Yeah." He gave her a crooked smile.

She smiled back at him. As cool as he had been under all that pressure, he wasn't unaware of the danger.

"I have some of those butterfly bandages in the first-aid kit," he said.

"Where is it?"

"In the luggage compartment, buried under your suitcases."

"Okay. Be right back."

She found the first-aid kit and rifled through it. It was well-stocked, and it even contained a bottle of penicillin, which would be good if Andreas's head got infected. Cat gave a shaky, loud laugh. They'd be rescued before it had a chance to get infected.

Of course they would.

She took the kit back to Andreas and finished cleaning him up. Then she carefully squeezed the edges of his cut together and pressed the bandages on.

"You should have been a doctor," he murmured.

"No way." She looked down to replace the unused bandages in the first-aid kit, fighting a wave of nausea. She hated blood and gore, but wasn't about to let him know that. Not right now, with all the blood-soaked paper towels strewn across the sand.

Anyway, she liked her career plans as they were. In the fall, she was headed to law school. She'd worked as a legal assistant for five years now, more than enough time to make her discover where her true ambitions lay. Because of Dave's moral and financial support, in just a few years she would achieve her dream of becoming an immigration lawyer.

The bottle slipped through her fingers, dumping onto the sand. Her bodice brushed against Andreas's knee as she lunged for it, capturing it just as it began to glug out precious water. Grabbing his leg for balance, she clutched the water to her chest and glanced up at him.

The expression on his face made her lose her breath. Andreas never looked at her like that—so direct, so openly hot. Sexy.

Like he wanted her.

She let go of him, lost her balance and landed on her butt in the sand, eye-level with his crotch. His erection bulged against the black material of his tux pants.

Oh God. Andreas? She clenched her hands over her knees.

"Cat," he said softly.

She tore her gaze away, biting her lip. He ran his knuckles over her cheek.

"I'm sorry for ruining your dress." His voice was a low rumble.

Her mouth was so dry, she wanted to gulp up the rest of the water. Was his head injury worse than it seemed? When she studied his eyes, however, she saw only clarity.

"It's okay," she mumbled, staring down at herself.

She was a mess. The relentless tropical heat made her sweat from head to toe. The dress had torn in more places, dirt and blood had smudged all over it, and it was sodden and heavy with sand from the knees down.

"You're beautiful," he said.

Her cheeks burned. What was going on? He'd never talked to her like this before. He'd never touched her like this before.

"And I'm sorry about today," he continued, his voice rising to a more familiar pitch. "I know you were looking forward to your wedding night. Dave told me—"

"What did he tell you?" Her words came out as a strangled whisper. She didn't know how to feel about Dave discussing their sex life with Andreas.

He opened his hand. It was so big it covered the whole side of her face. "He told me it was to be special."

His palm cooled her burning cheek.

"We only have an hour or so left of daylight," he continued. "We might have to spend the night here."

She nodded.

"If that happens, I'll leave you alone. I want you to have this night together."

She tried to laugh. "That's not what's important right now, Andreas. What's important is that we are safe, and we will be rescued soon. We can delay the wedding night."

He shook his head. "No. This is the most important day of your lives. I don't want you to forget it."

She did laugh, then. As if she would ever forget this day. It had been the strangest, craziest, most intense day of her life.

Chapter Two

Andreas found the oil leak in the line to the oil gauge behind the cockpit panel, an insidious place for a leak, where it wouldn't smoke or show a drip. Still, if he'd been paying more attention to the gauge rather than chatting with Cat and Dave, he might have had a few minutes' more warning.

Sunset came with no sign of rescue. They spent the final moments of daylight building a shelter of sorts beneath the sharp rock face at the end of the beach. Andreas planned to stay up for most of the night, keeping watch at a bonfire down in the middle of the beach so someone might see them if they happened to be sailing or flying by. He'd sleep there and leave Cat and Dave to their wedding night in the comfort of the shelter.

Cat unpacked the airplane, and, using their clothes and seat cushions, constructed a cozy room of sorts in a niche in the rocks. Dave found a tiny trickling stream at the edge of the tree line, good enough for fresh water, which Andreas would boil tonight to purify. While Cat and Dave set up the shelter, Andreas worked in the plane, building wire racks to support the cans of water in the fire.

They scrounged together what food they had for dinner: six protein bars, a bag of chips, a bag of trail mix and a box of Jordan almonds from the wedding. Andreas pulled a six pack of beer from the storage compartment, chuckling at their wide-eyed reactions. "I always carry it with me—for emergencies. If I'd known, I would have brought champagne instead."

"Better than nothing," Dave said.

Cat clapped her hands together gleefully. "Two for each of us."

Andreas snorted. Cat was so small, she was under the table after two beers. Two beers didn't affect him in the least.

He winked at her. "One for you and three for me, huh?"

"It's *my* wedding night, remember?"

He turned away, the smile falling from his face. Her wedding night. He'd almost forgotten.

They ate dinner under a vast blanket of stars, sitting around the bonfire. He stole glances at Cat throughout. She was more beautiful than ever at her wedding this morning, with flushed cheeks, a joyful smile and shining dark eyes. But after the crash, she had nearly knocked him flat—first with her tears, then with her brave face and shaking fingers when she cleaned his cut. He'd just wanted to hold her, to comfort her.

But she had married his best friend this morning. He would never get the chance.

He'd always felt a fierce attraction for her, but something about the stress of today, something about almost losing his life and causing Cat and Dave to lose theirs, had brought his feelings to the forefront. He just hoped he could find a way to suppress them. He hadn't been so subtle this afternoon. She'd seen his hard-on through those too-tight tuxedo pants.

Embarrassing. He downed his beer.

Dave leaned back on his elbows on the sand, protein bar in hand. "Ever read *Lord of the Flies*?"

"Yes." Cat shuddered.

Andreas remembered that story. A bunch of boys, crashed on a remote island, no surviving adults. By the end of it, they were killing each other like animals.

"Do you think that could happen to us?" Cat put her hand on Dave's knee, but she looked at Andreas. "I mean, if we're not rescued. Would we all go crazy? Forget to live like civilized people and end up hurting one another?"

"I read it in high school," Andreas said. "But someone will come tomorrow, so..." he shrugged, "...not to worry."

Cat bit her lip. "I don't know. People can go crazy when they're away from civilization. I heard one story of three couples who were sailing to Hawaii from the west coast. After a few weeks on the open sea, one of the women went nuts and flung herself overboard. They sailed around in the Pacific for days, but couldn't find her. When they got to Hawaii, they faced murder charges."

Andreas shook his head. "Not going to happen."

Dave clasped his hands behind his head. "I agree. First of all, we're grownups. The kids in *Lord of the Flies* were twelve years old and a figment of some writer's imagination. Second, who knows that woman's history? She could have been crazy before they set sail. Third, we know one another well. If we weren't rescued, we'd find a way to work together. We'd make it."

Andreas thought of the ELT, even now transmitting that signal at 121.5 megahertz. If they hadn't already heard it, someone would soon. Someone would come tomorrow. Cat and Dave knew it too. It was the only reason the conversation stayed light.

As he passed her the second beer, Cat snuggled up to Dave. "It's almost better than a resort, don't you think? Instead of strangers, we're with our best friend. It's beautiful here, and quiet. Not such a bad way to spend our wedding night."

Dave kissed the top of her head. "Not so bad," he agreed, looking over her head at Andreas.

Andreas forced a smile. His cock stirred again as he watched her, watched how she stroked Dave's leg, how her bare foot curled around his calf.

She'd called him their best friend. He knew he had Dave's trust, but had never known she felt that way about him. Did she mean it, or was she already drunk?

Dave still gazed at him, his eyes questioning. Andreas knew what his friend wanted. He flung his hand towards the shelter. "Ah, you two go ahead. I'll stay here and watch the fire."

"You sure?" Dave asked.

"Yeah. Go on. Have fun."

Cat giggled, then turned to Dave and punched him lightly on the shoulder. "You told him."

"Nah," Andreas said. "He just told me he wanted it to be special."

He lied. Dave told him everything. In fact, he had gone shopping with Dave for tonight. By the glint in Dave's eye, he was sure he still planned to dress Cat in the things they'd bought for her.

Andreas gritted his teeth against his tightening cock.

Grinning, Dave pulled Cat up. She snaked her arms around him and laid her head on his chest. Andreas wanted to press his body into her, grind against her butt cheeks. He wanted to make a Cat sandwich. Little Cat pressed between him and Dave. The thought made his cock twitch with anticipation.

He turned away, clenching his jaw so he wouldn't laugh out loud. He had lost his damn mind. The crash had rattled his brain.

He and Dave had almost shared a woman once before. It was a girl from work he'd dated a couple of times. One night, he took her to the apartment he and Dave shared. They had a few drinks before Dave showed up. The three of them fooled around a bit, but then Dave excused himself. Later, he and Dave had talked about it, and Dave said it wasn't doing it together that had turned him off, but the fact that he hardly knew the woman.

Small arms slid around his neck, and Cat's lips brushed the top of his head. "Good night, Andreas."

"'Night."

Before she left, she pressed her unopened second beer into his hand.

He opened the can and took a long draught of warm beer as he watched them stride hand-in-hand up the beach. He wished he had someone with him tonight, someone to hold, someone like Cat to have sex with on a warm, moonlit beach.

Dave was a lucky bastard.

Time passed. The moon blazed, full and bright. Andreas fed the fire and stared at it gloomily, punishing himself for allowing the crash to happen. In his logical mind, he knew it was a mistake and not his fault. Last week the flight school's mechanic had done some work on the oil lines. The innocent error of attaching an incorrect fitting could have been what almost killed them.

Still, he could not help but feel responsible for their current predicament.

Andreas stretched and checked his watch. A little past midnight. He passed his fingers over the cut on his temple. It hardly hurt anymore. Cat had a magic touch.

He walked down to the waterline and stared over the midnight blue of the ocean. The waves and wind had diminished since the crash, and now the water shimmered in the moonlight, as silky as Cat's thighs.

Stop. Stop. Stop.

Over the gentle roar of the surf, he couldn't hear anything from the direction of the shelter. He wondered if Dave and Cat were still awake—still making love.

Stop!

He went to the stream and filled the beer cans with water. Returning to the fire, he drew short, realizing he'd left the wire stands inside the plane.

They'd moved the airplane closer to the shelter. If Andreas went there, he'd risk disturbing Cat and Dave. Still, they needed the water, and he needed the stands in order to make the water safe enough to drink. He'd try not to disturb them.

Slowly, Andreas approached the airplane. He climbed on the wing farthest from the shelter, so they wouldn't see him if they were awake, opened the door and reached inside for the twisted wire on the backseat.

He heard a low groan.

There it was again. Unmistakably Dave. Andreas looked up through the window on the opposite side of the airplane and saw them.

Cat straddled Dave and was riding him hard, her black hair down and streaming, shining in the moonlight. She wore the white satin corset he and Dave had bought for her. It contrasted starkly against her cappuccino skin. The laces criss-crossed down her back and tied in a neat bow at the bottom. Dave must have helped her get into it. Satin garters curved in narrow strips over each of the round globes of her ass, attached to white lace stockings covering her legs. White spiked heels finished the ensemble.

Dave lay on his back on the cushions they'd taken from the plane, naked and pale beneath his wife, his torso heaving, his eyes squeezed shut, his hands clasping her waist, pushing her pussy down over him.

Andreas's cock jumped to instant, painful life. Almost without thinking, he moved his hand to his shorts, pressing his erection flush against his body. His polite mind shouted, *Turn away, go back to the fire*, but he couldn't move. He froze, watching like some voyeur, sweat breaking out on his temples, his pulse hammering in his hard-on. He ran his fingers down the bulging vein on the underside of his cock.

Dave said something. Andreas couldn't decipher what it was, but it sounded like an order, and in a flash, Cat moved off him and crawled down his body feline-like. Dave's cock looked just as hard and painful as his own, but it was flushed red, many shades darker than the skin on Dave's torso, and glistening with Cat's juices.

Cat turned so that she was on hands and knees alongside Dave, facing his toes. She tucked a lock of black hair behind her ear and knelt over Dave's groin, giving Andreas a perfect view of her generous cleavage and pretty face. She was totally focused on her husband. She knelt lower and took Dave between her lips. Slowly, she worked her way down, until the entire length of his cock disappeared into her mouth.

Dave moaned again. The side of his buttocks hollowed as he tilted his hips to give Cat better access. His hands moved all over her ass, caressing her cleft, sinking lower.

Andreas stroked his shaft. He could not see exactly what Dave's fingers were doing from this angle, but he imagined them plunging into her. How did Cat's pussy feel? Dripping wet? Tight? Contracting with every stroke of Dave's fingers? Could he feel her pulse in it, as Andreas felt his own pulse in his cock?

How deep was he going? Dave had long fingers. Was he thrusting them all the way in? One of them? Two? More? Was he fucking her ass and pussy at the same time?

Stifling his moan, Andreas sank to his knees on the airplane wing. He had to watch, to see what happened, to see how they finished it. He gripped the edge of the doorframe with one hand and tightened his fist over his cock. His palm felt cool over the burning, sensitive skin.

Cat wiggled her ass and slammed herself back over Dave's fingers, her cries muffled by Dave's cock. She popped her mouth off him and skimmed her cheek against his shaft to the base. Her tongue curled over his balls like a cat licking cream.

Dave twisted his fingers as he slid them inside her.

Andreas pumped himself in time with Dave's thrusts.

Cat stiffened, arched her back. "Yes!" Her eyes closed as she shuddered all over. Still, she stroked Dave with her fingers, pressing him against her cheek, rubbing her face against him as she came.

Andreas felt the build, the fire racing down his spine, through his balls, up into his cock.

No, not yet. It wasn't over. He had to give Dave a chance... He wanted to come with Dave, it was important that they come together. Andreas loosened his grip and closed his eyes, breathing through pursed lips. Control.

The tightness receded, and he opened his eyes and looked through the window.

Cat gazed straight at him.

He stared at her. *Shit.*

But then Dave said something and she turned and positioned herself on her back. Maybe she hadn't seen Andreas after all. Maybe moonlight shone on the window, creating a two-way mirror of sorts. He hoped.

She spread her legs wide so he could clearly see the swollen, pink folds of her pussy, glistening wet and waxed bare.

Holy shit. Andreas had never seen anything so inviting in his life. He wanted to suck her, to finger her, to make love to her all night long.

Dave moved into position over her, blocking his view.

She raised one leg up so her heel stuck straight into the air. Andreas pumped his own shaft as Dave pushed himself in, agonizingly slow, until she swallowed him whole.

Andreas wished it was his cock, not Dave's, penetrating her. He ran his fist up and down his shaft, imagining he was inside Cat. Inside her hot, wet, tight pussy. Buried to the hilt inside the amazing Catalina Hernandez.

Not Hernandez, no, not anymore. Robinson. His best friend's wife. He winced. What was he doing here? He was fucked up.

Dave said something, pulling Andreas's attention back to them. The only word he could decipher was "beautiful".

Andreas looked at her face. Damn right—she *was* beautiful. She smiled up at her husband, angling her hips for deeper penetration.

Dave dragged his cock nearly all the way out, then drove back in. Too slow. Andreas ground his teeth in frustration, but disciplined himself to pump his cock in time with his friend's agonizing pace.

Cat stroked her nipples over the corset. Andreas wanted to see them. He wanted to lick them. He imagined how they would feel under his tongue. Firm, ripe little nubs. She would squirm as he lapped at them.

Dave held her waist, his fingers digging into her flesh, finding his rhythm. Cat's head thrashed back and forth. She was panting—making little "hah, hah, hah" noises. Dave ground out another order, and one of her hands instantly went to her pussy, the other flicked her nipple over and over through the material.

Andreas couldn't see much more than Dave's profile, but he saw the tight line of his jaw and knew that he was barely holding on.

Good.

Sweat gleamed off Dave's back. He pumped faster now, driving into Cat with gusto, grunting at the end of every thrust. Andreas jerked harder, squeezing up and down his cock's length, brushing his thumb over the head with every stroke. His cock swelled. Every nerve came to life, blood rushed through every vein.

Andreas couldn't hold back. Dave ground into Cat with a guttural groan. His body tensed. Andreas's body tensed. Cat's back arched. She clutched Dave. Andreas clenched his teeth together. Come spurted from his cock, spattering on the seat of the airplane. Tremors rolled through his body. Tremors rolled through Dave's body. Cat screamed.

Andreas dropped his forehead against the doorframe, gulping air. His body felt like rubber. He wished he could stumble over to Dave and Cat, lie beside them, flop an arm over them and fall asleep.

But he couldn't do that.

Gathering his strength, he put his dick away, wiped up the mess he had made, grabbed the wire stands from the backseat and tried to escape back to the bonfire without them noticing his presence. As he walked away, he heard them murmuring words of love to one another.

He felt very much alone.

Chapter Three

Dave dragged a forearm over his sweat-soaked brow, dropped the armload of coconuts he had gathered into a hole in the sand and approached Cat, who stood outside the airplane with a pile of tools at her feet.

"Shit!" Andreas exclaimed from the depths of the cockpit.

Dave raised an eyebrow and slipped an arm over Cat's sandy shoulders. "Uh-oh."

She shook her head, rolling her eyes. "He's in a mood," she whispered.

Andreas crawled out of the cockpit, holding a yellow rectangular-shaped box, which he flung out onto the sand. "Piece of shit." He clambered out of the airplane and jumped down, separated from them by the wing.

Dave ground his teeth. The yellow box was the ELT—he knew it. He shouldn't be surprised—it was their third day here with no sign of rescue. Yesterday, Andreas had spent most of the day trying to get the radio working, with no luck. Seawater had shorted out the battery during the crash.

Cat released a breath. "Broken?"

"Yeah. Contacts are all corroded. I don't know how—I just had my fucking annual in January. It never turned on at all."

240

Andreas frowned at her, a deep crease appearing between his black brows. "We're stranded."

"No," Dave said. "Look, people will be looking for us soon. You filed a flight plan, right? So they know we went down somewhere between Miami and Barbados. Once the wood dries out, we'll keep the fire going day and night. They'll find us."

Andreas looked towards the sea and spoke rigidly. "I didn't file a flight plan."

Silence.

Dave released a breath. "Uh...why?"

"Not required for flights into Barbados."

So nobody knew where they were. Probably no one even noticed they were missing.

"It's Monday, right?" Cat leaned forward, her hands resting on the wing. "You didn't show up at work this morning. They'll—"

"I was going to take the week off." Andreas continued to gaze off into the distance, tight-lipped.

Cat stared at him. "People won't know we're gone for another week, then."

Dave shrugged. "Well. We'll survive."

"A week, minimum." Andreas crossed his arms over his chest. "And we're out in the middle of fucking nowhere."

"It's okay." Cat reached out to Andreas, as if she wished she could hold him. Dave shot his wife a curious glance. Was she thinking what he was thinking?

And what exactly was he thinking? He gave himself a mental shake. Ever since he'd seen Andreas watching them, he couldn't get a picture of the three of them together out of his mind.

"It's not okay!" Andreas paced behind the wing. "What if one of us gets sick? We're isolated out here. It could be months before they find us."

Dave squeezed Cat's shoulder. "We're healthy. We've got plenty to eat—"

"Hurricane season is starting. If bad weather hits, we have no shelter—"

"We'll do the best we can," Dave said. "That's all we can do."

Andreas spun on them, his hands cupping the top of his skull, his eyes wild. "The best we can? My fucking airplane had an undetected oil leak. The battery is fried. The ELT is a piece of shit. My best is a piece of scrap metal. Not fucking good enough, Dave! Keep with me, and I might kill you both."

With a ferocious kick at the plane, Andreas strode off down the beach, leaving a dent in the shuddering fuselage.

Dave watched him go, shaking his head. Andreas had a tendency to become overdramatic about things. Dave was more of a practical guy. This was the Caribbean, a populated place. They would make contact with civilization, and he strongly suspected it would be sooner rather than later. There was no question of their survival until then. This island was stocked with fish begging to be caught, juicy coconuts and water—not that he considered those ideal foods. But they'd survive. All they needed to do was sit back and wait to be found.

Cat hoisted herself up to a sitting position on the wing, tucking a stray strand of hair behind her ear. She wore the new black bikini top she'd bought for their honeymoon and tight jean shorts. She'd pulled her hair into a ponytail to keep it out of her face while she worked. Dave suspected she wouldn't wear much else for the duration of their stay here. It was too hot to wear too many clothes.

His dick was already at half staff. He sighed and leaned against the engine cowling. She was too sexy for her own good. Ten minutes didn't go by without him thinking of making love to her.

Cat's forehead creased with concern. "He blames himself."

"Yeah."

"What should we do?"

He thought about it. He'd known Andreas for ten years, since they were both eighteen years old and fresh out of high school. They'd been roommates through college, then moved down to Miami together and shared an apartment while Dave earned his M.B.A. and Andreas worked for a flight school. Despite their differences in appearance, they came from similar backgrounds and understood one another's ambitions. Andreas eventually learned how to fly and became a partner in the company while Dave found his niche in corporate finance. Last year, they had gone their separate ways—Dave and Cat bought their executive townhouse in South Beach, and Andreas bought land outside of the city, where he was building his own house.

Dave sighed. "He thinks he's let us down."

Andreas was the best friend he'd ever had, the person closest to him in the world besides the woman sitting in front of him.

And Andreas wanted her.

Dave had suspected it for a long time. Now he knew. He also knew Andreas would never make a move on Cat. Andreas took his friendships seriously. He was Dave's brother in every way but blood.

"He thinks he's messed up our honeymoon," Cat said.

That made Dave smile. He stepped closer to her and stroked her cheek. "He didn't ruin it for me."

The past two days had driven home what a lucky man he was to have Catalina. Cat was a city girl, born and raised in Miami. She was the type of woman who preferred exotic clubs and high heels to camping and rock climbing. He wouldn't have expected this level of toughness from her, but she had shown her adaptability in the past two days. She'd worked beside them to build their shelter, catching and gutting fish, organizing supplies, trying to fix the things that were broken. She'd had a sense of humor when they all huddled under the wing during the rainstorm last night. She'd laughed while eating her pathetic portion of fish this morning, and said that it was the best way to diet. All of it made him love her even more.

He was beyond lucky—he was blessed to have her. And he didn't know why, but she felt the same way about him. He was doubly blessed.

She smiled up at him with sparkling eyes. "It's an adventure. Not ruined. Something we'll tell our kids about. Someday we'll have fond memories of this."

He laughed out loud. "'Fond memories?' That might be stretching it."

If they were not sweltering hot, they were being rained on. He was hungry—not that he'd admit it—Cat and Andreas must be equally hungry, but neither of them had complained. He craved a burger. A big, dripping triple-decker burger, with cheese and bacon. Oh yeah.

Worst of all was the uncertainty. When would they be rescued? How would they be rescued? What should they do while they waited to be rescued?

He had a few ideas for the last question, anyway.

The image of him and Andreas on either side of Cat invaded his mind again, and his cock hardened painfully.

Damn. He wanted it.

He would talk to her about it. The worst thing she could do was say no.

She leaned forward and tugged on his arm, drawing him between her legs, flush against her body. "Yes. Fond memories. I already have a few of this island." Her voice lowered into a sexy purr. "Don't you?"

He laughed and slipped his arms around the curve of her waist. Her skin was so warm. "Yeah. I do." He nuzzled her hair for a long moment as she made sweeping strokes with her fingers over his back.

"Maybe Andreas needs some fond memories too," he murmured into the black curls.

She stiffened. Not much, but enough for him to feel it.

She pushed him away so he could see the serious expression on her face. "What are you saying?"

He took a deep breath. "I saw him watching us."

She licked her lips. "I...uh...I saw him too."

"Ah. I see." Dave remembered how she had paused after sucking him off. He could pinpoint exactly when she'd spotted Andreas, right when he'd asked her to get onto her back. What made it more interesting was that she had scarcely blinked, then had lain on her back on the mat and spread her legs, giving Andreas a clear view.

Dave almost smiled. This might be easier than he thought. Gazing down at her, he got straight to the point. "He wants you, Cat."

She swallowed. A look of panic crossed her face, followed by a wide-eyed look of distress. He swiped his fingers down the smooth column of her throat.

He fought the urge to kiss her, to plunge into her right here on the wing.

"Dave—"

"What do you think?"

Her eyes widened even more. "What do I think about *what?*"

He lowered his voice. "Don't play with me, Cat. I know the effect Andreas has on women. He wants you. Chances are you want him too."

His reaction when he'd seen Andreas watching had shocked him. He would have expected to be pissed off, or at the very least embarrassed. Neither had happened. Instead, it had made him proud of his woman, and proud of himself.

Damn, he was like some sort of caveman exhibitionist.

He shook his head to dismiss those thoughts. There was no need to psychoanalyze himself. He wanted what he wanted, and if Cat was interested...he knew Andreas well enough to know he'd take full advantage of the opportunity.

Cat frowned. "You're testing me. We've been married for one and a half days and you're testing if I'll stay faithful. Do you have that little trust—?"

He pressed two fingers over her lips. "No. I'm not testing you. I—" He took a measured breath. "The way he was looking at us—watching us—watching you. I want this. For all of us."

"I'm married to *you.*"

"I know."

"You're the one I love."

"Yeah." He cupped her cheek in his hand and tilted her head up to face him. "You're mine, babe. I trust that. I *know* it. If I was insecure, I wouldn't want to share, I'd want to keep your hot little body all to myself."

"So, you're so secure with me, you're suddenly willing to pass me around like your own personal sl—"

He kissed her before she could finish it, yanking her body tight against him, snapping her head back with the force of his mouth. Her hands dove beneath his shirt, pulling him closer, and her torso wiggled, creating friction between his dick and her stomach.

He pulled back, threading his hands into her hair, holding her face. "You love Andreas in a way too. I know you do."

She gripped his upper arms. "I'm not about to break my wedding vows to...to make Andreas happy."

"You wouldn't be breaking your wedding vows. I'm still your husband—you're not going to leave me for him, right? You wouldn't be cheating on me. And why not make Andreas happy?" He pulled her close again and stroked her ponytail, pressing his erection against her belly. The thought of her and Andreas...and him... He nearly groaned aloud.

"You... Dave, are you serious?"

"He's my best buddy, my lifelong friend. You're my wife, my lifelong companion. We trust one another. I want all of us to be happy. Satisfied."

Her chest raised and lowered with shallow breaths. "Have you shared women with him before?"

They'd come close, but... "No."

"You mean to say, I'd stay with you one night, and the next I'd stay with Andreas, and so on?"

He chuckled. "No. I want us all together. I want to watch. I want him to watch. I want us both fucking you at the same time, both working to make you come. I want you sucking my dick while he fucks you, and then I want to fuck you while you suck him."

He loved her reaction when he talked dirty. He watched her carefully. Her eyelids grew heavy. Goose bumps rose across the bare skin of her forearms. He slipped his fingers to her throat, feeling the race of her pulse.

It would happen. His own pulse sped to match hers.

She was silent for a long time. Then she ran her teeth over her lower lip. "All three of us? Together?"

He stroked her arms. "Yeah." He wanted to add "right now", but it would probably be better if she took some time to wrap her head around the idea first.

"Okay." She blinked and looked up at him, grinning, her eyes sparkling mischievously. She wiggled against his cock. "When?"

He took a startled step backwards, then laughed. She would never stop surprising him.

ଔୠଔ

They found Andreas skipping stones at a tide pool on the far edge of the beach. He sat on the edge of a rock, his feet immersed in water.

Dave moved beside him, gathered a handful of stones and began to throw. Cat lingered behind, watching them. They sat wordlessly beside one another, tossing stones. It became a silent contest. How many skips before the rock sank? Who could skip the farthest?

Would they compete over her in the same way?

Andreas was starting with a huge handicap. She was married to Dave, happy with him. They were great in bed together. It was hard to imagine that Andreas's presence in their sex life could change any of that.

It might change everything, though. She didn't really believe threesomes could work. Someone always got hurt.

But Dave was confident enough in her love to share her, and Andreas wasn't just some sex partner they'd picked up in a swinger's club. Both of them trusted him with their lives. He would never hurt either of them.

She knew Andreas wanted her, from his erection on the day they had crashed, and then she'd seen the look in his eyes as he'd watched her and Dave make love—that hot, dark look, potent with lust. But when she heard Dave say it aloud, *He wants you, Cat,* her pussy had clenched so tightly, she thought she might come on the spot.

And that was the most surprising thing of all. She wanted Andreas. Badly.

Andreas's bare back rippled with muscle every time he tossed a stone. Dave's allure was more subtle, with his torso hidden beneath a white T-shirt. She was more accustomed to seeing him in a suit and tie, but right now all he needed was a pack of cigarettes rolled up in one of his shirtsleeves and he'd look like one of the Jets from *West Side Story*.

Both men had broad shoulders, tapering waists, thick thighs. Gym workouts every day after work had honed Dave's body, and the manual labor of building a house had honed Andreas's. Compared to her soft curves, they might as well have been made of stone. Both were much taller than her—Dave was six feet even and Andreas just a fraction of an inch over that. Compared to her, at a little over five feet, they were giants.

Cat stepped around them and lowered herself into the pool. Water came above her knees, bath-warm, lapping softly against her overheated skin. She wiggled her toes in the silky sand of the pool's bottom.

She looked at Andreas. "Hey."

"Hey." He turned a rock over in his hands, not meeting her eyes. Guilt rippled off him. She wanted to tell him how stupid he was—that it was because of him they were alive at all.

She glanced at Dave, who had nothing more to offer than an encouraging nod.

Oh, nice. He was going to leave this up to her. She subtly bared her teeth at him, then turned back to Andreas. She moved around them slowly, until she stood in front of them both. Very deliberately, she placed one hand on Andreas's thigh and one hand on Dave's thigh. Andreas's thigh twitched under her palm, rock hard with tension. Dave's wasn't relaxed either. She glanced at him furtively once again. His blue eyes darkened, narrowed. A thin sheen of sweat broke out on his forehead.

Lust or anger? Hard to tell.

Well, he had gotten her into this. It was too late for second thoughts. She wasn't going to turn back now.

She added pressure to Andreas's thigh. "This isn't your fault, you know."

He cocked his head at her. "It was my airplane, my radios, my ELT. At least I should have told you to make sure you'd have cell phone coverage, but I didn't even do that, did I?"

She shrugged. "We wouldn't have done anything to our cell phones. We weren't planning to use them on the honeymoon. We wanted a complete escape." She smiled slyly. "Looks like we got it."

"Huh." Andreas flung his stone past Cat. They all watched it skip three times before hitting a rock at the far end of the pool.

She turned back to him. "Stop being so angry with yourself. We don't blame you for any of this."

"You can say that now—it's only been two days. How are you going to feel in a week when we're hungry, sunburned and bored? If we're not dead of some tropical infection, that is."

"We'll work through it together. And we're not going to die of an infection—you've got antibiotics in your first-aid kit."

Andreas snorted.

She squeezed his thigh. "We're together," she whispered meaningfully, knowing he felt like an outsider.

He wouldn't anymore. Not if she could help it.

Taking a deep breath, she moved to stand directly in front of Andreas. Slowly, she reached up to stroke his cheek, gliding her fingers over his lips. He had such a gorgeous, wide mouth, such full lips, so soft. She kept her eyes solidly on his, but felt Dave watching her. Heat resonated from him, swirling between the three of them.

Andreas's eyes narrowed. He flicked a glance at Dave. "What are you doing?"

Courage, Cat. She swallowed the lump of anxiety in her throat. "Kiss me."

"Hell, no!" Andreas jumped to his feet into the pool in front of her. Water splashed, wetting her shorts.

Andreas's head swung from Dave to her, and back again. "What the fuck is this? Is this some kind of test?"

Cat took two shaky steps backward. "I'm sorry, I— No, it's not a test."

Andreas turned to leave, but Dave captured his forearm. "Stay. We have a proposition for you."

Andreas stopped, breathing heavily, staring at Dave. The muscles in his torso were so tense, they rippled with every breath. "What?"

Dave's Adam's apple bobbed, the only hint that he was nervous. He didn't beat around the bush. "I want you to sleep with Cat."

Goose bumps rippled over Cat's skin.

"What?"

Dave's voice lowered. "Come on, man. It's stupid for you to jack off in the corner while we're having a good time."

Cat didn't think skin as dark as Andreas's could flush, but he proved her wrong. His cheeks reddened. He pressed his lips together and didn't speak.

Dave held out his hand. "Come here, Cat."

Shakily, she took her husband's hand and moved to stand between his legs. He turned her to face Andreas. "Look at her. She wants this." Dave stroked her hair. "I want it. You want it. Why deny it?"

Cat's nipples ached. She didn't dare cast a glance at them, but feared they must be poking out like marbles against the shiny material of her bikini top. Resisting the urge to cover herself, she raised her gaze from the rippling water at Andreas's shins, up his strong legs, his gray surf shorts, his rippled abs and muscular torso, his strong chin and nose, sculpted cheekbones. She stopped when she saw the fear shining in his eyes. He looked more fearful now than he had sounded in the moments before the crash. He shook his head minutely.

Dave flicked the clasps at her neck and behind her back. She stood very still as the bikini top slithered down her body and slid into the water. Still as a statue, Andreas watched her. She gazed into his eyes, saw his pupils dilate.

"Dave," he groaned.

She was on display. Her husband was the one putting her on display, showing off her body like a trophy. His trophy.

God, it made her hot. Her pussy was on fire. She wanted Dave's mouth on it. She wanted both their mouths on it.

Dave pulled her close into his body and licked up the curved side of her breast. "She tastes good, my friend."

She stared at Andreas. He didn't move.

Dave stroked down her shoulder blade, resting his palm on the small of her back.

A muscle in Andreas's arm quivered.

Cat licked her lips. *Now or never.*

She moved out of Dave's embrace and took two long steps through the knee-deep water. She felt Dave's presence just behind her as he jumped into the water and stepped forward with her.

"Please kiss me." She pressed her breasts against Andreas's chest, wrapped her arms around his neck and pulled his head down to hers.

He froze, but he didn't jerk away. She'd never kissed such an unresponsive mouth. His lips felt like velvet against hers, so soft. She kissed the corners of his mouth, then a little higher at that place that dimpled when he smiled. She returned to his lips, brushing them over and over with hers. Dave held her from behind, running his hands up and down the sides of her waist.

Andreas's cock pressed against her belly. Dave's rubbed against her lower back.

Cat's knees buckled. It didn't matter. Dave held her up.

She nipped at Andreas's lower lip. She could feel his tension, streams of electricity buzzing beneath his skin. She willed him to relax, to set himself free, to open to her. She traced his lips with her tongue, and then tried to nudge them apart. Suddenly, she was no longer in control.

Andreas was.

One of his arms wrapped around her waist, drawing her tightly against him. The other held her by the back of the neck. All she could feel were the two men's hands everywhere, moving over her, making her weak with desire. And his lips. They opened, hot and strong, and his tongue insinuated into her mouth, thrusting and retreating in the rhythm of sex, making her think of his cock hardening against her stomach.

She wanted to taste him.

"That's right," Dave murmured. His tongue traced the shell of her ear. His hands slid over her hips to work the button of her shorts.

She skimmed her hands down Andreas's sun-heated torso, over his small, tight nipples, down further to the waistband of his swim trunks. She pushed against his hips until he backed away, sitting down hard on the rock he'd used as a seat before. She found the snap of his swim trunks and tugged it loose.

He wrenched his lips away. "Shit...I can't...I can't..."

"You can," Dave said.

But Cat hardly heard them. Dave slipped her shorts down into the water and she kicked them off. She knelt, gasping as the coolness washed over the overheated skin between her legs. She yanked open the fly of Andreas's shorts, and his cock sprang free.

Dave knelt behind her, his chest pressing against her back. His fingers glided down the crack of her ass, past her pussy, stroking the folds of her labia, making her shiver. The water washed away her natural lubrication, and when he stroked her, every nerve jumped and quivered. Her pussy contracted.

"She loves to give head," Dave informed Andreas over her shoulder, as if talking about the weather.

She almost laughed. It was a joke between Dave and her. Cock—her favorite popsicle. And this cock... She took it in both hands and smoothed her fingers up it reverently. It was big and dark and beautiful, rippled with veins, velvety smooth like his lips, but so solid, with a plum-shaped head. Just right. She brushed her lips over it. As she did, Dave's fingertips brushed over her clit.

"Mmmm." A pleasant tingle ran through her body.

"Cat...Cat," Andreas whispered.

She looked up into his eyes. He squeezed her upper arms. "Do you really... Is this what you really—?"

"Please, Andreas," she said. "Please, please let me suck you."

His shoulders shook. "I... God, you know I want it. But Dave...you— Shit this could—"

"Stop fucking analyzing this," Dave growled. "Let her do what she wants to do."

Andreas made a sound low in his throat. His fingers relaxed on her arms in silent acquiescence.

She opened wide and took him into her mouth. Dave's breath hitched behind her. He grabbed her hips with both hands, lifted her in the water and impaled her over his cock. A startled cry erupted from her throat.

"Ah!" Andreas responded. His fingers tangled in her hair. She loved it, loved the tension in his fingers, the pleasure-pain as he pressed her mouth down over his cock, the feel of Dave's cock buried deep inside of her.

Dave stilled, holding her butt against his hips. "That's right, babe. Take us deep. Yeah. Good girl."

As her husband watched from over her shoulder, Cat worked her way down Andreas's shaft, so deliciously salty and rock hard and silky soft at the same time. When he reached the back of her throat, she forced it to relax and pushed him deeper.

"Holy shit," Andreas groaned.

"Yes," murmured Dave. As if to reward her, Dave drew out slowly, and then drove back in. She cried out again, trembling all over, and slid Andreas in and out of her mouth, basking in the moans and muffled curses her actions elicited.

There was nothing like this. Nothing in the world. Two men she loved, two beautiful cocks pumping into her. Each of them watching her pleasure the other.

Water lapped against her hips as Dave thrust into her from behind. The position might have been difficult, but the saltwater buoyed her hips, giving him easy access to her pussy. She knelt between Andreas's thighs, working his shaft and balls with her mouth and hands.

She and Dave made a rhythm of it. He thrust into her, pushing Andreas deep down her throat, and then he'd release, and she'd move her mouth up to swirl her tongue around Andreas's cock head.

She wanted to tell Dave how good he felt inside her, fucking her the way he was, with water swirling all around them. She wanted to tell Andreas how gorgeous he was, how hard. How close she was to coming, just from having him in her mouth, just from the sounds he was making. She couldn't talk with her mouth stuffed full, but Dave did it for her.

"It feels good, doesn't it?"

She moaned her assent.

"You like his big dark cock thrusting deep into your throat, don't you?"

"Mmm."

"You like me fucking you from behind, don't you? Harder, babe? You want it harder?"

She whimpered. A deep shudder spread from her core through her body. It made her wild when Dave talked dirty.

Shaking, she pressed the tip of her tongue into the slit at Andreas's head. She knew he was close. He came alive beneath her lips, heating, growing, dark, pulsing veins standing out in relief.

Dave thrust hard, stroking a sweet spot within her, and she drove her mouth down over Andreas. Together they pumped. Andreas thrust into her mouth. Cat tightened her hands and lips around him, applying as much pressure as she could. Dave hammered into her from behind. Cat lost herself in the wetness, in the sensations. She was one giant, flaming nerve. It felt so good. The only sounds were wet sounds. Her mouth working Andreas's cock. Small waves slapping around their hips.

Then Dave reached around to brush his fingers against her clit, and she was lost.

She exploded. Her back arched. She held on to Andreas for dear life, trying not to clamp down with her teeth. She cried out, her body spasming with every contraction. As if in a dream, she felt Dave stiffen behind her. "Fuck," he gritted, and then louder, "Fuck!"

Then he started pulsing within her, sending off a round of shattering aftershocks in her body. Andreas thrust his hips, pushing himself down her throat. His fingers curled in her hair. And then his come flooded the back of her throat. He came and came, giving a feral grunt with every burst of his cock.

Suddenly, everything was very still. Cat loved this moment of savoring, right after someone came in her mouth. She moved her tongue lazily over Andreas's softening shaft, lapping up every creamy drop of him. Dave leaned against her from behind, breathing harshly, still inside her and pressing her against Andreas's body.

Keeping Andreas in her mouth, she laid her cheek against his thigh and looked up from under her lashes. He stared down at her, eyelids heavy, lips parted, temples shimmering with sweat. She pulled off and kissed the head, then smiled up at him, reaching behind to search for Dave. His fingers threaded with hers and squeezed.

Love for both of them washed over her like a foamy wave. It was so liberating, knowing Dave would approve.

"I love you," she whispered.

Chapter Four

June 21—Thursday

Dave didn't have the attention span to work for hours on the airplane with Andreas. Obsessed with finding a way to communicate with the outside world, Andreas spent most afternoons working on the radios. During those long hours, Cat would sit in the shade under the wing or in the cabin and help him whenever she could, but mainly just keeping him company. Dave grew restless and explored the island.

He had it mapped out in his head now. They had landed on the best, longest, flattest beach on the island. Deep crags and jagged rocks featured in all the others. Despite Andreas's unending fury at himself for being responsible for their situation, he had saved their lives with his cool decision-making under pressure. Dave had done nothing but sit helplessly in the backseat.

He climbed over the rocky coast on the windward side of the island. Ahead, a thick thatch of trees blocked his path, hanging heavy with green fruit. He went towards them to investigate.

Soursop! His heart quickened. The trees were laden with the spiny fruit. He tore one from its stem, ripped it open and sucked at its insides, his mouth puckering from its sour, slimy flesh. It was something new, something they all could enjoy.

And there was plenty of it. Spitting out seeds and whooping with glee, he picked as many as he could carry, and, arms full, trekked back across the island.

Tomorrow, he'd bring a bag. Then he'd explore more. Maybe he could find something else to eat.

He saw Cat and Andreas as he approached camp. They were standing beside the airplane, arms wrapped around one another. Cat's head rested on Andreas's bare chest.

Jealousy stabbed at Dave, drawing him short, but then Cat looked up and saw him. Grabbing Andreas's hand, she ran towards him, a silly grin spread across her face.

He dropped the soursop fruits and met them halfway. "What? What's going on?"

Cat flung herself into his arms and showered kisses over his cheeks and lips. Andreas held back a few paces.

Dave was stupid to have been jealous. Stupid, stupid, stupid. Nothing could come between what he and Cat had for one another. Their relationship with Andreas would only help it grow.

"I think I can fix it," Andreas said.

Dave glanced at the mangled airplane and raised a cynical eyebrow.

"Not the plane!" Cat smiled up at him. "The radio."

"Really?" He swung his gaze to Andreas.

"Yeah." Andreas reached up to scratch the scab on his temple.

"Stop," Dave and Cat commanded together. Andreas's head had started to get infected on Tuesday. They'd dosed him up on penicillin and it seemed fine now, but the last thing it needed was for him to pick at it with greasy fingers.

Smiling crookedly, Andreas dropped his hand. "The battery shorted during the crash, but if I use the ELT battery in combination with a couple of flashlight batteries, I think I can rig them to create a makeshift twelve-volt battery for the radio. Then we'll be able to call in some maydays."

"Apparently nobody heard your distress calls when we were going down." Dave surprised himself. Usually Andreas was the cynical one.

"Yeah, but that was a fluke. We've seen airplanes overhead. If we can catch one of them monitoring the right frequency—" Andreas shrugged, "—it'll be over."

"Wow," Dave said.

It hit him that their days here were limited.

It hit him that he was having a damn good time, despite the constant hunger gnawing at his stomach.

It hit him that things would change once they got home to Miami. They would go back to their old lives. Their old lives had been full...but they were fuller now. There was more of a purpose when you strived so hard simply to survive.

Cat sensed his feelings. She put one arm around him and reached out for Andreas.

They stood for a long moment, looking out over the ocean. Dave slung his arm over Cat's shoulders, Andreas slipped his around her waist. She pulled both of them close.

"It'll be good to be rescued," she murmured. But the catch in her voice told Dave she had reservations too.

"The first thing I'm going to do when I get back is go to Clarke's for a burger and an ice-cold beer," Andreas said wistfully, staring at the horizon.

Cat grinned. "I'll go with you."

Dave smiled and kissed the top of Cat's head. "Me too. But in the meantime...we've got soursop."

CRROR

Andreas licked his fingers. Soursop was a refreshing change from their diet of the past five days, but if he ate another bite, he'd be sick.

As it was, he was sticky and messy. He'd washed his hands in the stream, only to have the airplane grease replaced by fruit slime.

He stood, stretching his arms overhead. "It's hot. I'm going to go in the water, start spearing before it gets dark."

He had taken his spear to the coral reef for the past few days and had done better with that than he had with the fishing pole. He'd caught five grouper fish yesterday alone—big ones.

"Sounds good, but..." Dave slid a sly glance to Andreas, then flicked his eyes meaningfully to Cat, who was wiping soursop from her face with a little grimace, oblivious to their exchange. "Let's all go in."

"All right," Cat said. "Gotta go change. My bathing suit is hanging—" Dave and Andreas broke into peals of laughter. She looked up at them. "What?"

"What do you need a bathing suit for?" Andreas asked.

"Oh." Cat blushed a pretty pink shade. "Well, I suppose I don't. I guess."

Dave pulled her to standing. "Here, let me help you."

He took the hem of her shirt and tugged it up, exposing a lacy bra. Every muscle in Andreas's body tightened in anticipation. Cat bit her lip. The way she looked at them with her shy bedroom eyes made his pulse race.

"You know—" she unclipped her bra and tossed it away, "—just because we're sleeping together and we're alone here doesn't mean I'm going to start running around like I'm in some nudist colony."

"Why not?" Dave and Andreas asked in unison. Cat snorted, and with a haughty raise of her eyebrows, dropped her shorts and panties, and ran off towards the water. Dave and Andreas shared a glance and then sprinted after her.

Andreas walked in slowly, savoring the feel of the cool water stroking his skin. Just ahead, Cat dove underwater, coming up right in front of Dave. He took her in his arms. She wrapped her legs around his hips and her arms around his neck, and kissed him on the mouth.

Andreas had never seen anything like them. They shared such unabashed love for one another, they virtually oozed sex. He came up behind them and pressed his body into Cat's naked back. Her head dropped back on his chest, her eyes closed, and he slipped his arms around her waist, caressing her stomach. She made a purring noise in her throat. "Mmm, that feels good."

He rinsed her shoulders and neck as she relaxed against him and Dave held her. Then they set her gently down and cleaned themselves.

Andreas was the first to leave the water. He strode purposefully to their comfortable shelter. It was so hot out, he was almost dry by the time he got there. He leaned against a rock and waited, watching the beach.

Cat tugged Dave out of the water, following Andreas. But Dave stopped just as they stepped out of the shallow water onto the hard-packed wet sand.

"Let him wait." Dave twined his arm around her stomach, holding her back possessively. "I want to be inside you here. Now."

She glanced up at the rock overhang. She could see Andreas's silhouette just beyond the wing of the plane. "He's watching."

"Yeah," Dave said into her ear. "Get on your hands and knees."

Her breath shallow, her heart racing, she lowered herself onto the sand. Dave was always dominant in bed, and she loved that about him. She loved doing the kinky things he asked her to. She loved the toys he bought for her, how he sometimes tied her wrists and ankles to the bedposts, how sometimes he spanked her during sex until her butt tingled.

But she'd never known he was such an exhibitionist—that taking her from behind while his friend watched would turn him on.

Dave went onto his knees behind her and entered her without preliminary. Her pussy was already dripping from the men's caresses in the water, and it swallowed his cock greedily.

He began to fuck her in slow, long strokes.

This was her favorite position, it always hit the sweet spot inside her, and she wriggled and moaned with the joy of it. The sand was cool and wet beneath her hands and knees. The sun beat down on her back. Salty water droplets rolled down the sides of her face.

"You have my permission—" Dave punctuated each word with a thrust, "—to fuck him whenever either of you wants it, understand?"

"Oh God, Dave," she whispered, meeting him thrust for thrust. Her climax was building, a sweet, intense pulse deep within her.

"Just tell me about it," he said. Thrust. Thrust. *Thrust.* Cat bit her lip to keep from crying out. "Tell me everything."

"Okay," she whimpered. "I just...I just..." Right now, all she wanted was for him to shut up and make her come.

"No games, Cat. We tell each other—" *Thrust.* "—everything. Everything, do you hear me?"

"Yes. Everything. No games. I love you, Dave. I love *you.*"

His hands gripped her hips now, jerking her body into his with every thrust. "Now you can come."

That was all it took. It overcame her in pounding waves, leaving her gasping and shuddering. Dave came soon after, his fingers sinking into the flesh of her hips, groaning her name as he spilled himself inside her.

She sank onto the cool sand and he came down with her, spooning her from behind. They stayed in that position, naked and wet, warmed by sex and sun, until Cat's eyelids grew heavy. Finally, Dave nuzzled her hair.

"Ready for round two? Andreas is waiting."

Chapter Five

June 24—Sunday

Cat shook out the cushions they'd been using for bedding and tidied their little shelter. It had rained nearly solid for the past two days. It was a good thing they had made the shelter weatherproof. Still, their palm-frond roof leaked. Everything was damp.

This past day had been the hardest for her. She couldn't help but think of their king-sized bed at home—soft, warm, dry, covered with fluffy pillows. Their kitchen fridge, stocked full of food. She missed people in general—the hustle and bustle of her cosmopolitan city. And she had started to wonder if they'd ever be rescued.

Dave had gone off on another of his island scavenging treks despite the rain, saying the wetness didn't bother him. Andreas was working on his radio rig inside the airplane. She was beginning to think nothing would ever come of his efforts to get the radio working.

A shadow fell over her. She looked up to find him standing in the makeshift doorway between palm fronds. His lips curled into a wide, sexy smile. "It's going to work."

"The radio?"

"Uh-huh." He took a step inside. "Where's Dave?"

"Oh, you know." She waved her hand.

"Hiking?" He lowered himself on a cushion. "Well, we should keep watch for airplanes. Whenever we spot one, we should try it. We'll keep doing it until someone hears or the batteries die."

"Sounds good." She reached down to brush a drop of rainwater from his nose.

He caught her wrist and looked up at her with serious, dark eyes. "Cat?"

"Yeah?"

"What's going to happen when we get back home?"

"You mean...with us?"

He nodded.

She blew out a breath. "I don't know." She didn't know where she wanted this to go. They were having a great time, but things were different here. Free. Without any of the restraints or demands of their real lives. When they got home, Cat and Dave would begin married life together. She would start school in the fall, while keeping her job part-time. Andreas was mired not only in work responsibilities, but in the immense project of building his house.

"So this is a temporary thing? We're together here, but once we go home, we go back to how it was?"

She shook her head, lowering herself beside him. "Back to the status quo? I don't know. Do we have a choice?"

He took her chin in his hand, turning her head to face him. "There's got to be a choice. I can't go back to the way it was before. Not now. Not knowing—" His voice dwindled.

He was so gorgeous, he took her breath away.

Before she knew what she was doing, she raised her lips, inviting him for a kiss.

267

He did not decline the invitation. They were all over one another in an instant, and within seconds, they were both naked, and Andreas lay on his back on the cushions, his hard cock in her hands.

The three of them had sex twice, sometimes three times a day every day since she and Dave had approached him. They were insatiable.

Like newlyweds.

She didn't want it to ever end.

"Suck it, Cat," Andreas demanded. Then, almost as an afterthought, "Please."

She pressed her lips to it and grinned. "Since you asked so nicely..."

Cat ran little kisses up and down its length. She nipped and nibbled and licked. Then she took him into her mouth, running her lips from the base to the tip of his long shaft, humming with pleasure.

His hand closed over hers, over his heavy cock. "Mount me."

She looked up at him. The plea had disappeared from his eyes, now he stared at her with a dark, intense look, and she dared not disobey. She did not want to disobey. At this moment the heat swirled in her, so insistent and greedy, she would do whatever he asked. In the end, she knew her own satisfaction required her compliance.

She crawled up him on hands and knees, and positioned his cock at her entrance. Both her men were so big, so masculine, so gorgeous and demanding. How had she gotten so lucky?

Slowly, she sank her body over him, reveling in the friction of him sliding into her.

"Yesss." The word came from her in a long breath.

"You're so good," he murmured through his tight jaw. "So tight and sweet. Better than I—"

"—imagined?" She leaned forward over him. Her nipples brushed his chest. "Did you fantasize about sleeping with me?"

He blew out a breath through his nose. "Oh, yeah."

She rocked her hips. "Even though I was marrying your best friend? That was naughty, Andreas. Very bad."

He cupped her breasts, running his big thumbs over her nipples. Hissing, she arched her back to give him better access.

"I'm a man," he said. "No control over fantasies."

She rocked over him again. Her clit rubbed against him, sending delicious ripples through her body. "Ahhh." She stroked the hard ridges of his chest with her fingertips. "Tell me your fantasy."

He laughed, a low rumble. "Why? I'm living it now."

She shivered. "Fuck me, then."

He took control, setting his hands on her hips and controlling the rhythm of her ride, forcing her clitoris to brush against him at every stroke.

Cat squeezed her eyes shut and focused on climbing the ramp to orgasm. Pants of pleasure erupted from her every time he pounded her over him.

Suddenly his hands relaxed, breaking the rhythm, breaking her from the sweet build. With a groan of frustration, she opened her eyes. Andreas was looking up, past her shoulder.

"Don't stop on account of me," Dave said from the doorway behind her.

Cat's heart pounded. Dave's voice sounded bland. Flat. Dangerously so. How long had he been there? Had he listened to their conversation?

Her face was hot—not with guilt, but of the sheer embarrassment of being caught on the edge of an orgasm. This was the first time she and Andreas had made love alone together. Dave had given permission, but it was in the heat of sex. Was he angry? She couldn't turn around. She couldn't face him.

Andreas's lips curled in a wicked smile. He lifted her slowly, until his cock barely touched her pussy, then pushed her down, hard, over him. Cat gasped.

"Lean forward," Andreas murmured. "Kiss me."

She hesitated.

"Do it," Dave said behind her, his voice still soft, still dangerous.

Leaning forward, she took Andreas's mouth. He was such a good kisser, she could almost forget that Dave stood behind her, watching. She could almost forget that her ass was tilted up in the air, open and exposed, with Andreas's cock buried inside her.

She could almost forget, but not quite.

Andreas's tongue swept into her mouth. He held her by the flanks, caressing her skin as if he felt her hammering heartbeat and tried to soothe it.

Dave's cold, wet hands massaged the cheeks of her behind. "My wife has such a fine ass." She wiggled involuntarily, which caused Andreas's cock, still rock-hard, to stroke her inside. She moaned against his mouth.

"So round and pretty." Dave gave her butt cheek a little smack. Cat flinched, more from surprise than pain. His sodden shirt landed on the cushion beside her head, and then his pants. He knelt beside her. His hand curled around her shoulder, lifting her mouth away from Andreas's, then tugged on her hair, turning her to face him. His eyes were narrow and intent, his hair dripping around his ears.

"Fuck him," he said harshly. "And kiss me while you do it."

Slowly, she began to move. Andreas massaged her legs, then his fingers glided back to her breasts to stroke her nipples. Cat held onto Dave's muscular arm with one hand, Andreas's chest with the other, and rotated her hips in little jerking movements.

She kissed her husband. He held her head, moving with her, biting and licking her lips and tongue. His kisses traveled across her face, down to her jawline and beyond, to the sensitive spot behind her ear. She looked down and saw his pale hand on Andreas's dark leg.

She came. Hard, pulsing bursts of pleasure rocketed through her. They raced through every nerve in her body, leaving her breathless, choking for air. She saw stars. Vaguely, she heard herself making noise. Dave and Andreas held her in the firm cocoon of their arms, and Dave kissed her, murmuring words she didn't understand into her ear.

There was no rational thought for her beyond that. She fell into the sensations of making love to them, of them making love to her. They spoke to her, to one another, but she didn't hear. All she could hear was the roar of her arousal, the scream of pleasure as it raced through her veins. Her body wanted more, and she would not deny it.

Dave's cock pressed into the crack of her ass, sending a fresh orgasm rolling through her. He cradled her in his arms while she shuddered through the spasms, and then began to tunnel into her ass. She writhed against it, but Andreas held her firm. She whimpered, pleaded, begged for them to stop, or for them to give her more, she wasn't sure which.

She heard Dave's soothing words. "Relax. I love you, babe. Open up to me. Accept me."

And so she did.

Then their hands were all over her. Over her skin, her breasts and her clit. She came again. And again. And then both of them were fucking her vigorously, and all she heard were her own cries of pleasure and pain, and the sounds of two men, *her* men, making love to her as one.

Again, they spoke to one another, and she couldn't hear anything but one word, *"Together."* They both expanded within her, intensifying the pressure and the pleasure-pain. Everything. And through the fog of it all, she heard them say another word, this time in unison, *"Now!"*

They both stiffened. Andreas groaned, Dave yelled, and they burst inside Cat, sending her into yet another bone-melting orgasm. Her body tightened and coiled around them, milking their cocks until she was dripping, overflowing with a combination of their come and her own.

She sank onto Andreas's chest. He wrapped his arms around her, his breath warm in her hair. Dave fell to the cushions beside them.

Cat closed her eyes and sank into oblivion.

ଓଞୠ

Cat stretched her limbs. Ooh, she was sore. Pleasantly so. She rolled to her back, feeling the press of a man on either side of her. The intoxicating musky smell of their bodies, their sex, wafted through their cozy little shelter.

A shaft of sunlight pierced through the doorway. The rain had stopped.

Life was good.

If they got the radio working, life would be changing very shortly. Yet none of them wanted to live forever on this island.

Cat sat up, twisting her back to get the kinks out. The insides of her thighs were sticky. "Oh. I think I'm going to take a bath."

Instantly, both of them were sitting up beside her.

"You okay?" Dave asked.

Andreas's hand made little circles on the small of her back. A crease of concern appeared between his brows.

She smiled at him, then turned to kiss Dave softly on the lips. "Yeah. I'm okay." She shrugged her shoulders to her ears, then dropped them. "I'm more than okay. I'm..." What was the word? Oh, there it was. She giggled at the realization. "I'm happy."

Dave nuzzled her hair. "Aw, babe. I'm happy too."

They both looked at Andreas expectantly. His lips tilted and his dimple appeared. "Yeah. 'Happy' is a good way to describe it."

CBℵHരᎳ

Wires and tools were scattered everywhere in the cockpit of the airplane. Andreas sat in the pilot's seat, Cat sat naked in Dave's lap in the passenger seat beside him.

Dave had heard the plane first and called her away from her bath.

Cat craned her head to look out the door. She couldn't see the plane through the thick cloud cover, but she could hear the steady roar of its engines. It was growing fainter.

"Hurry," she whispered.

Dave touched a wire to one of the smaller batteries.

The light on the radio's display came on. Faint, but there it was.

"Not much juice," murmured Andreas, turning the dial to the right frequency.

Cat's heart sank. She bit her lip as Andreas pressed the communicator button and spoke into his headset. "Mayday, mayday, mayday…"

He announced that they'd gone down, gave the airplane's N-number, and their approximate coordinates. Then he released the button.

The three of them listened in silence. Nothing. Cat felt tears welling. She thought she'd been ambivalent about being rescued, but at this moment, she wanted nothing more than to hear another human voice on that radio.

Andreas released a breath between his teeth. "One more time. Then we'll try again later."

Cat and Dave nodded their assent.

"Mayday, mayday…"

This time at the end of his speech, there was some static. Then a tiny voice.

"This is American fourteen-oh-two en route to Miami International." *Static.* "We have your coordinates and will—" *Static.* "—as soon as we are within range. Is anyone hurt?"

Cat felt the air release from all of their bodies. A commercial jet had heard them. They were going to be saved.

Andreas went back on the radio and briefly explained their situation, then said their battery was dying and they wouldn't be able to communicate for much longer.

As the light flickered, they heard the small voice once again. "Search and Rescue gives an ETA at your coordinates in two hours. Good..." The voice faded.

They all sat silently for a long moment, staring at the radio.

"Guess we'd better pack," Dave said.

CʒՖԾ

Andreas watched Dave and Cat run along the beach, waving their arms at the advancing helicopter. The chopper was still far offshore, but headed directly for them. Cat grabbed Dave's hand and they stopped to watch it.

Andreas approached them, his hands thrust into his pockets.

"They're coming," Cat whispered as he moved beside her.

Andreas nodded. "Just a few more minutes on Fantasy Island, then we're gone forever."

He felt the little shiver go through her. "'Fantasy Island'. I like that." She glanced at Dave. "What do you think? Should we ask him now?"

"Now's as good a time as any," Dave said blandly.

"Ask me what?"

She turned to Andreas, took his hand and pressed it to her chest. "We don't want to be separated from you when we get home."

He raised his eyebrows.

"We were thinking...well, we were thinking that you might want to stay with us, at least until you get your roof built."

He flicked a glance at Dave. "Were you?"

Dave nodded. "Yeah. We—well, *I*, at any rate, miss having you around. Miss your dirty jockstrap on the floor. Miss your dirty dishes in the sink."

Cat scowled. "Hey. No dirty jockstraps or dishes in my house."

Dave shrugged. "She runs a tight ship, I've got to admit. But if you follow her rules..."

"...she'll be a nice kitty and try her best to make you happy," Cat finished.

Andreas looked down at her. "Will she?"

She bit her lip in that sweet, shy way she had. "Yeah," she whispered. "She will."

"Until my roof is built?"

"And your walls are up," Dave said.

"And you might want your plumbing in," Cat added.

"And electricity..."

"And all the fixtures."

The helicopter drew closer, its engine roaring. Dave raised his voice so they could hear him. "You'll want your flooring too."

"And you'll want to paint it first. It's nasty living with a fresh paint smell." Cat wrinkled her little nose.

"Of course, you'll need to move all your furniture there too." Dave made a grand, encompassing gesture with his free arm, as if insinuating Andreas had so much furniture that it would take years to get it all moved in.

The helicopter was almost overhead.

Andreas nodded slowly. Cat's heart beat frantically against his fingertips. She gazed at him in a silent, hopeful plea.

The three of them together. This could work.

"You know," he shouted over the sound of the beating rotors, "my house will be big enough for three."

"Me, Dave and you in your brand-new house?"

He looked down at Cat and saw the joy and trust in her eyes. Dave squeezed his shoulder and nodded, a grin playing about his lips. Cat slipped an arm around both of them and leaned into him to whisper into his ear, "Yeah, I think we might be able to manage that."

Smiling, all three of them tilted their heads to the sky.

About the Author

Raised on a boat in the South Pacific and in the quiet rainforests of Hawaii, Dawn Halliday had plenty of time to develop her overzealous imagination. Between exploring deserted atolls, swimming in churning seas, and exploring lava tubes, Dawn starting dreaming up stories of love and adventure before she could read them.

When she's not traveling to exotic lands (which she can always justify as "research"), Dawn lives with her True Love and three rambunctious children in Southern California. She writes passionate historical and contemporary romance, and loves every minute of it.

To learn more about Dawn Halliday, please visit www.dawnhalliday.com or send an email to Dawn at dawnjhalliday@gmail.com.

Discover Samhain!

THE HOTTEST NEW PUBLISHER ON THE PLANET

Romance, fantasy, mystery, thriller, mainstream and more—Samhain has more selection, hotter authors, and everything's available in both ebook and print.

Pick your favorite, sit back, and enjoy the ride!
Hot stuff indeed.

WWW.SAMHAINPUBLISHING.COM

GREAT CHEAP FUN

Discover eBooks!

THE FASTEST WAY TO GET THE HOTTEST NAMES

Get your favorite authors on your favorite reader, long before they're out in print! Ebooks from Samhain go wherever you go, and work with whatever you carry—Palm, PDF, Mobi, and more.

Samhain
Publishing, LLC

WWW.SAMHAINPUBLISHING.COM